THE EMPTY ONES

ALSO BY ROBERT BROCKWAY

Rx: A Tale of Electronegativity
You Might Be a Zombie and Other Bad News
(from the editors of Cracked.com)
Everything Is Going to Kill Everybody

The Unnoticeables
The Empty Ones
Kill All Angels (forthcoming)

ROBERT BROCKWAY

THE
EMPTY ONES

TITAN BOOKS

The Empty Ones
Print edition ISBN: 9781783297993
E-book edition ISBN: 9781783298006

Published by Titan Books
A division of Titan Publishing Group Ltd
144 Southwark Street, London SE1 0UP

First edition: August 2016
2 4 6 8 10 9 7 5 3 1

A CIP catalogue record for this title is available from the British Library.

Printed and bound by CPI Group (UK) Ltd, Croydon, CR0 4YY

You have always been there for me,
and I will always be there for you.
This book is dedicated to you,
whiskey.

THE
EMPTY ONES

ONE

1984. Lima, Peru. Meryll.

I messed up this poor girl's code, and now she's got teeth where her eyes should be.

I looked inside of her, and I saw hunger. Simple as that. You look inside some folks and you see this dense web of needs, desires, secrets, and regrets. It's all laid out like neurons. Maybe train stations is a better analogy. There's always a Grand Central. You just gotta find it.

You take a strand of somebody's personality—like, the way they always say "naturally" instead of "of course"—and you start feeding it back, through moments, through years, through whole lifetimes even, and you'll eventually find the source. They were watching *The Avengers* as a little kid, they saw Emma Peel say that, and they thought it was so sophisticated.

"Naturally," she said, like it was the most obvious thing in the world. And she laughed.

This person tried it on for themselves, and they liked it. It stuck. So much hinges on that moment. So many experiences, so many connecting points where if they'd said "yes," instead of "naturally," the ensuing sequence of events would've gone in a totally different direction. Because they start using this silly, meaningless little word, they develop an affection for what they perceive to be sophistication. They listen to classical music, not because they like it, but because they want to be perceived as the type of person who likes it. They go to the ballet when they're seventeen. They stay up all night reading about it first, so they can tell their mother "that's a pas de deux," and she would nudge her husband as if to say "See? See how refined our child is?" All of these little strings, hanging on other strings, wrapped around hubs, providing supports for the whole network. So you find them there, cross-legged on the orange shag in their living room, biscuits all over their face, watching *The Avengers* with eyes like glass, and you pull that out.

You show them that moment. They see that so much of who they thought they were was arbitrary—it all comes from here. And half their lifetime just goes away. You find another hub, getting felt up by Jaime in the locker room, and another, the spider crawling across their ear as a baby. You pluck out a few more of those, and pretty soon there's not much left to a person at all. They just . . . go away. And all that energy they were wasting by existing, it becomes yours. You can do whatever you want with it.

You can use it to knock an asteroid out of orbit. You can use it to blow up a city. You can shove it deep down inside of you and store it, like a battery. It decays some over time, but there's so much, and it's so easy to get.

But we're talking about a different girl: this girl here, in the wind-blown shack with the corrugated metal roof just outside of Lima.

Some folks need dozens of hubs plucked out of them before they're solved. Most just need three or four. This girl has only one main concern: hunger. She's always been hungry, and she's never had enough to eat. There were other elements to her personality, other things that made her who she was, but in one way or another, all of those strings led back to hunger. You can't pull just a single moment. You wouldn't even get any energy that way—there'd be nothing left to simplify.

So I plucked out all the other, smaller hubs around hunger. Getting beaten by the policeman behind the supermarket. Kissing her little brother on the head before a soccer game in an overgrown lot. And here she is, teeth where her eyes should be. Belly twice the size of her body. Huge hands, fingers curling into canines. Her tongue is six feet long and flailing about like a live wire.

Dang it. Three years, and I'm still making these mistakes.

Ah, well. I'll find a use for her.

Hi, my name is Meryll. And this is the story of how I became God.

TWO

The band sounded like a domestic violence case in progress. Couple of hoarse guys yelling over guitars so distorted they sounded like somebody rapidly flipping channels on a TV that only got static. The drums rolled out, all crashes and bangs—the catfight in the alley outside knocking over some trash cans. All the scene was missing were some police sirens, and by the look of the crowd, they wouldn't be missing for long.

My head hurt. I'd been wearing the same socks for about two weeks and was just starting to realize it. My beer was warm, stale, and nearly empty—just like the four on the floor at my feet. The blonde next to me elbowed me in the ear, again. She was blitzed. She'd bounced her tits out of her shirt two minutes ago, and hadn't even noticed yet.

It was about as close to a perfect night as you could ask for.

"Hey! Ho!" Joey Ramone yelled, and the crowd screamed in response.

It was New Year's Eve at the Rainbow Theatre. I was

doing everything I could not to be happy, and it just wasn't working. I would've spat in your eye if you'd told me this last month, and I'll do worse if you ever tell anybody I said it now, but god damn if the British punks couldn't teach us Americans a thing or two. There's an anger to the scene here that makes it feel fucking *vital*. It has to *do* something— succeed, or explode in everybody's faces, or dance a merry jig and poop in the corner. Nobody knows *what* it's doing, exactly, but "nothing" isn't an option, because the scene is the only damn thing the Brits have. I love New York like the filthy whore she is, but sometimes concerts there feel like fashion shows and the line out front of a venue is a place to be seen. Here in London, it's a place to be stabbed. I watched a man get his front teeth knocked out an hour ago, and his only response was to spit a mouthful of blood on the guy that did it. They both laughed.

It was a magical time.

I'm sure the coke was helping with the festive atmosphere some. Last time I went in the bathroom, people were pissing in the sink so folks had more room to do lines off the backs of the toilets.

Hey, I'm not passing judgment. At least it kept these fuckers dancing. I've been to a few shows where more people were sleeping than listening to the band. The only drug I'm against is heroin, because it keeps you from dancing, fucking, and fighting—and really, what else is there? I'm not crazy about acid either, but that's only because a dog lectured me about dropping out of high school for three straight hours the last time I did it. But if it peels your banana, you do it up. Just don't shoot dope into your arm and fall asleep on my shoulder on the way to the show, that's all I ask.

But energy wasn't a problem at the Rainbow tonight: Hundreds of young punks, all stinking of cheap cigarettes and warm beer and sweat, hopped up and down to the music like hyperactive rabbits. Their heads rose and fell in great waves. A swell of greasy-haired skulls broke against the stage, where three skinny, gawky boys stood—each looking for all the world like dirty mops dressed in leather jackets—and flailed at their instruments like the things had grown mouths and called their mothers a bunch of bitches.

Aw, there I go, waxing all poetic again. Give me a break: I'm four beers and two joints into the night. That's the poet's ratio.

I felt an elbow in my crotch. And not in a friendly way. I grabbed the attached arm and looked down into the raccoon eyes of a short white girl, just a touch on the pudgy side. She had a streak of crimson zigzagging down the back of her shoulder-length hair. It matched the smear of blood on her black-painted lips. There was a look in her eyes that said she hadn't gotten it in fun.

She was wearing thick leather bracelets, black-and-purple leggings—torn at the knees—under a tight black miniskirt, and dusty combat boots. A plain white T-shirt, just a bit too tight, read "Punk's not dead, it's just pining" in Magic Marker.

She sneered, flipped me a "V" with her fingers—I guessed that didn't mean "peace" over here—and wrenched her arm away from me. She swam into the crowd and I let her.

The Ramones were just launching into "Gimme Gimme Shock Treatment," my buzz was teetering on the edge, about to fall facefirst into a sloppy pile of drunk, and I was pretty sure this blonde with her forever-bouncing tits wasn't going to be exactly discerning tonight. I bet American boys pissed off her daddy.

I didn't want to go.

Fuck it. I wasn't going to go.

Then somebody passed by a few inches in front of me, and their face was like a library on a Sunday. Quiet, unassuming, forgetful. Nothing of note. Nothing to pay attention to. Look away. *You're not missing anything,* that face said to me, *go ahead and look at better stuff. I hear there are bouncing titties nearby.*

It had the opposite effect on me. It shook half the buzz right out of my head, replaced it with a surge of adrenaline. I stared hard at the person with the unnoticeable face, and felt the start of a focus headache build up behind my eyes. Their features blurred and shifted. Their face squirmed like wet soap under my stare and refused to resolve. There were too many people, too close together. You could never hope to pick out the features of an Unnoticeable in a crowd like this.

Shit.

I had to go.

I drained the rest of my beer, shaking the can to get at the last few drops. I ran my tongue into the narrow hole, cutting it a little on the sharp metal edges, and tossed the thoroughly empty can sideways into the crowd. It skipped off the skull of a kid with only the front half of a mohawk. He looked around to see who did it, didn't find anybody, and settled for punching the fat guy next to him instead.

I shoved my way toward the exit. I followed the red zigzag as it disappeared and reappeared. Ducking in and out of the crowd. It bounced merrily, like those little dots that highlight the lyrics in sing-alongs.

Behind me, the guitars died, and Joey's goofy, mooky voice rang out clear and alone against the silence:

"I saw her walking down the street
He jumped down and knocked her off her feet
And then I knew it was the end of her."

The chubby girl ducked under a purple rope and slipped into a darkened alcove. The Unnoticeable followed after. Somebody shouted *"1-2-3-4"* and the guitars blared back into life like antiaircraft fire. Joey screamed:

"He's gonna kill that girl
He's gonna kill that girl
He's gonna kill that girl tonight."

A bit on the fucking nose there, Joey.

THREE

The entire thing was filmed in such high definition that it looped back around to looking cheap again. A soap opera or a corporate training video. The carpet was a deep beige shag. The walls were beige, with some faded floral design worked into the wallpaper in slightly lighter beige. The fixtures were modern and minimalist: The lamps were a series of connected rods of burnished steel; the blinds were faux-Asian rice paper; the television was wafer-thin and huge, shining black like ice on a pond—and wherever possible, all of it was trimmed in beige. All except for a big, puffy, bright orange couch that sat obscenely in the center of the room.

The couch was absurd. The couch was out of character. The couch was a *situation*.

The couch seemed guilty and brazen all at once, like the 1970s had shat it out on the carpet while your back was turned, and it was now waiting in the corner, just daring you to comment.

Around a light beige table with ornate wrought iron legs,

there were four tall chairs with beige corduroy cushions. On one sat a woman with a fanatic's eyes, bright blue and perpetually wet, as if on the verge of hysterical tears. Her hair was blond, her skin was tan, her blouse was unbuttoned just slightly, and her pencil skirt looked as though it had been officially assigned at the graduating ceremony of Sexy Journalist Academy. Her unwavering smile could have blinded a welder. In another sat a handsome Latino man. His muscles barely fit in his shirt, which was both a testament to his workout routine and his wardrobe consultant, who only bought him shirts that were two sizes too small, in order to better emphasize the man's impeccable workout routine. He, too, seemed physically incapable of not smiling. His immaculate teeth, their edges squared off by a ruler, were as orderly as a military parade. They stretched from one ear to the other and possibly beyond. You got the irrational impression that those teeth would continue right on into the back of his head, wrapping about the skull and out the other side in an unbroken ribbon of enamel. He wore a smile like an ordinary person wears underwear—just a fact of life, something you put on first thing in the morning and only take off at night—but his eyes did not smile with him. They were small, black, and just a touch too close together. They reflected no light. Two bottomless pits dug into his face.

The woman laughed. She stretched out a hand and laid it on the man's knee. You could be forgiven, at this point—given the setting, the cast, and the artless resolution of the camera—for thinking that you were watching the start of a porno. One look into the desperate yearning of the tanned blonde's face, and you might reasonably assume you were only two innuendos away from full penetration. But you are, instead, watching *Access Hollywood*. You have made better decisions in your life.

. . .

Nelly:—and you've got some experience with . . . *sticky* situations, I hear?

Marco: Haha, you mean my little *hombrecito*? Enrique— Kiki—he's a gem, Nelly, truly he is. I tell this funny story about him. He's gonna hate me for it when I'm older. Sorry little dude! So we were at SeaWorld watching the *delfines* and *ballenas*—that's "dolphins" and "whales" in Spanish, Nelly. . . .

Nelly: Fantasti—

Marco: And Kiki, that little goof, he leans over too far, and plop! His ice cream drops right off the cone and into the water! *Ai yai yai!*

Nelly: Oh no! What flavor was i—

Marco: So I don't know what I'm thinking. I'm not thinking, I guess, and I just reach right in there and go to scoop it out. But, uh oh, here comes the delfín—right for my little hombrecito's ice cream!

Nelly: Who even knew dolphins liked ice—

Marco: So I'm in one of those dad moments, you know. I want to do right by my Kiki, but at the same time, I don't know what this crazy delfín is thinking, man! He could be coming for my hand. I'm leaning in there, trying to reach the ice cream, the delfín is swimming right toward me, faster and faster, and I'm leaning farther and farther and— well, let's just say now we know little Enrique doesn't mind wet ice cream!

Nelly: You're one *cool* dad!

Marco: Haha, you got that right!

Nelly: Speaking of temperatures, I hear the next season

of your show is going to be *sizzling*. You're headed down south of the borde—

Marco: To Tulancingo! We're headed down Mexico way, my hometown—*mi cuidad natal*—for my next project.

Nelly: Tell us a little abo—

Marco: Well, you remember the first season I tried to teach some inner-city Latino kids that there's a better way. This time, I'm returning to my roots—you know, small-town boy made good—to give a little something back to *mi pueblo*. It's going to be great. Really great. *Super great!*

Nelly: I hear you had a little trouble with the kids on the first season—

Marco: The Rollerblading! That's right. Some of these kids, you know, they get themselves into bad situations. They steal, they do drugs, they get into gangs, so I thought—if you're gonna get them out of something bad, why not get them into something good, like Rollerblading? We had some spills along the way, but they got pretty good by the end. We're gonna have some fun on this next season, too! I'm thinking bungee jumping! Haha, scary!

Nelly: But you ran into a little trouble with at least one teen last year who—

Marco: The only trouble we had was finding a nice smooth spot for Rollerblading! I love LA—*amo mi cuidad*—but they gotta work on those roads, Nelly!

Nelly: I was referring to the incident with—

Marco: Haha!

Nelly: I . . . yes, it does sound like a . . . *rough situation*.

Marco: You got that right!

Nelly: Haha, okay. Thanks for coming down to talk to us today, Marco.

Marco: Thanks for having me. *Muchas gracias!*

Nelly: And be sure to check out the second season of Marco Luis's *From the Barrio to the Bellagio,* only on E! But first: Up next, how low can J. Lo go? It's a Lo down dirty shame, and we've got the pictures to prove it. Jennifer Lopez does the limbo—commando—and shows her no-no. Oh no! Back to you, Tad.

. . .

You could feel the tension break as soon as the camera flicked off. Nelly let out a sigh that lasted for an entire minute. She wiped at her watery eyes, blinked her contacts back into place, and smiled at Marco. Genuinely, this time. It was a more subdued expression. No more cheeks stretched taut to show off the glimmering wall of teeth. It was a small, nervous smile. A little sad.

"So how did you stop that dolphin?" she asked Marco. Her voice was twenty decibels lower off camera. A slight southern accent chased about the edges.

"What." Marco responded. There was no intonation at the end to mark it as a question. His voice was flat and still.

He had also lost his camera mask, but while Nelly's had been replaced with a version of herself ten years older and a hundred IQ points brighter, Marco's was replaced by nothing at all. A mannequin sat in his place, perfectly still, just waiting for somebody to come and put him away.

"The dolphin?" Nelly tried again. "The one that wanted your son's ice cream? How'd you get it away?"

"There was no dolphin," Marco stated. When she looked confused, he continued: "It was a cute story. People like cute stories about famous people. It makes them feel like they are like us. Like we are just the same as them. I have people that write down cute stories for me to tell. That was one of them."

"Oh . . ." Nelly tried to think of something else to say, just to keep the conversation going, but she came up blank. She pulled at a thread in her tight pencil skirt instead.

"If I had to stop a dolphin," Marco continued, seeing that something more was expected of him, "I would hook my fingers into each of its eyes and push up and in until they popped."

Nelly's mouth went dry.

"Everything has eyes," Marco said. "Eyes are always a weakness."

Marco stared at her, unblinking and unmoving. Nelly got the sense he was not awaiting a response from her, or even trying to discomfort her. It was just that his face was already pointed in her direction, and he saw no reason to look elsewhere. She felt sweat spring up on the back of her neck. She tried to think of a polite reason to walk away. Then an impolite one. Then she just tried to get her legs to work. They would not.

Steele, her wardrobe assistant, paused as he walked by them. He frowned deeply at Nelly and made an extravagant series of noises.

"Now why do you have to pick at your skirt like that, Miss Nelly? Nasty habit. Nasty! Here, come on, that was the last reel for today. Let's get you in your civvies and out of my damn expensive clothes before you do any more damage."

Steele grabbed her by the wrist and pulled her to her feet. She let him lead her across the set like a blind woman. He pointed out the various cables and rigs so she didn't trip on them, and only released her when they were safely around the corner and out of sight. She slumped into the beaten and stained break-room sofa while Steele filled a Styrofoam cup with stale coffee.

"Miss Nelly, I thought you were supposed to be a smart girl."

"What's that?"

"Smart girls know better than to keep talking with the Empty Ones once the damn camera stops."

"I didn't know . . ." Nelly said, "I didn't know he was one of them. I've never met him before. Just seen him on TV. He always seemed so . . ."

"Nice?" Steele laughed and handed her the tiny, wholly inadequate cup of coffee. "You sound like one of the rubes, Miss Nelly. You know they like to put on a show."

Nelly made an affirming noise, and sipped at her terrible coffee. It burned her tongue, but she didn't really notice.

I flicked the television off, then decided I didn't like the silence. It would just give me time to think about what I saw. Digest it, swallow it, and let it slowly poison my thoughts until I'd lost another night to sweat and anxiety dreams. Instead, I flipped the channel a few times and dropped the remote onto the duvet cover that the '90s forgot. It was pale pink, shot through with pastel blue fractals and little squiggles of orange. It looked like the cover to my old Trapper Keeper. The Trapper Keeper I had in fifth grade. The same one that used to hold my embarrassing pictures of Marco Luis, in his role as hunky jock J.C. Sable on the teen sitcom *Home Room*. I had three pictures, I think, and all of them were as precious as fine art to my childhood self. I had lovingly cut them from those preteen girl softcore porno mags—*Tiger Beat, Seventeen, Teen Vogue*—with a pair of blunt scissors, and got them laminated in the library. The librarian laughed at me when

I made the request, and my ears had turned red, but I braved the embarrassment, shoved the glossy papers across the desk and waited.

They were worth it.

There was Sable in the pool, shirtless and staring back at the camera with his self-satisfied "I know you want me" smirk. Sable dancing with Kristi at the prom, her head leaning on the shoulder of his sleeveless white tuxedo. Sable with Mack, the two of them posing against an old cherry-red Impala. God, I couldn't count how many times I'd stared at those pictures and imagined myself as Kristi, my great big puffy '90s bangs crushed up against the wide lapels of Sable's tuxedo/vest. Imagined myself in the backseat of that Impala, belting out all the wrong lyrics to classic rock songs while Sable drove and Mack played air guitar. How many times I pictured myself in that pool, Sable's strong hands lifting me up and swinging me around, entwining in my bathing suit and . . .

And then I met him.

I actually met him!

Jackie had dragged me to an industry party in the Hollywood hills—the kind where underpaid waiters wander around with trays but everybody's on some specialized diet and nobody takes the food. You know how those things go. There's never anybody to talk to at those things except the people you came with, and they always ditch you in the first fifteen minutes. And then out of nowhere, there was Sable.

Marco Luis.

He was funny. He was self-deprecating. He was a little odd. He was also so goddamned pretty it hurt to look at him. He should have been in a museum, surrounded by little velvet ropes and a stern-eyed guard that would clear his throat at you if he saw you start to reach out to try to touch him. We had an awkward conversation.

Obviously.

What do you even say to somebody like that?

"Hey, funny thing—I learned to pleasure myself to your poster above my bed. You know, back when I was twelve. I used one of those squiggle pens with the battery-powered motor. Working on anything interesting lately?"

Jesus Christ, it was a nightmare. I tried to bail, but Jackie volunteered him to take me home, and I very nearly stroked out from embarrassment. But then the impossible happened: He said yes.

What?

Nobody gets that chance. Nobody gets to slip out of some glitzy showbiz party with their teenage crush and glide away into a masturbation fantasy turned reality. Well, nobody except me.

All of my preteen puberty dreams—those confused young fantasies that kept cutting out right as they got to the good parts, all stuck partway between disgust at the gross mechanics of sex and the desire to finally experience them firsthand—they were going to come true. I was there, in Marco Luis's expensive exotic car, and he had his J.C. Sable smirk on when he leaned over to kiss me.

It wasn't exactly how I'd pictured it. I had imagined some rock ballad blaring softly from the stereo while the full moon cast a pale and romantic light through the foggy windshield, his lips just brushing me at first, and then harder. . . .

I did *not* picture Marco then trying to drain the humanity out of me because he's some kind of immortal sociopathic monster. Didn't imagine the army of faceless people at his beck and call, and the screaming balls of light they worshipped as "angels."

Haha, listen to me! This is my life. This is what I would say, if I ran into an old acquaintance at the supermarket and they asked what was new.

"Oh, you know, just running from a former teen heartthrob and his army of half-people because I somehow managed to kill one of their energy-gods. How about you? Got rid of the braces, I see . . ."

Of course it has occurred to me that I'm completely, gibberingly, smear-my-crap-on-the-walls-to-insulate-against-the-government's-thought-rays insane. It occurs to me every single morning, when I wake up in another scabby anonymous motel and briefly wonder where my life went. I had a good one, you know—not great, but waiting tables and doing low-grade stunt work on the side was better than huddling behind the closed drapes in a Motel 6 by the highway. It occurs to me that I've gone mad every single time I step into the stained and forever broken shower to stand under five minutes' worth of tepid water that smells like pennies. It occurs to me when I eat my breakfast of stale chips from the vending machine—maybe fast food, if Jackie or Carey weren't too hungover to go out in the morning. The notion is occurring to me right now, as I'm narrating my own life to myself, swaddled in a scratchy comforter that looks like something Vanilla Ice would have worn. But if I'm insane, the pills aren't working. Maybe I'm not crazy. Maybe this is all just some impossibly elaborate prank.

It would be really funny, if it was.

"You got me!" I yelled, louder than I meant to. "You got me good! Come on out now. Come on, guys—I see the camera. Right there in the sad plastic fern thing. Pretty sneaky!"

I waited for a response. I rubbed at the sixth finger on my left hand. The ugly, malformed little extra digit that had hurt me every day of my life, except for three: The night my sister died, the first time I saw an angel . . . and the first time I killed one. It hadn't hurt for a single moment since.

"—she's never going to come," said the TV. A scrawny, weaselly-looking dude moped into a bowl of cornflakes.

"I bet *that* sounds familiar," Charlie Sheen quipped back at him.

A fat child looked at the camera, smiled and shrugged like, "what are ya gonna do?" The only sound in my room was canned laughter.

A drink.

I need a drink.

But the thought of joining Carey and Jackie at the bar of the chain restaurant in the far corner of the motel parking lot (Was it a Chili's? Might have been an Applebee's, or a T.G.I. Fridays, or a Fuddruckers—or one of any other million identical buildings full of identical people only temporarily joined together by their lack of a better idea when somebody said they didn't feel like cooking tonight) only made the anxiety worse. Carey didn't exactly fit in with drunken middle America—in his ancient, patchwork leather jacket, grinning through a broken face and slurring through a Brooklyn accent—but he seemed able to tolerate just about anything as long as the drinks were free. Which they were, if he agreed to go and keep Jackie company. She actually seemed to like the chains. She got some perverse satisfaction from trying to "pass" as a local.

She never did.

I did not have the energy for that. But I still wanted that drink.

My motel room was too crappy to have an overpriced minibar full of little liquor bottles, and the thought of going to the store—out there, alone, in a world full of teen heartthrob monsters and screaming orbs of light and people without faces—well, even sober reruns of *Two and a Half Men* seemed better than that.

Marginally.

I changed the channel. A man with a bumpy stomach screamed something about abs and held up a device that looked like a torture implement designed by Nerf. I changed the channel. Four women sat around a tiny table in a hip, modern-looking bar. One of them said something slutty and the rest crawled all over each other trying to out-slut her. I changed the channel. Synth-pop covers of Mozart. A clean blue grid, broken up by white blocks of text forever scrolling by at a snail's pace. A picture of a resort in one corner.

The local channel guide.

Thank god.

Wherever you go, anywhere in these great United States of America, you will find a local channel guide that always looks and sounds exactly the same as the one you know. An unadorned grid of text-boxes listing the day's programming on an eternal loop, one portion reserved for pictorial advertisements for local restaurants and bowling alley specials. The local channel guide plays music rejected from elevators for being too boring. The listings scroll by like cold molasses, so that you always forget what was on the first channels by the time the last ones pass through, and you end up watching the whole thing again. This is how we meditate, in Motel America: to the tune of an all-saxophone "Moonlight Sonata."

I stared at the channel guide, unfocused my eyes, and let it wash over me. The grid calmed my psychic wounds. The synthesizers refreshed my soul. I was very near to a state of adequate numbness when Carey kicked the motel door open, sang six consecutive refrains of "I'm Henry the VIII, I Am"—each somehow louder than the last—and then passed out at the foot of the bed, curled into a ball like an old hound. Jackie stumbled in after him, wearing a children's activity menu that she'd folded into a paper cowboy hat.

"K!" She said, then started laughing. "I'm wearing a cowboy hat! And I'm so happy! I'm a jolly rancher!"

Jackie fell on the floor beside Carey, and giggled herself to sleep.

I got up and closed the door behind them. I slid the dead bolt. I fastened the chain. I dragged a chair underneath the knob. Then I sat on the edge of the bed and watched it until the sun came up.

FOUR

1978. London, England. Carey.

A girl with frizzy green hair and black tape over her nipples danced in front of me. It was only when she flailed into my chest that she looked up long enough for her bleary eyes to focus. I gave her the widest, most earnest smile I could muster and waited for her to flip me off.

I did not wait long.

As soon as she lifted her hand from her side to give me the finger, I reached into her purse and snatched the can of hairspray that I'd seen poking out.

"The fugg you lookin' at, mate?" Green Hair slurred at me.

"My future wife," I answered.

She spit in my face. I wagged my tongue at her. She laughed and danced a bit closer.

God damn it! Here I am clearly meeting my soul mate, and I have to ditch her—and the no doubt beautiful moment we'd share in the men's bathroom later—to save some stranger's life? It just ain't fair.

I slid away from Green Hair, ducked under her spiteful

kick, and made for the alcove that the chubby girl and her faceless pursuer had disappeared into. The Rainbow was a weird place for a punk venue, but then, that's all we usually got—the weird places. Abandoned factories, condemned restaurants, old pharmacies converted into concert halls with huge bars and tiny stages. The Rainbow used to be a theater, I think. Maybe even in the proper British sense of the word—like, live-action, guys in wigs and makeup saying shit like "forsooth"-type theater. I don't know, maybe it was just a holdover from the times when movies were a big affair you dressed up for, and not someplace cheap you went to sleep it off for a few hours.

Either way, the Rainbow was huge—it was Grand Central Station compared to the clubs I was used to in New York. If the main hall hadn't been jam-packed with drunken flailing punk rockers, I could have thrown a football around in there.

Well, if I could have thrown a football.

The inside of the Rainbow was old, gold, and decaying: Flaking paint, crumbled plaster, faded spray paint in the corners. Looked like a set from one of those cheap '60s horror flicks. These big, ornate pillars lined the lobby, surrounding a giant sculpted fountain that looked like it should be attended by chicks in poofy dresses holding little umbrellas, instead of six fat skinheads huddled together to block the view of whatever it was they were smoking. They looked at me like wolves spotting a lone hiker—not sure if I was a threat or dinner. I locked eyes with the biggest one and ran my tongue across my lips seductively.

He looked away.

Where did the hell did the unnoticeable girl go?

I swear I saw her duck behind the musty red curtains

after the chubby English broad. I followed right after them, went down the short, smelly hallway and got spat right out into the lobby. No other doors. No other way to go. She was here. She had to be here.

I scanned the room, found nothing of note, and started to turn around.

I stopped myself.

God damn it, they can do it even when you know they're doing it.

I scanned the room again, slower this time, carefully cataloguing what I saw in my mind.

Pillar. Pillar. Slashed painting. Pillar. Girl in torn tights giving a painful-looking blow job to a skinny guy with a death grip on a bottle of cheap gin. Pillar.

Nope. Nothing out of the ordinary here—

There.

I looked at her twice before I could convince my mind she wasn't just part of the scenery. Brown spiked hair, black lipstick, short black skirt, and combat boots. It wasn't that she was invisible, or faceless. She had normal, maybe even pretty features—but you had to squint to make them out, like putting on somebody else's prescription glasses. And the second I looked away, my brain shuffled her face off into the "irrelevant if she's not going to fuck me" folder.

That is a *huge* folder. Bursting at the seams. There are subfolders. *Indexes.*

The unnoticeable girl slid through the heavy glass doors. They let a brief howling wind into the lobby, then clipped it off short so I could once again hear muffled drums, twangy guitars, and that girl's teeth scraping on dick.

"Jesus Christ, woman, it's not corn on the cob," I said, as I stepped over the pair and made for the door.

"A-fucking-men," the guy agreed in a pained voice.

He raised his bottle to me as I heaved open the double doors and stepped out into the wet, cold piss of a British night in winter. I blinked the rain away from my eyes, only to find it immediately replaced by more rain. I held my hand up to block the downpour—had to make a little gutter with my fingers to redirect the torrent—and looked around the street. If this had been New York, I'd have seen little pockets of punks huddling on every corner. No matter how great the show was, or how cold the night was, there would be just as many kids hanging around outside as there were watching the band. If you really pressed most punks, they'd admit that drugs and the privacy to do them are every bit as important as the music. Not here, though. There were people on the street—it was New Year's Eve, after all, people had places to be and pints to pound—but I didn't see any smoky clusters orbiting the venue like junkie moons. The rain changed the story. Whatever the kids here needed to do, they did it inside, and if you walked in on it, well, you were welcome to either join in or fuck off. Nobody wanted to be out in this mess. A big red bus kicked half of a puddle in my face, and I blew oily water out of my sinuses. When my vision came back, I saw the chubby girl's face backlit by the wan yellow light of the bus's interior, as it pulled past me and disappeared around the corner. I did my best to peer into the other windows.

Pay attention pay attention pay attention—

Nothing. Too far away, too much rain, going too fast. I couldn't tell if the Unnoticeable had followed her onto the bus or not.

Shit.

She was probably fine.

Shit.

She'd take the bus home, trudge into her house or flat or whatever all wet and track mud everywhere and her mother would scream—

Shit.

—and she'd flip her mom the bird and storm upstairs to play *Never Mind the Bollocks* too loud—

Shit.

—and I could go back inside with a clear conscience and fuck the holy hell out of the green-haired girl in a bathroom stall like God intended because—

Shit.

—she was probably completely okay. Right?

Shit shit shit. Even I don't believe me.

I looked for a cab. Nothing. I looked for another bus. Nothing. I looked for anything—a bicycle, a helicopter, an uppity horse with digestive problems—literally any vehicle that was not a cute little red-and-white scooter covered in obnoxious punk rock bumper stickers. But there it was, propped up against one of those old-timey-looking British lampposts. Taunting me.

No keys in it, but no chain around it either.

Shit.

I flipped my switchblade open and jammed it into the ignition. I grabbed the opposite handlebar and yanked, while kicking the front tire. The steering lock broke. I mounted the torn pink seat and twisted the switchblade hard. It snapped clean at the hilt, nicking my thumb. Oh well, I tried—

Shit.

The little headlight flickered. The ignition was on. I held my breath and kicked the starter once. I gritted my teeth and prayed it wouldn't turn over. It sputtered politely to life with a sound like somebody clearing their throat in an elevator.

I sighed.

God hates me. Small wonder, with all the shit I've said to the guy over the years.

I pushed off of the curb and twisted the throttle, for the first time noticing the multicolored ribbons jutting out of either handlebar that danced merrily in the wind as I picked up speed. Well, what the scooter hilariously thought passed for speed, anyway. Between my weight, roads that were more water than asphalt, and an engine roughly the same size and ferocity as a fairy fart, it was slow going. I managed to keep the double-decker bus in sight, but just barely. I would twist the grip and wait for the subtle signs of acceleration (basically just those dorky little streamers twisting about a bit harder), but by the time I got up to speed there was a corner, or a pedestrian, or a roundabout full of psychotic cabdrivers weaving in and out of lanes like Ali dodging punches—and I was back on the brakes again. Luckily, the bus was making regular stops. Unluckily, since I was tailing it, I had to ride right past the disembarking passengers. I kept thinking one of those oblivious, probably drunk, and certainly deranged London cabbies was going to run me over before I'd catch the damn thing. . . .

But no such luck. I just kept right on puttering by, wholly intact, while people pointed and laughed.

Let's make something clear: I don't give a lackluster fuck what people think about me driving a girly scooter. I'd put on a dress and pretty bows just to spite the people who'd laugh at an ugly mug like me dolled up in a dress and pretty bows. But these goddamned bumper stickers were killing me.

PUNK AS FUCK, one read.

PUNK OR BUST, said another.

PUNK ROCK FOREVER, one insisted; POP MUSIC NEVER.

I knew the girl who owned this scooter. Or girls like her. They went to maybe one show a month, but drew Xs on the backs of their hands with markers to make it look like they went every night. They collected empty beer cans after parties and put them in their bedrooms for their parents to find. They practiced flipping people off in the mirror. For them, punk rock was an easy way to fake a temporary personality. Which is fine.

Normally.

Normally you listen to how much they hate their dad, maybe slip them a Schlitz or two, and they might show you their tits later. That's the way the drunken punk rock economy works.

But there's nothing saying I have to ride their poser scooters around in public and like it.

Luckily, salvation was at hand: The bus stopped at the next corner, letting an old man with a cane and a buzz I could smell from a block away wobble off it. I hit the brakes, but the scooter took that to be a friendly suggestion and chose to ignore it.

Fuck it. Not like I was setting any land speed records anyway.

I put both hands on the seat and reverse-leapfrogged right off the moving bike.

I did not plan this well.

Neither one of my worn-smooth ancient Chucks found purchase on the slick asphalt. I started to slide, fell over, slid some more, then managed to get my feet, only to find I was still sliding, and finally had the good fortune to slam headfirst into a mailbox. I stood, feeling about as wobbly as the old guy a few feet away looked, and stumbled up beside him. Shoulder to shoulder, we watched my riderless scooter disappear into the night.

"Godspeed," I said, and gave it a mocking salute.

After a short, confused moment, the old guy raised a hesitant hand and saluted with me.

I was still laughing as the bus pulled away.

I plunked fistfuls of those silly British coins into the slot until the driver finally nodded at me to stop, then headed down the aisle. I only made it a few steps before he buried a foot in the gas pedal, sending me stumbling sidelong into one passenger, then rebounding into another. I pinballed my way down the bus until I found my prey: Chubby English Girl.

She was staring out the window in an aggressively apathetic way. I could hear her thoughts, and they were all screaming: "Please don't sit next to me, please don't sit next to me, there are like twenty open seats why are you sitting next to me *oh god*."

I gave her my widest, most obnoxious smile, then flopped wetly onto the seat beside her.

"Hi!" I waved. "I'm Carey. I'm drunk *and* American. Let's have a long and detailed conversation!"

She closed her eyes, took a deep breath, and let it out over a span of about two minutes.

"Not in a place tonight, yeah?" she finally said, when it became apparent that her prolonged groan wouldn't actually make me magically wither and die.

"What kind of place is that?" I said, working to keep my tone casual. Friendly.

The driver. A passenger.

"A friendly place," she answered. "Mate, I'm knackered.

I've got a headache. I'm not the least bit interested."

She nervously tucked her hair behind her ears, and reached down to paw through her purse. Her fingers found something in there and wrapped around it. Keys, if she was a smart girl. Something bigger and sharper if she was a fucking genius.

"That's all right," I said. "You don't have to be in a friendly place. I'm in a place friendly enough for the both of us. All you have to do is keep talking to me all casual-like until I figure out a game plan."

Her eyes went dark when I said it. I don't know what she thought I meant, but hell, if an asshole that looked like me sat across from *me* and said something like that, I'd be worried, too. She shifted the purse over a bit, getting ready to whip out whatever was in there.

"See," I continued—*super big smile, hushed, friendly tone, all buds here*—"you're worried about me, and that's fine. I'm downright worrisome. That's what my mom always said. But you and me share a bigger problem right now."

Her eyebrows knit together. She was actually kind of pretty when she was preoccupied like this, trying to decide between confusion and rage.

"Which is?" she asked.

"When I got onto this bus, I paid the driver and bumped into a passenger. That's exactly how I thought of them: *The driver, a passenger.* Now, I'm a few beers deep into what I call 'a working drunk,' and I'm not the sharpest knife in the rack on my best days, but I've learned to be pretty good with faces. I'm sitting here, trying to figure out—why did I think of them like that? I didn't see a fat lady, or a black guy, just 'a driver,' and 'a passenger.' I'm looking for them right now, hard as I can, and I can't seem to find them."

"I think you're a bit past 'working drunk,' mate."

"Just do me a favor. Real quick. Do this one thing for me and I'll get up, stumble up front and fall out at the next stop."

"What's this favor, then?" she said, clearly expecting me to suggest some lewd sexual act.

"Take a good look around at our fellow passengers, and tell me anything about any one of them. Something specific—what color their hair is, their race, if they got stuff stuck in their teeth—anything at all."

She looked around dutifully. Her hair slipped from behind her ears and fell about her rapidly widening eyes.

"No? Nothing?" I said, "Well, let's try something easier—tell me how many of them there are. . . ."

She was silent.

"I can't count them, either, but it looks like a hell of a lot, to me."

The cheesy smile was starting to hurt my face, and I guess I don't have a lot of practice at faking small talk, because we were starting to gather some unwanted attention. I couldn't pick out details on their faces, but I could tell they were all pointing at us now.

"I know this is going to sound crazy," I said, "but I think we're the only people on this bus."

"Bollocks," she said.

"No, it's true—" I started, but she cut me off.

"Bollocks! I just had to go and get on a bloody bus full of Faceless, didn't I?"

"Wha—You know about them?"

She shoved me out of my chair and stood up, pulling her hands out of her purse. I saw what she'd been holding onto in there: two sets of viciously spiked brass knuckles, one wrapped around each fist.

She was a fucking genius!

FIVE

2013. Tucson, Arizona. Kaitlyn.

Sometime around 4:00 A.M., I slipped into a sort of hypnotic state. The channel I'd left the TV on started playing back-to-back infomercials around two in the morning, and the easy cadence of the host's pitch-voice mesmerized me. I watched the light around me change from the diffused harsh white of a parking lot streetlamp, to the hazy crimson of sunrise, to the muffled clarity of day. Whatever the source, the light always felt suppressed. Probably because it had to filter through two sets of thick, scratchy motel curtains, and had an even harder time squirming past my itchy, burning eyes and into my muddled brain.

I was pretty rough on my body back home, doing grunt-level stunt work on whatever B-movie was willing to hire me. I had shattered elbows, broken teeth, twisted fingers, and sprained knees. But I always came home to my bed, which had a truly excessive California King memory foam mattress. It filled every inch of my room, which was my sleeping space, and only my sleeping space. I *adored* my sleep. I could come home limping, picking sugar-glass out of my hair, covered in fake, caked-on blood, and it just didn't matter. Because I knew I could always swing open my bedroom door and fall facefirst into a deep syrupy slumber, my body utterly absorbed by that gorgeous hedonistic slab of heaven. Down comforters. Big fluffy pillows. It was the one thing I had.

Now I slept in musty hotel beds with springs poking through the fabric, dried blood—not mine—on the jagged ends. Probably some sort of exotic mite infestation in the fabric. A whole alphabet of hepatitis just waiting for me to snuggle on up.

Wait, no, I'm being unfair: I didn't sleep in them at all.

Another night gone. How long can a human being function without sleep?

I thought I heard somewhere that a person can only take a week of sleeplessness before insanity sets in. That's probably a rumor or something, right? Yeah, it's like "mixing Pop Rocks and Coke will kill you." Just stuff kids say to each other because school is boring and lies are fun.

It has to be.

I mean, look at me. I wasn't crazy. And I hadn't slept for a second since that night three weeks ago, when I dive-tackled the angel—when I leapt headfirst into a ball of sentient light that was burning my best friend's brain from the inside out. I don't remember much of what happened to me in there, just a few vague notions. A feeling of misplaced nostalgia, like re-watching a show you loved as a kid only to realize, as an adult, that it's total garbage. A void. Whiteness. The number six?

And then I woke up in my apartment, and heard Carey and Jackie laughing in the living room. I thought we beat them. We won. I forgot about Marco for one beautiful, simple afternoon.

Then he started sending the Unnoticeables after us. A guy from the gas company knocked on my door, all bureaucratic smiles and shrugged apologies. I let him into my apartment—he had the paperwork. I didn't read it, but it was paperwork. You don't have that stuff unless you mean business. He needed to do an inspection. There was a leak. He made it all the way to my bedroom before Carey flushed the toilet, came out of my bathroom, spotted the guy, and stomped his head into pieces all over my hallway.

We ran, after that.

We'd been running ever since. We holed up at a friend of Jackie's house at first, until her friend went to the kitchen to make dinner and Carey asked Jackie what her good friend looked like. She couldn't remember.

We burned the place down to cover our tracks. It was shitty motels and sleeping in the car ever since.

Haha. Sleeping.

It was me, staring at the clock on the dashboard, watching the glowing green digits tick over one by one while Carey snored in the passenger seat and Jackie kicked my chair, trying to get comfortable in the back.

It was nighttime TV. Watching until the channels ran out of programming and just started playing terrible orchestral music and pictures of waving flags. It was flipping to deep cable, and rewatching cheap action flicks.

I watched every Van Damme movie ever made. They were all on TBS. He did the splits in every single one. Even if it wasn't appropriate, even if he was just standing in the kitchen in his underwear, a bad guy would run in with a Taser and they would find a way to make Van Damme do the splits.

I saw it so many times, I could write a thesis on it: *The*

lateral extension of Belgian appendages in male power fantasies and its greater impact on archetypal roles in society.

That was where we were now. But that didn't answer the question: Where did it go wrong? It started with Marco, but did it end there? Thinking back, I'm pretty sure it was Jackie who first asked him to take me home. I don't think it was his idea. What if she had never asked? Would we still be here? What if I had said no? What if . . . God, I shouldn't even think it—what if I hadn't gone looking for Jackie? What if I'd taken the hint at the police station and let it drop? What if I hadn't chased Marco when he showed up at my apartment that night? What if . . . what if I'd seen Jackie being hollowed out, and I didn't help her? What if I had just run?

Nobody could have blamed me. Most people, I think, would have bolted. It's too much to handle: caustic monsters; immortal, soulless things that only look like people; girls being mashed into jelly by giant gears; angels that rearrange people's souls, getting rid of the pesky inefficiencies like humanity and morality and personality, and burning everything human away, like fuel. That's enough. That's enough to break somebody's mind and send them running for the hills, no matter who might die because of it.

I should have run. But I didn't. I turned, and I jumped headfirst into the burning ball of light.

Why the hell did I do that?

But here's the really disturbing question, the one I really don't want to ask, the one that keeps me up at night, desperately trying not to answer it:

How did they know I was going to do that?

The Empty Ones, the other things like Marco standing around in the church that night—they were all waiting for me to do it. They celebrated when it happened. That's what Jackie and Carey said. They flipped out. They clapped with their bloody hands and cheered with their broken mouths. They wanted me to do it. No, they didn't just want it: They knew it would happen.

But it was such a stupid thing for me to do. How could they possibly count on it?

I knew the answer. I could feel it creeping up on me like some big, unseen predator. I couldn't fend it off forever. I sat there running down recent history, night after night, like I could have found the answer in those events. But that wasn't right, because it didn't start with Marco. It started a long time ago. It started the night of the fire. The night my sister died, and I saw—

"The fuck off my stuff!" Carey hollered, bolting awake.

He looked around the room with sleep-blurred eyes, expecting to see another hobo making off with his shoes, or his booze, or his shopping cart full of recycling, or whatever it was he valued. When he didn't find one, he turned and spat on the floor, then rubbed his tongue against his filthy T-shirt.

"Gross, dude, come on," I said.

"What?" he asked, with utter innocence.

"You can't just spit on the floor."

"Haha, yeah? That's what you're worried about? You know how many truckers fucked some cheap trick right there, on that exact spot? That's pretty much all places like these are used for. I bet somebody even died there. I bet somebody died there *while* getting fucked by a trucker. My spit is the cleanest thing that will ever touch that carpet. My spit is practically shampoo, as far as this poor bastard carpet is concerned."

"You believe all that, and you still slept there?" I watched Carey executing his morning wake-up routine: A series of stretches, like hobo yoga, seemingly designed to get the kinks out after sleeping a night on rough, flat ground. It was punctuated by occasional coughing fits and some gagging.

"'Slept' is a stretch. I passed out here. And sweetheart, I have passed out on far worse. I once passed out on top of a sick horse, when I woke up there was this black spray ev—"

"God! No! I do not want to hear any of that!" I threw the pillow I'd been clutching between my knees at his head.

He was far too slow to duck it. He laughed after it hit him, then you could practically see the room swim behind his eyes, and he crawled desperately toward the bathroom. He bumped Jackie's leg as he crawled over her. She stirred.

"Noooo," she groaned. "Just noooo."

"Wake up, sleeping beauty," I said. "You've probably got super-lice from sleeping on that floor."

"What? Dammit!" Jackie jumped to her feet and fell facefirst on the bed. "Why did you let me sleep on the floor?"

"Let you?"

We both tried to ignore Carey dry-heaving in the other room.

"If it was you, I would have dragged you up onto the bed," Jackie said. She tried to slap at me, but was unwilling to open her eyes. She missed by a mile.

"No you wouldn't." I'd had the TV on so long I stopped noticing the sounds it made. It was playing cartoons now. Maybe it was Saturday.

"I would too," Jackie protested. "I would have tucked you in and brought you water and bacon, a cool compress for your fevered forehead . . ."

"A nice tall glass of straight vodka," I filled in for her,

and she groaned. "Some cottage cheese, maybe a side of raw salmon . . ."

I started bouncing in place on the bed.

"God damn you," Jackie spat, and stumbled wildly into the bathroom. There was a commotion as she and Carey fought for the toilet. I turned the TV up. I didn't need to hear the details. It was playing some crazy anime thing. All children screaming and rapid flashing— something about collecting a bunch of Super-Tongpus to defeat the Octopus Who Lives at the End of Time or other such nonsense.

I shouldn't have taunted Jackie like that. She wouldn't be mad at me or anything—she does worse to me all the time—but I needed her in good shape this morning. I needed both of them as clear as possible. I'd had nothing to do all night but listen to the pair of them snore, and think. I came to some conclusions. Serious ones, and we needed to talk about them as soon as possible. I couldn't do that if she and Carey spent all morning fighting for toilet space and yelling for me to go get them increasingly stupid hangover cures.

"Kate," Carey yelled, as if on cue, "run down to the corner store and buy us a loaf of plain white bread."

"No," Jackie slumped backwards against the bathroom door and made a valiant effort to look in my general direction. It was a failed effort, but she made it. "No bread. Meat. Get beef jerky and, like, the biggest thing of water. Do they sell barrels? Buy me a barrel of water."

"Make it two barrels," Carey added, "and the bread. And a tallboy of PBR."

"I'm not going to the store," I said, and they both instantly started whining like children being denied a snow day.

"But I'll tell you what: If you get yourselves together enough to move, I'll buy you both breakfast at that shitty diner across the street."

"Oof. Moving," Jackie said.

"They'll have bacon," I told her, then to Carey: "And bread, and unlimited tap water. Sweet, sweet tap water."

The Bearly There Diner seemed to have been based entirely on bear puns, and not at all on food, service, or atmosphere. It looked like a hunting lodge drawn in crayon by a meth fiend. Our waitress was named Sally, and she looked like she'd been born an orphan, got divorced this morning, and accidentally backed over her cat on the way to work. She had deep frown lines etched permanently into her face, and big, watery gray eyes. But then she opened her mouth, and it was all bubbling enthusiasm and "honeys" and "sweethearts." She looked like that sad donkey from Winnie the Pooh got his wish and became a real person—but she was friendly, happy, and very understanding about hangovers.

She brought water, first thing, without even being asked.

Carey hadn't stopped talking about wanting to fuck her since. Jackie joined him, after Sally set an extra-large plate of bacon down in front of her with a knowing wink. I let them get a few mouthfuls in before I started:

"We're going to Mexico," I said.

Jackie blinked, but continued silently tucking neatly folded wads of bacon into her mouth.

"Fuckin' A," Carey said. "About time we got serious about the fugitive life. We'll head down south. Pound cervezas on the beach and throw bottles at the tourists."

"We're going to Mexico because Marco's down there," I said.

"How do you know that?" Jackie asked, barely audible through a mouthful of fried meat.

"I saw him on TV last night. He was talking about a new show he's filming right now in his home town. Tulancingo, I think it was called."

I sipped my watery coffee. At least it was hot. At least it was caffeine.

"Why do you want to *find* Marco? All we've been doing the past few weeks is trying to put as much distance between us and him as possible. Those schoolgirl hots come back or what?"

"I haven't slept in weeks, Jackie. Not since . . . whatever it was that happened in that church. I can't do it anymore. I can't keep running. I need it to end."

I fixed my weariest stare on her. I wanted to let her feel how utterly beaten I was. I put all of my exhaustion, fear, resignation, and hopelessness into my eyes. I needed her to look, really look, and understand how raw I was—realize that I had considered every option and settled on this only as a last resort.

"You're serious?" Jackie asked.

"I am. This isn't going to stop. Not on its own—that much has become clear. If we ever want to have anything like a normal life again, we can't just hope they forget about us. We killed their god, or whatever that ball of light was to them. People don't generally just let that type of thing go."

"But that can be good too," Jackie said. "I mean, yeah, they'll hunt you to the ends of the Earth and beyond, hoping to pull out your guts and hang you with them while—"

"Jesus, Jackie." I set down my coffee, momentarily

overcome by the mental images.

"But I'm saying: You killing their god pisses them off, sure, but it leaves them directionless too, right? I don't remember much, but Carey said that Marco was taking orders from some chubby guy, that night in the church. That dude made like Silly Putty in a microwave when you nuked the angel. Say what you want about him—he's a freak, a pervert, an inhuman monster with absolutely killer abs—but Marco does not strike me as the thinking or leading type."

"But what about . . ." I started to protest, but couldn't come up with anything.

Why couldn't this be the end of it? Who says I didn't already win the big boss fight, and now it's just a matter of cleaning up the little guys?

When Marco first started coming after me and Jackie, his little band of freaks wouldn't shut up about gears and angels and the turning of the universe. Crazy, pretentious gibberish, obviously, but at least it all sounded like real big picture stuff. The Unnoticeables we'd seen since the angel died hadn't said anything like that. They just seemed to want us dead. I'll admit it: At first, I just wanted to go after Marco as the last act of a desperate woman. If only because death sounded pretty close to sleep, and I could sure use a nap. But now, I was starting to think we had a chance. Then something occurred to me that I should have thought of sooner.

"Carey," I said. He stopped ogling Sally the Saddest Waitress's saggy ass to point his bloodshot eyes in my direction. "Why did Marco let me live, after I took out the angel? You said he wasn't hurt when the angel went up, and it's not like any of us were in any shape to fight after that. Why not just kill me then and there?"

"He ran," Carey said. "After the angel shattered like a dropped disco ball and his psychopath pals starting melting, Marco took one look at you, screamed like a little girl, and ran away as fast as he could."

I didn't have anything to say. Jackie smiled, then it spread to Carey.

"Wow," I finally managed, and downed the rest of my mug of what I could only call "flat coffee."

"Let's do it, then," Carey said, waving Sally over for either the check or a filthy proposition. "Let's go kick the devil's ass."

SIX

There were two Unnoticeables coming toward us down the aisle from the front of the bus, a couple more from the rear, and maybe a half dozen still in their seats and just starting to move. The girl with the striped leggings was fixing the ones ahead of us with a stare like Clint Eastwood after somebody shat in his cornflakes, which I guess left me with the ones behind. I uncapped the hair spray I'd lifted from the girl at the Rainbow and flicked my scarred and singed bumblebee Zippo once, twice. On the third time it caught. I tried to think of something clever to say to the blurry face nearest me, but I wound up going with "Here's fire in your face, fucker."

I hit the little tab and shot out a fucking monumental gout of flame. It was like watching a volcano orgasm.

Holy shit, girls put this crap on their heads?!

The Unnoticeable on the left seemed more startled than hurt, but the one on the right was wearing some bullshit polyester disco blouse. He lit up like a roman candle.

Serves you right for having no class, you molten bastard.

I turned around to reap some cool points with the little

punk rock chick, only to find that she'd already bashed one of her guys' heads nearly off his neck and had the other in a leg lock, using her brass knuckles to pummel him into a refreshing mist.

I would not be scoring anything today.

Somebody seized my arms from behind, and the can and lighter scattered down the aisle.

Oh right, the other one.

I tried to get my feet up to kick off of one of the benches, but the guy was strong. He was hefting me right up into the air, and I couldn't find purchase. He couldn't hurt me without letting me go, and I couldn't do anything to get away until he did. It was a stalemate. But his eraser-faced buddies were coming to break it for us. An old lady to my left with a ratty gray shawl; a muscle-bound guy in a too-tight tank top to my right. They were closing in, and all I could do was flail and kick at the open air.

Then the girl saw us, dropped the Unnoticeable whose face she'd turned into a meaty pudding, and came hurtling down the aisle like a bowling ball. She scattered the old lady and knocked the 'roid-head down so hard he left a dent in the metal pole with his skull.

Nobody is that strong. Much less this short, chubby, couldn't-be-more-than-seventeen-year-old chick. What the hell is going on? Oh shit, is she going to . . . ?

I ducked just in time as she sent a full-body rocketing jump kick into the guy holding me. I hope he enjoyed the time he'd spent with his ribcage, because those days were over. The few faceless passengers left didn't look afraid, exactly, but even they seemed to acknowledge that they wouldn't be taking us in a fistfight. Still, the driver showed no signs of slowing, and there was no way to the doors without wading through the bastards.

"Up the stairs," the girl in the striped leggings said, to the empty air.

I'm no dope; I was halfway up them before she opened her mouth. The second I crested that last stair I was looking for an emergency exit, which I guess was stupid. Even if they installed doors on the second floor of a city bus for the more thrill-seeking passengers, what were we gonna do? Jump off the second story of a speeding bus onto another car?

Holy shit, how cool would that be?

The girl came booking up the steps a moment later. She wasn't much to look at before, and now her spiked brass knuckles were dripping blood, her clothes were ripped, and I think she had somebody's ear sticking to her shoulder. She was getting hotter by the minute.

"Here, kick out this window and let's jump off the second story of this speeding bus onto another car," I told her. "It will be amazing."

Stop: I'm not a psychopath. I mean, I'm kind of an idiot, but I am aware of the limits of the human body—especially *my* cruddy human body—and though I frequently ignore them (because they're bullshit), I'm not suicidal. Sometimes, when things look bad, I suggest the stupidest plan I can think of, because the people around me will always roll their eyes, call me a retard, and then suggest a better one.

"Sounds good," the girl in the striped leggings said.

It is so goddamned unfair that I'm going to die on the day I meet my second *soulmate.*

She was trying to get the right footing to bash out the glass when I spotted a pair of owl's eyes in the dark outside the bus. Two darting little lights swerving erratically and quickly toward us.

"Down!" I said, though that was redundant, because I was already tackling her.

We both hit the floor, me on top of her. I managed to get my arms and legs hastily wrapped around the benches in front of and behind us. I barely had enough time to register how her tits felt pressed against my chest (pretty good!) before the car T-boned us, and the speeding bus wobbled crazily up onto two wheels. It rocked back the other way, and I could hear shouts from below as the Unnoticeables were whipped into the walls. Then the wheels caught, and the world went sideways.

I didn't actually manage to hold on to both of us through the whole crash. I would love to say that I did, and that I saved us both, and that the girl took off her shirt and jumped around in pure giddy celebration at the gift of life I'd bestowed on her, before giving me a hand job with the brass knuckles still on, which is a weird thing I'm apparently into—

I got slapped awake.

A guy with an Elvis sneer and a hot pink T-shirt with the words LEFT IS RIGHT across the front was staring down at me. He smiled when I opened my eyes. Well, the one that worked, anyway.

"Get up," Randall said. "Time to run."

"Fuck you," I answered, more by reflex than anything else. "Do I even have legs anymore? Where's the girl?"

"My name is Meryll, I'm right here, and I'm not bloody carrying you any farther, so get up."

One of her arms looked bent a bit funny, but she was apparently in good enough shape to haul me out of the wreckage of that bus. I was laid out by the side of the street, propped up against a little aluminum food cart that smelled like fish farts. I tested my limbs one by one. They weren't happy about it, but they worked. I held out a hand for Randall to help me up. He high-fived me.

Bastard.

I got to my feet. Behind us, the double-decker bus had mostly merged with a smear of blue plastic that I could only guess had once been the car Randall used to ram it.

"How the hell did you survive that?" I asked him.

"I just bailed before it hit," he said, and showed me a pair of scraped and bloody elbows. "Always wanted to do that. I uh . . . I wouldn't advise it."

Meryll laughed, that lilting girlish laugh that sounds too good to be genuine.

"Hi," Randall said to her, after being reminded of her existence. "Randall."

"I'm Meryll—oh, but I just said that! How funny." She laughed again.

God damn it, Randall, I heroically pancake a girl in a bus crash and you still stroll in to snake her from me.

"I like your shirt," Meryll said. Suddenly all bashful and girlish and awkward.

"Thanks," Randall said. "I got it off a dead guy."

She laughed that show-laugh.

Why do chicks always find his accuracy and honesty so hilarious? I helped him yank that damn thing off the corpse myself. He hasn't even washed it yet.

"Hey," I said, sick of the show, "aren't we running for our lives right now? 'Cause it looks like the fuckin' eighth-grade prom out here."

Randall shrugged and looked around, trying to get his bearings. Meryll didn't say anything, but the death glare she fixed me with said a bunch of nasty stuff about my mom.

"I have no idea where we are," Randall finally admitted.

"I think just 'away' is good enough for now," I said.

"I've got a place," Meryll said. "It's safe. Well, safe as you can get these days, anyway. We just have to get to the Underground. Come on."

She set off down a mostly submerged sidewalk, each stomp of her big burly boots sending up watery haloes. Randall smelled girl-meat, so he happily went jogging right after it. I took some time to sulk about how little recognition I was getting for saving the day and nearly getting myself killed in the process. Well, myself and others, I guess. I nursed my wounded pride for a solid five seconds before it got boring, then limped along in the lovebirds' wake.

"—ever met somebody you forget while you're still looking at 'em? Sure, sometimes those are just dreary numbskulls talking about the weather, but sometimes they're what we call . . ."

I'd apparently caught up right as Randall was launching into Monster 101.

"Faceless. Yeah, we got those here too."

"Shit," Randall blinked. "That is a way better name. We call 'em Unnoticeables. You know about them?"

"You could say that," Meryll said.

She was walking a bit too close to Randall for him being a total stranger. Maybe it was the rain, or maybe it was a cultural thing, or maybe she wanted to twirl about on his dick like a helicopter.

The bastard.

"Well, that's not the end of it; there's these big black things—"

"The Sludge," Meryll finished, laughing. "What do you call them, Tar Babies?"

"N-no . . ." Randall protested. But he didn't tell her what

we do call them. Probably too embarrassed. So I helped him out.

"We call 'em tar men," I said, and Meryll snickered again. "Pretty sure it was Randall came up with that name."

He glared at me; she avoided eye contact altogether. Stared down at the sloshing urban sea beneath our feet.

"I, uh . . ." Randall was defused, all hands-in-pockets awkward now. "You know about the rest too?"

Meryll nodded. "There's the Husks, the ones that look like people with normal faces and voices and all that, but they got no life in their eyes. And the Flares."

"The Flares?" I butted in. "That's new. I don't think we have those."

"They're the big baddies," Meryll said. "They start it all. There's not much to them, just a big bright empty spot in your eyes, and static."

"Oh," Randall said. "The angels."

Meryll stopped so quick I ran into her from behind. I didn't even have time to cop a quick feel before she wheeled on Randall. "Angels? You call them fucking angels? Jesus, but you Yanks really are stupid. They're not angels. They're not anything like angels. They're pure bloody evil, through and through. At least with the Faceless and the Sludge and the Husks, they got something they want. Maybe that's just to snatch you up, or melt you, or fuck your eyeholes from the inside out—but it's still an agenda. The Flares don't want a thing. There's no reason to them, no telling what they'll do or why—they show up, and people just stop being and then they're gone, and they don't even care. They're the farthest thing from fucking angels you could possibly get. Jackass."

Randall was holding his hands up like an old-timey bank robber, trying to figure out how to apologize for something he didn't understand that he'd done.

"I think it's ironic," I said, not trying to help. "Like calling a big guy 'Tiny.'"

Meryll glared burning holes into my brain.

"Randall named them, too," I said.

He started to say something, decided on a more effective means of communication, and slapped me upside the head instead. I jumped up to get a headlock on him and we tumbled into the flooded gutter. I pushed his head down— you know, just a bit of playful drowning—and the dickhead punched me in the kidneys. Totally uncalled for.

"Idiots!" Meryll shouted, booting me in the side.

Oh hey, wonder why you didn't kick pretty lil' Randall with those fucking hobnails?

"Couple of drooling damned cavemen, playing grabass when an army of Faceless are probably on their way here right now."

"Relax," I said, dragging my thoroughly soaked butt out of the chilly, greasy water. "They're not exactly the Green Berets. Got no organization. They usually just go away for a while after a good old-fashioned ass kicking."

"Maybe where you're from," Meryll said, and she—*you won't believe this shit*—she offered her hand to help Randall out of the puddle.

And he fucking took it!

"They've got their act together on this side of the pond. If you see one, there are more around. If you get away from them, you've got a bloody army coming your way. So would you two morons"—she shook Randall's hand away, a little display of self-conscious toughness—"put off humping each other long enough for us to get somewhere safe?"

"I'll try," Randall said, sheepish grin nudging its way

onto his face. "But you see the way he's dressed. He's asking for it."

Meryll laughed. I gave him the finger. He gave me two back. I went to unzip my fly, and Meryll rolled her eyes and walked away.

It was a few biblically flooded blocks to the train station. I wasn't much interested in watching their foreplay, so I hung back out of earshot. Either Randall was killing it, or Meryll was harder up than I could have imagined. She laughed at every other word out of his mouth. They bumped into each other a little more than Randall's six-beer buzz would account for. If they hadn't just met in a brutal bus wreck after nearly getting abducted by faceless attackers, the scene would be downright romantic.

I turned my head to look at a chick passing by on the other side of the street—*damn the hippie movement all you like, but I'm all for the lack of bras*—and when I looked back, Randall and Meryll were gone. Just vanished. My guts clenched up and I went into fight mode, looking around for body snatchers. I didn't find any. I jogged up to where I'd last seen them and spotted the culprit: A set of stairs, each a tiny waterfall in this downpour, leading down to the trains. They were halfway to the landing already. I thought about riding the wet railing all the way to the bottom just to beat them there—*surely that'll prove me a worthy lay*—but my hip and shoulder throbbed just thinking about taking another fall. I decided to walk instead.

Must be getting old.

The stairs were slick, and the torrent of water pouring down from above made just keeping on your feet a chore. It took forever to get to the bottom, and my hip ached with every awkward step. I thought I'd probably lost Meryll and

Randall in the crowd—there weren't many people up on the street, but this was still New Year's Eve in London; the tube *had* to be crowded—but no such luck. They were stopped right there in front of me, blocking the stairs. They were staring at a solid wall of punks. The whole station standing room only, and every last occupant was wet and nasty and riding the climax of an amped-up drunk.

The fucking show had just let out. I had forgotten all about it. And judging by the impending violence in the air, The Ramones had either done the best set of their lives, or personally pissed in the nostrils of every one of their fans on their way out the door.

It was mostly reflex. I can't see a crowd and not look for things I'm not supposed to look for—the faces I skip over, the people I forget, the overpowering urge toward inattention. I couldn't pick out individuals. There were too many people, too much anonymity—but I recognized that feeling in the pit of my stomach. Those hairs on the back of my neck.

We were stuck underground in a dismal concrete cave rapidly filling with water, surrounded on all sides by pissed-off punk rockers itching for a fight, and at least some of them were Unnoticeables. And we had to wade right through it all to get to the train.

Well, only one thing to do, really.

"Let's start a riot," I said to Randall's back.

He turned around to look at me, feigning shock for the benefit of the girl.

You goddamned phony. Wait until the punches start flying and you just fuckin' try not to have some fun.

"Hell of a show, right?" I practically screamed it, at a slab of beef wrapped in a leather jacket with a picture of the queen on the back. Her eyes were blacked out and somebody had drawn a crude dick slapping against her mouth.

"Fuckin' right," he answered. And that was all I needed to know: English accent.

"There's nothing like good old-fashioned American rock and roll," I said, feeling a twinge of mania building in my chest.

You are my favorite vice, adrenaline. Well, behind beer. And whiskey. And sex. But definitely ahead of cigarettes. Okay, maybe slightly behind cigarettes—but only slightly.

"Some of it's pretty good, yeah," the slab of meat agreed, hesitantly.

"I mean, what's it got?" I turned to Randall, snapping my fingers, looking for help with the word. "What am I thinking of, that American rock has and British doesn't?"

He glanced over to Meryll, who shook her head. My heart sank. I was going to have to do this one my own.

I was turning back when I heard him chime in: "Authenticity," Randall said.

I smiled with every inch of my face. "Thaaaat's it. It's got fuckin' *authenticity.*"

The slab of meat was making a face like he was trying to hold in farts with his mouth.

"Not like this British bullshit," I said, louder and louder, "all wrapped in politics, tryin' to pretend they're about something they ain't. It's pretty . . . what's the word?" I snapped my fingers again, not looking back.

"Pretentious," Randall supplied happily. I could hear Meryll sigh.

Ooh, we had an audience now. All eyes watching, even the ones too far away to hear the conversation. They could just feel it crackling in the air. Confrontation. Sweet lady fistfight dancing around in her low-cut shirt. Everybody just watching, hypnotized, wondering when something was gonna pop out.

"You don't know what the fuck you're talking about, mate," slab of meat said, and tried to turn away.

What the hell, man? Nobody that big and ugly gets to be a pacifist.

"You motherfuckers should get down on your knees and give us Americans a nice, wet, sloppy blow job of gratitude for inventing punk in the first place. Gave you lovely boys an excuse to play dress up for a while."

Slab of meat swiveled around slowly. I could see him trying to process what he was hearing—*Surely nobody is this stupid? Couldn't he see he has a whole train station of pissed-off drunken English punks in front of me? I'll never live it down if I don't kick his ass now.* By the time he'd wobbled all the way about to lock eyes with me, I could see the resignation in him. He'd run the scenarios, and there was no way he was getting out of this without punching me in the face.

My hip throbbed. My shoulder ached. I really hoped I could at least keep my feet.

Motherfucker hit me like a rocket ship.

I have no idea what happened next, exactly. I picture myself flying cartoonishly through the air, body stiff as a board, hitting the ground and sliding to a stop, my head pushing up a little mound of dirt that covers my body, then a little gravestone and a pretty white flower popping up above the spot where I finally settle.

You're never knocked out for long. Movies get that shit wrong. It's a second or two if it's anything, but by the time I opened my eyes, the train station had already gone full Vietnam.

Randall had slab of meat in a leg lock, and was pounding

on his thick white dome with both fists. I couldn't see Meryll, but there was a section of crowd substantially more screamy than the rest, so I assumed she was there. A busty blonde arced up out of that spot like a bottle rocket and slammed into the concrete next to me. Her leather jacket was open to the waist, and she wasn't wearing anything underneath. I could vouch for that, because she rolled straight out of it when she landed, and just sat there, tits-a-heaving, a big red welt already covering half of her face.

Holy shit, Meryll, you slapped that girl topless.

I jumped to my feet, intending to get a bit of momentum for a nice, hearty two-footed dropkick.

Gotta make an entrance.

But my body had other ideas. My hip flared, the world swam, and I fell straight on my face. I tried to rally my balance, but no luck. I settled for a slow crawl instead, and started biting knees. It was not going to be a dignified night.

I sunk my teeth into some stovepipe jeans that tasted like fried chicken and motor oil. There was a yelp and a swat from above, so I moved on to the next. Loose black trousers. Recently washed. They tasted a little like detergent, but were otherwise a pleasure to bite into. I felt blood well into my mouth, and spat it out right onto the trousers' bright white loafers.

"Aw, my damn shoes!" somebody moaned.

I moved on. Bit into a couple more greasy blue jeans; bit into a bandana with the Jolly Roger flag on it; bit into a nice bare kneecap under a dark purple skirt (but not before stealing a quick look). I caught a couple of knees to the head and got hit with a few decent smacks, but everybody's mind was mostly on the greater riot. I went largely unnoticed, and chewed my way across the platform until I hit an empty space. I crawled out into the clearing on all fours, and saw a dozen swollen punks trying to leave plenty of space between Meryll's fists and their faces. She was squaring off in a vaguely kung-fu stance, but you could tell it was more an impersonation of Bruce Lee flicks than any actual training. Still, she'd provided plenty of evidence of ass kicking, and nobody seemed in much more need of convincing.

"I'm sorry," said a voice like gravy thickened with sawdust. "Stop! Please stop!"

It was the slab of meat. Peering through the gaps in the crowd, I could see Randall still had him in that leg lock, and was drumming on his face with open hands now. Randall had his eyes closed, lost in the rhythm.

"Randall!" Meryll hollered. "Get over here. We gotta go before the Faceless get their shit together!"

No response. He was tweaking the slab of meat's cheeks now, laughing as the ugly man blubbered and squealed.

"Randall!" I tried. "Come on, man. Your pussy's getting cold."

He heard that.

He let the slab of meat go, and the guy seemed to think of reprisal for a second. Randall pointed sternly at the stairs, and the slab of meat slunk away like a chastised puppy.

Meryll was already making her way through the motley crew of beaten, bloody punks. They parted like the Red Sea. I crawled after her, trying to look like I just happened to be sauntering in the same direction . . . on all fours.

Who, me? Nah, I'm a fuckin' man. I ain't following some chick in the desperate hope she'll keep me safe. Just crawling over here to check out the newspapers. Grab the sports page. You see the game last night?

Nobody was buying it.

I wasn't really buying it either. With each shuffle my hip let out a dull, nauseating throb. I was getting dizzy, which was either from an acute lack of beer (ain't a good idea to stop drinking once you've gotten a nice running start at it), or maybe a mild concussion.

Do concussions come in "mild"?

Shit, even my thoughts are crawling. I zeroed in on Meryll's ass, giving myself a point of focus.

Just follow the ass. It will lead you to safety.

The ass was my everything. The world around it was turning fuzzy and red, but that didn't matter. The ass was all. The ass was me, and I was the ass. Its cheeks wobbled a bit with each footfall. Each step sent one buttock into the fabric of the miniskirt, highlighting its contours. The ass was confident. The ass was sure. The ass knew where it was going. The ass stopped, jiggled a bit, and then disappeared altogether. I was left alone in an assless world.

So this is what it feels like to lose your faith.

I blinked. I swallowed hard and looked around me. Meryll was gone.

Randall bumped into me from behind. Nearly sent me sprawling into the shadowy ditch directly in front of my filthy hands that I was just now noticing.

"Mary went down there?" Randall asked.

"Meryll," I corrected him. *The rat bastard.* "And I guess so. You first."

Me and Randall stood at the edge of the subway platform, unwilling or unable to move.

Do they even call them trains here? These Brits all have weird cutesy terms for normal shit. They probably call them "wonkers" or "moveys" or "side-lifts." I bet this is a "movey-cliff."

Concussion was seeming more and more likely.

We peered down the tracks in either direction, into the absolute darkness there.

Last year I threw a beer can at a living monster of tar because it cockblocked me, then jumped into a sewer to fight an immortal Iggy Pop wannabe. Just last week Randall trapped an Unnoticeable in a Dumpster and pushed it down a hill just because he thought it would be funny (it was).

We do not have a firm concept of mortal danger, is what I'm saying here.

But neither one of us wanted to jump down onto those tracks. Me and Randall and Jezza and Wash and the goddamned parasites used to get hammered at the South Loop some nights, but we knew that station was shut down. If there was any possibility a train could have come through there, we would've found a different drinking spot. Because, growing up in New York, every one of us had heard the stories: Some hobo pissed on the rail and got himself electrocuted. Some stoned girl passed out down there and they had to identify her by the teeth they picked out of the wheels. A secretary slipped and fell right as the train was coming in. It split her in half, and then stopped right on top of her. They couldn't move it or her guts would spill out. They brought her family in to say good-bye first.

Who knows if that shit is true? But you hear it enough as a kid that it gets inside you.

Staring into the darkness there, I couldn't help but think a train was idling just out of sight, sitting with its lights off, waiting for me to jump down so it could cut my damn legs off.

"What are you boys scared of, ruffling your Sunday best? Let's fucking go, already," Meryll said.

She was straddling the tracks and looking up at us with disapproval.

"Maybe we'll just keep kicking these guys' asses," I suggested, helpfully.

Meryll scoffed.

"Carey, I think we should go," Randall said. He hopped down onto the tracks and instantly looked like he was gonna be sick.

"What, really?"

"Look behind you," he said, already backing away toward the westbound tunnel.

I knew it was standing-room-only at this station. I expected to see a few score of pissed-off punks waiting to give me a firm kick in the ass. I turned my head, though every inch hurt, and behind me I saw . . . nothing. A blank wall of disinterest. It felt like looking at fifty solid feet of DMV pamphlets. I couldn't have paid attention if I tried. There were dozens upon dozens of faces staring at me, and I couldn't make out a single one. They must have been pushing up past the normals this whole time, just behind us.

Meryll was not kidding.

The Unnoticeables were different here. Back home they accepted a good beating with grace and tended to scatter. Here, they went and got reinforcements.

I flung myself down onto the tracks headfirst. I hit my back on one of the rails, and the irrational fear grabbed me instantly.

You're paralyzed. Just gotta wait here for a train here to pop you like a goddamned sausage.

But no. Gun beats knife. Rock beats scissors. Adrenaline beats pain. I got up. I stumbled a little when I first put weight on my bad hip, but it held, and I started running. Straight into the darkness of the westbound tunnel—which I now saw, too late, was moving.

"Tar men!" I yelled.

Randall pulled up short just this side of where the lights went out. But Meryll was already in there. I hobbled up beside Randall, and noticed he wasn't staring at the wriggling dark. He was staring back over my shoulder.

The Unnoticeables had made it through the crowd, and were just standing there in a line, toes at the edge of the train platform. Dozens of them, still and silent. Shoulder to shoulder. A shifting mass of blank faces. I couldn't even tell you if they were watching us.

They were waiting. They knew it. There was nowhere left for us to go.

"A trap, then?" Randall spat. "Pretentious bullshit. What is this Sherlock Holmes crap? Who sets fucking *traps*?"

"I don't think it is," I said.

I stared at the shadows that Meryll had vanished into. She hadn't shouted, hadn't sworn or screamed. I couldn't tell if that was a good sign, or a very bad one.

"What do you mean?" Randall said. "If this isn't a trap, then, what, there's just so many of these things down here that you can wander into any random train station and trip over a small army of the bastards?"

"Yeah, pretty much."

"Oh. Shit. I liked it better when it was a trap."

"Me too."

"You uh . . . you think Marie's dead?"

"Meryll," I corrected him. *Again.* "And, yeah, probably."

I was locked onto one of the Unnoticeables' shoes. Hot pink with blue laces, like a little girl's. It was giving me a migraine just to keep them in focus. I inched my gaze up, keeping all my focus on just this one small part of the crowd. I made it to the knees, knobby and thin. The hem of a black pencil skirt. White blouse with tiny intertwining flowers. My eyes crawled all the way up to her face, and got just an impression—plain, mousy, maybe part-Indian or something—before my peripheral vision got caught on a little piece of the faceless crowd around her, and the whole thing washed out like the tide coming in on a sand castle.

"I think we have to go after her anyway," I said.

I turned to Randall. And he was gone.

"No shit," he yelled from somewhere in the dark. "What are you waiting for, a red carpet?"

God dammit, Randall. Making me look like a pussy in front of the girl.

It would be pretty generous to call what I did next "running." I mostly just fell in a forward direction and did my level best not to eat shit on the train tracks. The tunnel was black. Black like velvet. Textures in there somewhere. Things moving. Then, light. Faint, intermittent flashes. Little sparks, drifting on cold, damp air. Then one stopped in its arc, pulsed, and went supernova. There was a sound like a jet engine exploding in a day care, and I went from night-blind to staring at the sun.

The tar men were catching fire.

Another spark. Then nothing. Another and another, nothing and nothing. Then, finally, that old tea kettle scream, followed by a flash and a wave of warm air pressure. In the spastic light, I saw Meryll crouching beside the rails. Those nasty brass knuckles of hers on each hand. She held one fist blindly in front of her, trying to ward off something she couldn't see. The other was scraping along one of the rails, a hail of tiny sparks trailing after it. Most of them died out instantly—the dark ate them. Some survived for a crazy second or two, spiraling madly into the black before fading away. But if a spark got lucky, it perched itself on a solid, glistening patch of shadow, and it got to go out like a rock star: burning, screeching, putting its foot through the bass drum, shoving the guitar through the amps, hurling the mic stand out into the crowd, and just generally putting on a hell of a good show.

The burning tar man gave off a flickering light, turning reality into stop-motion. I could see it coming. Meryll could take down a few more of them, but there were hundreds of the damn things down here. It was standing room only for tar men. Their brass gears turned slowly in their faces, like they were thinking.

Spark. Steam whistle. Strobe.

A scene: Meryll with her teeth bared.

Black.

A scene: a glistening arm reaching for a young girl's neck.

Black.

A scene: dark, greasy fingers embedded in soft pink flesh.

Black.

A scene: melted skin running down a pale neck, pooling in the space between collarbones.

Black.

"Meryll!" I tried to hobble toward where I'd last seen her.

I wasn't sure what I was going to do when I got there, but I could at least ruin somebody's shirt with my liquidized flesh. I heard a thump, some swearing, another thump, and then a million-watt spotlight exploded to my left.

"Train!" I screamed, and threw myself to the ground.

"Get up, jackass!" Randall hollered. "Grab the girl, and let's go!"

No train. The million-watt spotlight was a waxy yellow

bulb suspended from the ceiling of the maintenance stairwell, which Randall had just kicked open the door to. In the weak and wobbling light, I could see Meryll crouching there, a tar man standing over her, its fingers sinking into her throat. I got a good hobbling start, slid to my knees beside her in the gravel, and reached into my hip pocket.

I would only have a second.

I pulled out my battle-scarred bumblebee Zippo, said a silent prayer to the lighter gods—*grant me fluid, though I have sinned and not bought any for weeks*—and flicked it open. I hit the wheel, and a teardrop of flame hovered there.

I made a mental note to come back down here after all this was over and see if I could find her again. You don't leave a good soldier behind.

I wrapped one arm around Meryll's waist and whipped the Zippo up toward the tar man's face. I dug my heels in. I heard the rumbling inhalation, felt the tar man's hand slacken, and pushed us away. We rolled to the side just as the fucker went up like a tenement building.

Don't look at her. It's not that bad. Just get her moving. Don't look.

I was dragging Meryll toward the stairwell. The tar man still burned, and by his light I could see the others, turning in slow motion, regarding us with those glinting gears.

I'm an idiot. I looked.

The burns looked more like they'd come from acid than flame. Raw, cauterized networks of pulp cut into her skin in the shape of a massive handprint. They were deep. The thumb crossed the artery in her neck on one side, sealing it shut. The pointer crossed the other.

Don't think about what that means. Just move.

We were out of the gravel, but moving slow. The burning

tar man had gone out. I couldn't see the others, but I knew they were there. We made it to the raised concrete platform. Just a few feet from the door now. Every inch of black in that dark tunnel reaching for us. I crossed the threshold backwards, dragging Meryll in front of me.

Okay, at least your ass is safe.

I had her almost entirely in the stairwell. *Just her ankles left out there—all right, those are in; now just get enough room for Randall to swing the door shut. Please don't let there be a big black hand reaching in here at the last second like some goddamned B-movie horror—*

And we're through.

Randall slammed the door and slid to the floor beside me. We both let out deep breaths we didn't know we'd been holding.

. . .

"Shit," he said.

"What?" I said.

"Do tar men know how to work doors?"

SEVEN

I flexed my sixth finger. I curled it into my palm as tightly as I could. I contorted it. I wiggled it. I could not get it to hurt. It's not like I missed the pain, but it had always been there for me. A constant. Something that would never leave me.

My apartment was gone.

I didn't own it or anything. By now the landlords would have rented it out again. Somebody else would be in my bedroom, sleeping where I slept and never thinking about the life I'd lived there. They would put the couch in a stupid place, and everything would face the TV, and they'd put plants on the sidewalk out front, and it would not be my home anymore.

All my stuff was gone.

It's not like we had time to pack a U-Haul. We left most of my things behind when we ran. My bed. My glorious, massive bed—so disproportionately huge that it literally filled every inch of the bedroom. You opened the door and had no choice but to crawl right into it. It was made entirely of foam, so it bent, but only under extreme duress. Jackie helped me move it in there. It took us two hours of wrestling. Toward the end, that got literal: Jackie slipped the last corner past the doorjamb with a flying elbow. We collapsed on the floor, laughing and covered in sweat.

I bet they threw it away. Those new tenants. Those invaders.

They probably chopped it up into little pieces to get it out, shoved it alongside the Dumpster with the broken box fans and old TVs.

My job was gone.

Fuck that job, anyway. It was just waiting tables, mostly for wannabe or has-been Hollywood types who tipped really well, but always made sure everybody at the table knew it. I wouldn't miss the job itself, but Carl, my boss—he was a great guy. He really wanted to be something like a vulgar father figure to me. To all of the waitresses, actually. Some guys are into that. Some girls, too. I was not. My dad was amazing. He died when I was a teenager, but he was there for me my whole life. I didn't need or want another dad, but Carl needed as many daughters as he could get. We didn't know if he actually had kids, or what. The other waitresses and I, we made up stories about sterility, tragic deaths, kidnappings gone wrong—romantic tales that justified his compulsive need to dote over young girls in his gruff, harrumphing way. I never played the role for him, but he was still nice to me.

My other job—my real job—was that gone too?

It was only ever freelance. That's the nature of stunt work. To be honest, I wasn't making much headway. I did my gigs well, better than most, but I was crap at networking. I can jump a flaming motorcycle into a helicopter on cue, but I can't schmooze. I never made enough connections to

get anything regular. I could probably pick it back up when
I got back home.

. . .

When?

If.

I spent the first few hours of the car ride pretending to
sleep. I didn't feel tired, but I felt like I *should* feel tired. Back
when I pulled doubles at the restaurant and had to be on set
later the same night, I'd survive on adrenaline and caffeine,
trying to sync the crashes with my downtime. No matter
how tired you were, there were always moments when you
could ride a wave of alertness. Up there at the crest,
skimming along and feeling great, but always with the
knowledge that exhaustion lurked just below you.
Eventually, the wave would hit a break and send you
hurtling into sleep.

I felt like that right now. Like I was up on that wave. But
it wasn't crashing. It hadn't crashed for weeks.

I gave up even pretending to rest. I was holding my left
hand out the passenger window as we drove, catching
patterns in the wind, using my fingers like a sail to make
rolling arcs through the air. Jackie was driving. She had been
since we left the motel this morning. She'd driven through
two countries today. We crossed the border into Mexico late
this afternoon. I freaked out a little about passports.

We didn't have any. That's a big deal, right?

But the guard just looked in the car, made sure we were
all white, and waved us through. Getting back would
probably be another matter.

Jackie had to be getting tired by now. "Driver calls the
music" was her rule. We'd been listening to her iPod all
day. Real yelpy indie stuff. High distortion and quavering

falsettos. Carey rode shotgun, rolling his eyes so hard you could hear it from the backseat, over the guitars.

"I'm changing it," he said, poking at the iPod. "How do I work this thing?"

"You know the rules," Jackie said.

Carey prodded and swore, but it made no difference. Jackie had locked it. It was just a simple swipe-to-unlock deal, but that was apparently like a child-safety cap to the elderly.

"Fine! Then just let me fuckin' drive already!" he said. "If I have to listen to one more of these pussies compare a girl to the ocean, I'll grab the wheel and swerve us into traffic."

Jackie beamed at him. The track changed.

"Is that a fucking harp?" Carey screeched. "Is that a fucking harp?! No, pull over. I'm serious!"

Jackie laughed. I knew her. I knew she was tired hours ago, but she wouldn't stop until she broke Carey.

Anything for the joke.

She finally tapped the blinker and guided her sun-faded white Jetta onto the shoulder. The tires crunched rocks against the pavement beneath us. Jackie opened her door and spilled out the side in an avalanche of empty Red Bull cans. She'd bought two cases before we left, and they had been smoldering in the trunk ever since, the afternoon Mexican sun slow-cooking them in that enclosed space. It hurt just to hold them, they were so hot, but Jackie didn't care.

"Sure, it tastes like somebody-spit-in-your-cough-syrup soup, but it's better than drifting into a ditch," she'd said, before downing her fourth of the day.

Carey opened his door and carefully stretched. It looked painful, and sounded worse. Even his hips cracked. I tried to remind myself that he was only in his late fifties. He looked twenty years older, and acted forty years younger.

He spat onto the ground and the pavement swallowed it right up. He squinted up at the sun. Directly at it.

"You're not supposed to do that," I said. "You'll go blind."

"That's what they told me about jerking off," he said, "and if they were right about that, I'd have gone blind twice this morning."

"Bullshit." Jackie laughed, kicking her Red Bull cans under the car like a little boy kicking errant toys under the bed instead of cleaning his room. "We've been with you the whole time."

"Not in the men's room at the gas station." Carey smiled. It looked like a catcher's mitt splitting open.

"Grooooss," Jackie sang, and pushed past him into the passenger seat.

I sighed, opened my door, got down onto my hands and knees, and started scooping the cans out from under the car. I looked back over my shoulder and saw Carey standing in the middle of the empty highway. We were surrounded on all sides by a western movie. Literal cactuses out here—for some reason I always thought that was just in cartoons. It was a beautiful, dangerous, and lonely place. Striated foothills loomed over squat green trees—the only spot of color in a world of dusty browns. Sagging power lines and the cracked pavement of Highway 57 South were the only man-made things around. It was like walking on another planet.

Yet Carey had eyes only for my ass, stuck up in the air as I scooped Red Bull cans out from underneath a busted-up 2001 Volkswagen Jetta.

I whipped one at his head, and tucked the rest under the front seat.

"You're picking that up," I said, slamming my door.

After another series of painful stretches, he picked up the

can, then threw it as hard as he could out into the desert. He sat down in the driver's seat and started fumbling with the adjustment levers.

"You're a fucking asshole," I told him.

"Stop the presses," he replied.

Carey spent a moment carefully tweaking the mirrors, checked his blind spot, then stomped on the accelerator. We went nowhere. The Jetta screamed like a castrated robot.

"It's in neutral!" Jackie yelled, slapping his arm.

"Oh right, and that's . . . bad?" Carey asked, wiggling the shifter.

"You need to push the clutch and—holy shit, you don't know how to drive!"

"Never stopped me before," Carey said. He jammed the knob into second gear and we took off with a massive lurch.

Jackie spent the next ten minutes desperately trying to convince Carey that he needed to shift out of second at highway speeds. He reluctantly agreed, but only on two conditions. One, that she show him "where the highway gear was," and two, that she work the "music dealy" for him. Jackie spent the next thirty minutes explaining to Carey that the Music Dealy did not contain all of the world's music. Just the stuff she put on it. She did not have any Stiff Little Fingers. She did not know who The Stranglers were. She did, however, have some Gang of Four. A compromise was reached, and Carey agreed not to shift out of fifth without permission so long as we listened to *Entertainment!* on repeat for the next five hours.

We ate miles.

We passed through small towns now and again. "Towns" is probably the wrong word.

Settlements? Outposts? Is that racist, if I don't call them towns?

Mobile homes with tarps for roofs. Cinder-block structures whose only adornments were a propane tank and a massive Coca-Cola sign. The occasional wooden church, rotted dry and peeled clean by the sun. But mostly, it was desert. Desert that blew in through the gaps in the windows, even if you had them closed. The dull green of the sagebrush melted into a solid band of color that ran alongside us as we drove. I watched the hills on the horizon swell and dip like massive waves, and the sky slowly dim from burning pale blue into a gemstone sunset. The world outside the window flowed by, broken only by telephone poles and cactuses that acted as vertical barriers, forming the edges of the frames as they flickered, like a film reel played at half-speed. The constant drone of the tires on pavement became static, merged with the guitars as they burped and squealed. A British man's voice, deep and apathetic, droned tunelessly across backing vocals that emoted for him. The songs repeated. Blurred together. I watched a painting of the desert slowly dissolve into faded blues to a soundtrack of cosmic radiation. The monotone voice assured me of something, and it didn't matter what, just that it was something, and it was assured.

And then Carey screamed.

We were sideways, airborne, upside down, sideways again. I tried to pull back from the window, or duck, or something—anything—but then we hit. The moment froze. I saw the bubbling pattern of the asphalt, with little flecks of sand pooling in the pockmarks. An old beer cap, pressed into the road by years of passing tires. The latex of the passing lines—up close you could see them peeling up at the edges, trying to unstick themselves from the carried heat of the road—and then time caught up to me, and my head bashed into it.

An abstract impressionist painting. A muted Pollock number. Sun-faded white, denim blue, and bright shining red sliding together across a patch of black.

I was standing at the edge of a great river, on the opposite bank of consciousness. If I squinted really hard, I could see things happening over there, but they were impossible to make out. I thought I heard my name carried on the wind, but it was impossible to be sure. I could only get a general sense. Swearing, screaming, panic. Something bad was happening over there. Something to do with the shadows, and the way they moved even though it was dark over there, and there was no light to cast them.

But that wasn't my problem. I was safe here, on the other side of the river.

EIGHT

1998. Barstow, California. Kaitlyn.

The first thing I do when I get home from school is I take my shoes off. Something about being at school makes me hate shoes. I kick them off right in the hall, as soon as I get in the door. I dig my toes into the backs of them, and I pry them off without using my hands. I have very flexible toes. When Jackie and me went swimming at the pool over the summer, Sierra saw me grabbing the pool floaty with just my feet and said I was weird, so I swam over to her, and grabbed her hair with my toes. I clenched my toes like a fist and she couldn't get away. She cried *a bunch*.

The second thing I do when I get home from school is I go to the fridge and I get out the jug of SunnyD and I drink it as fast as I can. I drink it until the top of my mouth gets so cold it hurts, and I can't feel my throat anymore, and my stomach feels like a water balloon that got filled too much. Tara came over to my house once, and she said it was gross that I drank right out of the container. I said that she was gross, and she said that I was gross again, so I pushed her, and she went home. Except for Jackie, none of the other girls at school had come over before that, and they wouldn't come over after that.

They didn't like me, and it was because of my finger.

I wasn't supposed to have that finger. I had six on my left hand, one too many pinkies. It wasn't a full finger, just a little one, and it didn't bend. I couldn't really use it for anything, and it hurt all the time. Just a little, *but all the time*. Plus, the other girls said stuff to me about it.

Brienne was fat, and even *she* made fun of me. She called me a platypus. I thought that was stupid. I went home and I looked it up in the encyclopedia, and platypuses don't have extra fingers. I told Brienne the next day, and she said "That sounds like something a platypus would do" and all the other girls laughed. All the other girls were dumb, and Brienne was fat *and* dumb. I told her so and she pulled my hair, so I punched her in the arm. They sent me home. Then they called my mom. They told her I was starting fights at school.

If you ask me, calling somebody a platypus is starting it.

Today was an okay day, though. The girls don't make fun of me so much anymore, mostly because they don't talk to me. Except for Jackie, who's my best friend. The other girls mostly just make fun of me when I can't hear it—they laugh after I walk by, in that way that you just know is about you. None of the boys talk to me, either, but that's okay—none of the boys talk to *any* of the girls. Boys and girls used to talk to each other in second grade, but now it's third grade and we don't talk to each other anymore. I've heard that in seventh grade we'll start talking again, but if you ask me, we won't have much to talk about.

The only bad thing that happened today was that I heard Emily tell Sarah that her brother told her people with sixth fingers used to be burned at the stake, and they drew a picture of me tied up and on fire, and left it on my desk when I came back from recess.

I crumpled it up in a ball and I threw it at her during class, but she was too scared to look at me.

The third thing I do, now that I am barefoot and so full of SunnyD that I can hear it slosh around when I walk, is I go out to the garage to find my dad. I only do that when it is Tuesday or Wednesday, though, because he is off work early on those days. Every Tuesday and Wednesday afternoon, my dad works in the garage. He's got the door opened all the way, and a big yellow light shining down on the stripped frame of a Honda Elsinore. I know that because I asked him what he was doing last week, and he said "stripping it down to the frame." I asked him what it was and he said "an Elsinore. That's a Honda." I was getting okay at knowing motorcycles, but the Elsinore was new. I had never seen one before. I liked the front fender. It was pointy, and up way higher than fenders on other motorcycles. That made it special and cool.

Dad was holding a beer and just kind of looking at the Elsinore in a disapproving way. If he looked at me that way, it would mean he was going to explain something that I did wrong. He hadn't seen me coming yet, so I ran up behind him and punched him in the butt.

"Hey!" he said, and tried to swat me, but he missed.

"Too slow!" I said, dancing around so I could hear the SunnyD sloshing.

"What're you doing now?" I asked him.

I went around to poke at the pointy end of the fender. It made a *boing* sound and flicked up little clouds of dust.

"I'm about to grind the extra tabs off the frame," my dad said.

He picked up a tool and showed it to me. It was squat and round. The plug came out of one end and the other had a big wheel on it.

"Why are you doing that?"

"I moved some parts around, so now I don't need the tabs. They don't do anything but look ugly."

I felt something build up inside of me. It pushed at the edges of my body and made me feel like I was going to pop and spray SunnyD everywhere.

"What's wrong?" he asked.

"Why do I have to keep my finger, then?" I yelled, too loud. I didn't mean to, but it flew up out of my insides like a slippery bar of soap.

"K, we've talked about this. . . ."

"But you said! You just said you didn't like the tabs and they don't do anything anyway except for look ugly. Just like my finger! Sierra said her dad is a plastic doctor and he makes people look better. She said if we paid him some money he could take my finger away!"

I held it up in front of him, just in case he forgot what we were talking about. I wiggled it. Surely he could see what I meant now, right?

"You don't need it taken away, honey. It's . . . it gives you personality. It's part of you. And I think you're just fine."

"But why are you—"

My dad held up his hands in surrender and laughed. He put the tool down on the floor of the garage.

"You're right. I don't need to grind down the tabs. I'll leave them just how they are."

But that wasn't what I wanted. I didn't care about the tabs. I wanted normal hands so I could go back to school and show Brienne. I would hold them up in her face, and I would tell her

that now I'm normal, but she's still fat, and I would use my
normal hands to slap her right in her fat face.

Well, no. I wouldn't really do that. But I liked to think
about it. Even if I knew it was mean and wrong.

I didn't know what else to say to my dad. So I said: "I like
the pointy fender."

"It's up high because it's a dirt bike," my dad said. "Here,
do you wanna help me change the grips?"

"Maaaybe," I said.

He handed me a can of WD-40. I loved it because it had a
bright red straw coming out of the front. It felt like
something you would use at a party. My dad picked up a
pair of skinny pliers and grabbed the edge of the grip. He
pried it up and held it there.

"Here, you spray inside of it while I hold it open."

I put the end of the straw right up inside of the grip and
pushed the button until stinky metal liquid flowed out onto
the ground.

I looked up at my dad to see what we were doing next,
but he had that look on his face. It was the same look he was
giving the bike when I first came out. Something was
wrong, and he wasn't sure how to fix it.

I didn't want to help him anymore. I put the WD-40 on
the ground next to his beer.

"I'm going to see what Mom is doing," I told him, and I
started running before he could say anything else.

He didn't.

I hadn't closed the kitchen door all the way when I went
out to the garage, so I kicked it open without slowing down.
It banged against the fridge, and my mom jumped. She was
reading a magazine at the table by the kitchen window.

"Kaitlyn!" she said, sternly.

"Sorry!" I said, "but I was in a hurry. This is *important*."

I had never said things were *important* before. That was something my mom said to my dad when she wanted to talk about something. Then they would come in here and sit at the table and talk quietly in different voices for a very long time. *Important* things are taken seriously.

"Oh my," Mom said. She tried to sound serious, but I could tell she thought it was funny. "Well, if it's *important*."

She said it the exact same way I said it. That's how I knew she was making fun of me.

"Dad said I could go to a plastic doctor and get my finger removed," I tried. Then added: "Today."

I knew it wouldn't work, but the garage was pretty far away. Maybe she wouldn't check.

"He did?" she asked.

"He did." I nodded seriously in an *important* way.

"Well, plastic doctors are expensive." My mom laughed.

That's why I didn't like her as much as dad. She was my mom and I loved her, but she always laughed at me.

"What's he going to do that I can't?" she said, and stood up. She went to the drawer by the sink and got out a big shiny butcher knife. Then she slid out the cutting board. "Just hop on up here and I'll take it off right now."

Making fun.

I walked up right next to her at the counter. I put my hand on the cutting board, and pushed my extra pinky out as far as it would go. It wasn't very far. I couldn't move it much.

"I'm ready," I said.

Mom stopped smiling. She put the knife away and crouched down.

Here it comes. Here comes a speech. She only crouches down when she's going to give me a speech.

"Kaitlyn," she said, "I want you to know it's okay to be different. It doesn't make you worse than other kids. If anything, it makes you speci—"

But I was already running. Through the kitchen, the bare skin of my feet squeaking on the linoleum. Into the living room, past my kid sister Stacy watching her cartoons, up the stairs, down the hallway, and into Stacy and me's room. I shut the door as hard as I could. Then I thought it might not have been hard enough. So I opened it and shut it again. I sat down with my back against the closed door and thought about crying. I thought about it for a long time. So long it started to get dark.

I was thinking so hard about crying, and whether or not I should do it (sometimes my mom and dad see me crying and they do things to fix it. Other times they just get mad at me for doing it and tell me to stop) that I didn't realize I had fallen asleep. I woke up. Something was wrong. My brain was playing catch-up with my body, so I couldn't figure out what it was yet.

I held my hand up in front of me. I didn't have any lights on in my room, so it was lighter outside than it was inside. I moved my hand between me and the window and stared at the outline of it. I wiggled my extra pinky. I clenched my fist—that's what made my finger hurt the most—and I didn't feel anything. I did it again. And again and again. I clenched my fist so hard I could feel my fingernails digging into my palm. The palm hurt, but not my extra pinky.

It had stopped hurting.

It had never done that before.

Not *ever*.

I jumped up and threw my door open and ran into the hallway and down the stairs and through the living room and right into the kitchen. Mom was making something on the stovetop, so the whole house smelled like burning pans. I ran up to her and grabbed her from behind.

"It doesn't hurt anymore!" I yelled into her butt.

She turned around and laughed. She grabbed me under the armpits and lifted me up in the air. She put me on the dining room table and I couldn't stop giggling. I wiggled my skinny, single-knuckled little digit for her. Her eyes went wide.

"Are you kidding me? Is this a joke?" she asked.

I shook my head.

"That's great, baby!" she said.

Her voice was all thick, like she was about to cry or start yelling.

"I'll tell you what," she said, and she smiled funny. "I *was* making tuna and mac 'n' cheese . . ."

I stuck my tongue out involuntarily. *Tuna tastes like Dad's feet smell.*

"But since it's a special occasion, and all," she continued, "why don't I order a pizza instead?"

I thought for a minute. I was supposed to be mad at her for something, or maybe she was supposed to be mad at me for something, but I kept opening and closing my hand and it didn't hurt and I couldn't remember what we were mad about.

I nodded a bunch. I couldn't stop smiling.

So we had pizza and it was really good. Pizza is always really good, especially when it has pepperoni on it, but not when it has olives. Stacy likes olives, because Stacy is only six and she's too young to know better. We got to order the pizza in halves, so half was mine. I said pepperoni only, but there were nasty border olives, sneaking over the cheese from Stacy's side into mine. I made her a deal: I'd pick off her gross sneaky olives and trade her for any pepperoni that tries to get across to her side. She agreed. She thinks the pepperoni is too spicy.

We even got to stay up an extra half hour watching *Power Rangers*. Stacy said she should get to be the pink Power Ranger and I had to be the yellow Power Ranger, which is dumb. Why would you want to be the pink Power Ranger? She's always getting beat up. I said I wanted to be the red Power Ranger, and she told me that was just for boys; so I said fine, if I had to be a girl I'll be Rita Repulsa; and I made my fingers into claws and chased her upstairs.

We brushed our teeth. Well, I brushed mine. Stacy just put her toothbrush in her mouth for a minute without moving it, then she spat it out. She said the new toothpaste is too spicy. I stared at her for a moment, then slowly explained to her that it was cinnamon flavored and cinnamon isn't spicy, like pepperoni. But she wouldn't listen.

We got into our pajamas. Mine had motorcycles and cars and trucks on them. Stacy's had stupid ponies and some stars. I don't really understand how we can be related. I heard from Jackie that there's a thing called an affair that means your sister isn't really your sister, even if your parents say she is. I'm pretty sure Stacy is an affair. But I still like her okay. Dad says I was pretty dumb when I was six, too. Maybe she'll grow out of it.

I fell asleep when I wasn't paying attention. But I woke up because it was too bright. Even for morning. I thought somebody had turned on a light, so I shoved my head under my pillow and looked out through the gap between the pillow and the bed. There was a light out there, all right, but it wasn't like any of the ones in our room. I tried looking at the light, but it was like looking at the sun. I couldn't see anything, I could just feel it hurting my eyes. But there was something behind the light, or maybe in it. I knew it was there even if I couldn't see it, like when you're playing hide-and-seek and you just know somebody's in the closet. It was like a bunch of lines that lined up wrong; like corners that ended in themselves, and squares that were bigger than they looked. I don't know. It was just weird, I guess.

I poked my face farther out the gap between the pillow and the bed to get a better look at what was making the light, and I saw Stacy sitting upright. Her feet were dangling over the edge of her bed, and she was sitting up way too straight. She never sat like that. Her head was bent a funny way, too, like she was listening for something. Now that I thought about it, I could almost hear it too. It sounded like the ocean. Or maybe a bunch of oceans, all together on top of each other. And you could even sort of hear seagulls screaming, or maybe something else screaming, but it was also part of the waves. I closed my eyes and the noise stopped. I opened them and it started again.

I figured I had to be dreaming. But I think in Freddy Krueger movies they say you can't be dreaming if you know that you're dreaming? I don't know, I always close my eyes when Jackie watches those kinds of movies at her house.

I decided that I probably was dreaming, so I took the pillow off my head, tossed it on the floor, and sat up all the way.

The light moved. Or maybe it just changed shape—it was hard to look at it to tell. It seemed confused about the pillow on the floor. It moved toward my bed. I put my hands up in front of my eyes, to block the light but also to push it away if it came too close. But it didn't seem like it was paying attention to me. Just the pillow, and my bed, and everything around me *but* me.

Stacy shook her head, like she was trying to clear water out of her ear. The light snapped around and moved back over to her real quick. She sat still again. I could hear part of a song coming from somewhere. It sounded familiar, like what Mom used to sing to her when she was real little. But it wasn't in the same language, and that wasn't Mom's voice. It smelled like pancakes. Stacy flinched like somebody had slapped her. Then her eyes got bright, like there were little fires in there. My stomach started to feel funny. I got the feeling this was about to go from a weird dream to a bad dream. I stood up and crossed over to Stacy, making sure to give the light extra room. But it still didn't seem to care about me.

I put my hands on her shoulders, and she screamed.

I jumped back, and I screamed some too. She was screaming way too loud; I didn't think she could make that sound. But she was also trying to make words. She was yelling about the air in the forest and our old address. She laughed and cried at the same time, and then her words started bubbling. Clear, thick liquid that shimmered like a rainbow came out of her mouth and spilled down her chin, but it started turning black after a couple of seconds. Now it looked like the road when they first pour it out of that truck that builds roads. The road stuff ran down her neck, and where it touched her pajamas, they crinkled up like plastic in the microwave. The whole room smelled like a burning action figure. The black syrup stopped around her chest, and then it started going backwards.

This had to be a dream. Liquids can't go up.

But this stuff did. It climbed up her neck, and around her face, and now there was so much of it. It was all over her. I pulled my hands back before it reached her shoulders. Stacy wasn't making any noise anymore, but I was. I guess I hadn't ever stopped screaming.

The liquid was on the bed now, and little flames danced around Stacy's blanket. It went up so fast. When we went camping, it took Dad forever to light a campfire. He should just use whatever Stacy's blanket was made out of, because the whole thing was on fire now. I wanted to grab Stacy, but I somehow knew I shouldn't touch that black stuff. I wanted to run, but the light was between me and the door, and it was singing its screaming ocean song, and everything was too much. I couldn't do anything but scream, so I closed my eyes, and I screamed.

I don't know how long I was like that. Our room smelled like smoke so strong I could feel it filling my nose like water. Big hands grabbed me hard and yanked me. Then something was carrying me, and I could hear my mom yelling for Stacy. I tried to tell my mom that a light had come on and turned Stacy into part of the road, but only coughing came out. So much coughing there was no room for breathing. I fell asleep.

NINE

1978. London, England. Carey.

In case you're wondering: Yes, tar men can open doors. But they're shit at climbing stairs. Even dragging Meryll, me and Randall outpaced them easily. We took two landings for every one of theirs. There were too many of them in too narrow a space. They kept tripping each other, blocking each other, and slowly crawling over one another in their mindless desperation to reach us. By the time we made it to the street, we were soaked in sweat. Then we were just soaked.

I grabbed my crotch and gave the cabbie both fingers, but he still didn't stop.

How the hell are you supposed to hail a cab in this godforsaken country? Wait, hold on, here's another one. . . .

"Hey! Hey . . . fuck you!"

Nothing.

I tried jumping up and down; I tried throwing beer cans at their windshields; and, obviously, I tried swearing. I was all out of ideas, and I could not get these guys to stop for us. We had been standing out in the cold London rain, Meryll slowly dying in Randall's arms, for five minutes. They must have thought she was passed out drunk or high, and didn't want her puking in the back of their precious cabs. That's the only reason I could figure why they weren't stopping.

"Carey, come on, man . . ." Randall said.

He shifted Meryll in his arms. She was a little pudgy, sure, but she wasn't a big girl. Couldn't have been more than a buck fifty. But she still kept slipping right out of Randall's hands. It's harder than you think, dragging an unconscious person around. That's one thing I've had *a lot* of experience doing.

"Switch with me," Randall said.

"You think you can do this better?" I was almost offended.

But shit: I was getting nowhere. Might as well hold the chick for a while. Maybe she'll wake up right then and see me bundling her up like fuckin' Clark Gable and she'll fall uncontrollably in love with me and we'll fuck right on top of stupid Randall's ugly shirt collection.

Or she'll just die on the street. Then the tar men will come bustling up out of that maintenance stairway half a block back and melt you into a puddle of liquid asshole.

I looked down at her face. Her eyes were closed. Big fake eyelashes, one hanging loose from the edge of her eyelid. Too much mascara, the rain making it run down her cheeks and into her black lipstick. Her dark, wet hair matted to her skull. She had great skin. Pale, of course—she was English, after all; poor thing couldn't help but look like a sickly eggshell—but, you know, in a hot way. I turned her face a little and got another look at her neck. Maybe it was the dim lighting, or maybe I had been panicking back in the tunnels, but the burns didn't look so bad. I mean, they looked *bad*. They didn't look *good*. But they didn't seem as dire anymore. I swore, when I first saw them, that they were so deep I could see her fat and muscle bisected at the edges of those massive fingerprints. But I must have been hallucinating. They weren't much more than skin-deep. Just an angry pink sunken bit, not a gaping hole in her neck.

Shit. Maybe we can go back to the Clark Gable shirt-fucking fantasy.

A whistle loud enough to deafen God.

For a second I thought another tar man was going up, and all the muscles in my body knotted into tight little balls. Then I saw Randall with one hand in the air and two fingers in his mouth. One of those obnoxiously cute old-timey London cabs boated over to the side of the road, soaking Randall's legs in puddle-water.

Something croaked. It appeared to be coming from my arms.

Yes. She was awake!

"Hegh . . ." she said, and wound up doing a sort of coughing hiccup. She tried again: "He . . . got one. . . ."

Oh, no. Oh, god dammit, seriously?

"Yeah, but I softened them up for him," I pleaded. But she was already fading.

And I could see it now: Visions of heroic Randall wrestling cabs to the side of the road like a fucking horsebreaker. Pile-driving automobiles into submission and dragging her buxom body to safety. Then *they* would fuck on *my* ugly shirt collection.

Screw it. At least she's alive.

I dragged Meryll to the cab while Randall held the door open for us. The heels of her clunky black boots scraped along the pavement. I handed Randall her head, took her legs, and together we shoved the wad of girl into the far end of the backseat. Then we piled in after her and shut the door.

"You boys were at the show, eh?" The cabbie was a squat guy, face like somebody'd punched a potato.

"What?"

"The punker rock show, at the Rainbow? I been hearing about it all night. Heard you animals tore up all the seats and threw 'em at the band."

Fuck me. Is that what happened? And I missed it?!

"Yeah, just coming from the show," Randall confirmed.

He does this voice sometimes, mostly to cops or those half cops that try to bust you for jumping turnstiles. It was tired, a little respectful, and laced with just a hint of regret. Swear to god, boy deserves a gold statue.

"It got pretty out of hand at the end, and our friend wasn't feeling so good, so we figured we should get out of there," Randall finished.

I could see it working already. The cabbie's shoulders lost tension, he turned around in his seat, and looked Randall square in the eye. He laughed. "Eh, it's all right. I been known to bash it up in my younger years too. Where's home for you lads?"

"I . . ." Randall looked at me.

I gave him the hardest shrug I could manage. We'd been crashing at a hostel.

Oh, hey, yeah, sorry, Andrew: We know we're not supposed to be out past eleven and no guests, but we thought we'd bring this severely mangled girl back to our communal bunks at two in the morning for a bit of a good time.

"Hospital?" he whispered to me.

"I don't know, the burns don't look as bad anym—"

"No." Meryll slapped me weakly across the chest. "Bermondsey Wall West."

"You've gone insane. You're not putting words in the

right order," I told her, gently.

"I got it, boys," the cabbie said. "I know the place."

He pulled away from the curb. The world outside the cab was lights and blurry water. No radio on. Just the sound of tires pushing water around and windshield wipers thunking and squeaking like a drumbeat. Meryll's eyes roved around the interior of the cab—to the windows, to Randall, to me—but they couldn't seem to find what she was looking for, so she closed them. The adrenaline was starting to fade, and I could feel my hip burning again. I tried shifting weight off of it, but nothing doing. The bastard was determined to hurt no matter what I did. At least my shoulder wasn't quite so bad anymore. I rotated it—stiff, but nothing fucked up in there too badly.

Randall was staring out the window at nothing. At rain streaks and traffic lights.

"What?" I asked him.

"What?" he asked me.

"You're all quiet and shit. What's your problem?"

"Her burns aren't as bad."

"That's a problem? You and me, we got different definitions of problem."

Randall glanced down, made sure Meryll was still out. It was hard to tell, but she wasn't moving and her breathing was deep and regular. He risked it.

"I saw them too," Randall whispered, "down in the stairs. They were halfway to the bone. Looked like she got choked out by the devil."

"Ah. I thought so too," I said, barely whispering. If Meryll was awake, I was damn well planning on getting some points for defending her. "But we were freaked, and it was dark."

"No, man. That girl was *dead*," Randall said. He turned back to the window.

"Well, I'm glad she changed her fucking mind, then. I don't get what the problem is."

I reached down to push some of Meryll's hair off of her face, and she slapped my hand away.

I got them points, Randall.

Turns out Bernardsey Wall or whatever was a street. Or at least it used to be. It looked like somebody had dropped a bomb on a sadness factory and nobody'd ever bothered cleaning up the debris. Must have been a port or something in its heyday. Big brown brick buildings, lots of concrete, not a lot of windows. There were lights on in a few of them. Tinny music filtering through the bricks from somewhere far above. Somebody was living here. It smelled like water, and we'd crossed a bridge a ways back. Must be near the river, though I couldn't see it. The street was barely big enough for a single car, and the warehouses looming on either side of us made an urban canyon.

Randall and me had gone to drag Meryll out of the cab, but she was alert enough to take our hands instead. We had her in a soldier's carry.

"So . . ." Randall said.

"So we just stand in the street for a while?" I supplied.

I shuffled Meryll a bit, trying to rouse her.

"Rape office," she said.

I laughed.

"Girl's got a concussion," Randall said. "Knew we shoulda gone to the hospital."

Then I spotted it. Sure enough: Rape Office.

It was tall, four or five stories, but thin. Bricks that probably started off red, then turned to shit brown after somebody rubbed a few decades of shit on them. Every single window was broken and boarded over, but the doors were intact.

Above them, in severe metal letters: Rape Office.

It used to say "Trade Office." You could still see an imprint in the grime from the now-missing "T." The "D" had lost a few retaining bolts, so it hung upside down, now a lopsided, rusting "P."

"Huh," Randall said, now spotting it. "Good name for a band."

We hobbled Meryll up the steps. They were concrete, chipped damn near out of existence. Old newspapers and what was probably bloody fur splayed across them. I gave up counting after I spotted about a dozen needles. I didn't even try to count the crushed beer cans. You'd have to straighten the place up a bit to call it a squalid hellhole.

"You're sure this is where you wanna go?" Randall asked Meryll.

She pulled her arm from across my shoulder, and almost fell. I went to catch her, but she shrugged me off. She steadied herself against Randall with one hand. With the other, she knocked a pattern on the flaking metal doors. One knock. Slight pause. Four knocks. Long pause. Two knocks.

Shave and a haircut. Two bits.

Nothing happened for a long, suspicious minute. Two thrashed-looking American punks on an abandoned wharf, holding a beaten, nearly unconscious British girl between them, standing outside of a building called the Rape Office. I just knew a cop was gonna come by right then. Do they have the death penalty in England? If so, we would get it on general principle.

Finally, the door swung inward. A short, ugly guy with scars all across his lips wobbled in the doorway. He peered out at us with hooded little rat eyes. He belched, and I smelled cheap beer.

Well, hell, now I'm thirsty.

"We, uh . . ." Randall started, but there was no need to finish.

The ugliest man in the world had turned away and was already staggering down a short, narrow hallway filled with soiled mattresses and broken shopping carts. Halfway down, he looked over his shoulder at us, and gave us an exaggerated wave. Nearly knocked himself over doing it.

Follow me to my den, says the troll.

We did.

Meryll was walking on her own now. Not very well— she'd get booked for public intoxication if she went to the mall like that—but she was moving, and that was good. It was not at all disturbing for a girl to be moseying about an hour after getting strangled by an acid monster. Totally normal. So normal it would be stupid of me to think about it anymore.

The hallway ended in a soggy pile of T-shirts that reeked of ammonia. I could see Randall eyeballing them hungrily. The man just cannot turn down a free shirt. But the troll was moving along at an unsteady clip, down the hall to the right and nearly out of sight. We followed him, and wound up in a skinny room with a ceiling so high it disappeared into shadows. It looked like there had been floors to this building, at one point. But something came through from above, a long time ago, and blasted most of them out, one by one. The ground beneath our feet was one great big shattered crater, sloping from the farthest edges right down to the center of the room. Old, black water had collected at the deepest point. Somebody had posted a crude, hand-drawn sign that said *"Swimmin Pool."* The whole place was lit with gas lanterns. Some hung from hooks embedded in what little ceiling remained. Most were just shoved randomly into the debris. One corner had been given over entirely to band equipment—amps, guitars, a partially kicked-in drum set held together by duct tape. The other corners were filled with torn couches, broken recliners, and smashed TV sets. Kids sporting Mohawks and patchwork jackets were wrestling across the wreckage, passed out on the couches, and playing drinking games by the lanterns. A record player tucked into a broken safe was playing The Adverts' "No Time to be 21."

I was here. I was home.

I looked around for our guide-goblin, but he wasn't there. Took me a minute to spot him. He was climbing a ladder lashed up against one wall that looked like it had been part of a fire escape, once. It poked right up through the blasted ceiling. The light from the gas lanterns was thin and didn't carry far, so I couldn't see it until my eyes adjusted: Every floor, or at least what little that hadn't been caved in yet, was occupied. I could hear other songs from up above, tinny guitars rattling around unseen speakers, voices laughing and yelling. One was just making monkey noises over and over. Or shit, maybe they had an actual monkey!

Calm down, Carey. There's probably a very slim chance that you will finally be able to get drunk with a monkey tonight. Just concentrate on the task at hand.

I hollered up at the ugly guy, who was quickly ascending out of sight into the gloom above us. He turned around to glare at me.

"What are we supposed to do, drag her up there?" I asked.

He motioned for us to sit, then silently resumed his climb.

Me and Randall steered Meryll over to half a row of folding seats that had been boosted from some upscale theater. They smelled like ancient butts and dust mites, and they tilted crazily when we put weight on them, but they held. Meryll slumped gratefully, laid her head on Randall's shoulder, and closed her eyes.

I made up my mind to get over that shit as soon as possible. What good was fucking mooning over her gonna do if she's made it clear the only pole she wants to slide down is attached to that doofus Randall? I mean, so what if she could fill out a skirt *and* uppercut a guy out of his own shoes? I'm sure there are plenty of fish in the sea . . . with sexy freak strength . . . who'll jump out of a moving bus with you. . . .

Fucking Randall.

I looked around for other chicks to annoy with my presence, but there were only guys around. Not even particularly girly ones that I could ogle if I squinted hard enough—they were all ropy boys with broken teeth and black eyes. I held out a thin sliver of hope that they segregated the sexes by floor, and the second story was all slutty punk rock coeds with low standards. But that seemed about as likely as the monkey fantasy.

Not impossible, but no sense counting on it.

I watched the punks hollering, throwing cans at each other, and making a huge point of ignoring us. I was waiting to see which foolish cub would unwittingly lead me to their beer stash. The one who finally did it was a kid, maybe sixteen or seventeen, with a head shaved like a monk and two front teeth missing. He stumbled toward a kicked-in TV set, reached through the shattered glass, and pulled out two cans.

"Wanna beer?" I asked Meryll.

She struggled one eye open a crack, sighed, and closed it again.

"So . . . is that a yes?" I asked, confused.

"I'll take one," Randall said.

I pushed up out of the folding seat and a cloud of gray dust followed me. I crossed the room, skirting the Swimmin Pool, which was full of the most poisonous-looking water I have ever seen, and reached into the set as casually as possible.

Something ate my fingers.

"Motherfuck!" I yelped, and drew my hand back too fast. My wrist scraped on the broken glass, drawing neat and precise lines of blood.

All the punk kids bust out laughing.

There was a mousetrap closed across three of my fingers.

Out of obligation, I swore at them for a good twenty seconds, but I couldn't really blame somebody for protecting their stash. I'd just never thought to use mousetraps, myself. Good idea. I'd have some new tricks when I got home— travel really *does* teach you things.

When I finished calling their mothers my usual laundry list of filth, I pulled the trap off my hand and reached back into the set.

The kids stopped laughing.

Keeping eye contact the whole time, I felt around inside it. *You watch me, motherfuckers. You watch me steal your beer.*

I was all Clint Eastwood on the outside, but inwardly I dreaded that metallic snap with every movement. None came. I emerged intact with three room-temperature cans of something called "lager." Weird name for a beer. The punks glared at me while I crossed the room, took my seat, and handed out drinks to my friends.

Meryll looked down at her hand, surprised to find a beer in it.

"I didn't want one," she said.

"What? Seriously? You should have said something."

"I glared at you when you asked."

"But you didn't say no . . ." I eyeballed the unwanted beer, waiting to see if this was a trap.

"It was implied."

"Listen, girl. Unless you specifically say 'please do not get me a beer' I am always going to assume beer. It's the only reasonable assumption to make."

I snatched the can out of her limp hand just seconds before Randall got to it. He snapped his fingers.

Finally, a point for Carey.

I cracked open my pilfered can, stuffed the reserve in my jacket for emergencies, and killed half a beer in one long pull The bubbles bit pleasantly at the back of my throat. It was as bitter, thin, and warm as the embrace of an ex-lover. It was the best beer I'd ever had, just like all the rest. This one maybe a little better than usual. It was coming at the tail end of an aborted buzz, just as the headache was starting to set in. There's no way I could have felt it that fast, but I swear my hip stopped hurting quite as much after the very first taste. Pictured those beer molecules down there, fizzing about, knitting up bones and sewing back together the torn muscles. My little doctors.

"Ahhhh . . ." Randall and I said, practically in unison.

"I'd tell you to make yourselves at home, but you seem to have gotten that message already," a voice like wet sandpaper came from above.

A really old guy (like, probably *at least fifty*), was climbing down the ladder. He took it slow, both legs on one rung before he moved to the next. He was wearing a faded green jacket that I associated with the army for no particular reason. Gray trousers, baggy. Didn't look intentional, like for style or anything. Seemed like he just used to be a bigger man and had held on to the pants. He was thin now, but still solid. You could tell by the way he heaved himself down that ladder. He was moving carefully, like he had something wrong with one leg, but the rest of him worked smoothly and easily to compensate. He reached the floor and turned into the light. Now I could see he was more beard than man. A big, poofy gray nest took up most of his face. Eyes like metal were set deep into dirty wrinkles. He unhooked a nasty-looking piece of rebar from its resting place in the crook of his elbow. It was three feet long, rusty, and curved at one end to form a handle. He used it like a cane.

He crossed the room quicker than I would have thought. Definitely favored that right leg, but it looked like he'd had a long time to get used to it.

"The name is Tub," he said, and offered a hand.

Without thinking, I reached out and shook it with fingers still stinging from the mousetrap. He mashed them into dust with his handshake.

"What kinda name is 'Tub'?" Randall asked.

"Got a big old tub up there on the top story. I sleep in it," he offered. That was plainly the only explanation we were going to get.

Tub offered Randall his hand, but Randall saw through that trap and just raised his beer a bit in greeting.

"Randall," he said. "That's Carey and this is—"

"He knows who I am, dipshit," Meryll croaked.

"Girl's slept in the bathtub with me." Tub laughed. "I don't think we need to stand on formality."

Randall made a face like somebody had slipped shit between his lips while he wasn't looking.

"Not like that!" Tub whapped the frame of the theater seats with his cane. "She's practically my daughter."

"Tub . . ." Meryll warned.

"I said practically, didn't I?" he protested.

Tub eyeballed Meryll's neck. He took her face in his hand and turned it this way and that.

"I don't like the look of that burn. Better get Annie to take a look."

"I'll be fine," Meryll said, but the words died in the air.

"Beaver!" Tub yelled, and the monk-headed kid with the missing teeth jumped to attention like an army private caught napping. "You help Meryll over to Annie's place. Get her fixed up. And make sure she gets the good pain pills."

"I don't need any pain pills," Meryll whispered, fading.

"Yeah, but I might like some." Tub laughed. He slapped Beaver on the ass with his cane as he passed. Beaver winced.

Tub sure liked to gesture with that thing, which would be fine if it wasn't *fucking rebar*. I sure hoped he never needed to emphasize a point for me.

"Now, you boys," Tub said, settling into Meryll's empty seat, "are gonna tell me what happened, and how much you saw."

Randall sighed. "No," he said. "I don't wanna do the recap again. Carey?"

I took a long pull from my beer. Then I burped as loud as I could. That was my answer.

"Long story short: There are monsters. We know all about them. We fuck 'em up," Randall said. "Why don't you give us the rundown instead, while we sit here and get shit-faced off your beer?"

I think Tub smiled back behind that deep dandelion puff of a beard.

"Right!" He snapped his cane against the concrete, sending little chips flying. "A couple of professionals. About bloody time."

I laughed.

Professional! Never heard that one before. At least, not without "asshole" or "cocksucker" at the end.

"Usually I have to spend the first hour just fighting disbelief. 'There's no such things as monsters.' 'You're just some crazy old hobo.' 'You have to let me go or I'll call the police.' Good to be able to cut to the chase. You boys have seen it all already, so I won't mince words. It's bad. We think Meryll's candidate cycle is almost up, and we've neutralized twenty-eight of them, but have no leads on the last seven. Not to mention that we have no idea where the Faceless are planning to summon the Flares. There are Sludges in greater numbers than we've ever seen—maybe hundreds of thousands, all waiting in the Underground for . . . something. Who knows, with them? Now, we always had our fair share of Husks here, but it seems like we're bloody importing 'em these days. They're coming in from all over—you know, one of my boys said he saw the Council of Six in the West End? The Council itself! You know it's bad when those tepid old child-eaters all gather in the same city. I mean, clearly we've got the mutation in our ranks, and she's training up fine. But this doesn't look like another run-of-the-mill Division. We haven't seen anything like this since the Trial of the Blitz. And I don't need to remind you boys how that turned out. . . ."

I stared silently into the opening of my beer. I figured I could just crawl in there and go to sleep if I tried hard enough. I looked at Randall, and he silently mouthed "W-H-A-T?!" I shrugged wildly in return.

Tub looked at each of us, then frowned. Or I assume he did. His beard drooped. "Were you not following?" he asked.

"I uh . . . I understood some of those words as words that I know," Randall said carefully.

"I got 'bloody'—that's how you Brits say 'fucking,' right?" I added.

Tub exploded out of his chair, spun, and lashed his rebar cane down at my leg. I dodged, but only by flailing so hard that the row of theater seats tipped backwards. The rest of my open beer emptied onto my face. Me and Randall scrambled to our feet and tried to get between him and the door.

"You think this is a game?!" Tub hollered, his colorless eyes boring into each of us in turn. "You think we've got time to hand-hold idiots while our people die in the dark by the bloody hour?! You're useless, the both of you. Get the hell out of our house before we string you up and use you as Sludge-bait."

Randall was already turning to go, and it was a good move. We came here for Gus, to end the thing that killed our friends, not to volunteer for some wacky Brit's crazy magic war.

But if you stay, Meryll will be here. She'll see how Randall wanted to go, but you bravely volunteered to stick around, and she'll leap on your dick like an offensive tackle.

Not good enough, brain.

They also have plenty of beer and a place to sleep that's not filled with German tourists.

Shit.

"Wait!" I said, sheltering behind the overturned folding chairs, my eyes glued to the wavering piece of rebar. "We didn't understand pretty much all of that. True. But we

been through this shit. We've taken out tar men—Sludges—
and we've tangled with the Unnoticeables plenty of times
and came out on top."

"Faceless," Randall clarified.

"Right, Faceless. We've only messed with one uh . . .
Husk. We call them Empty Ones. His name was Gus, and
he killed our friends. All because some fucking lightbulb
wanted to jump in my head and—"

"What?!" Tub lunged at me with his cane. I hurdled the
seats, took several desperate strides, and jumped over most
of the Swimmin Pool. One of my Chucks slipped and slid
right into the black water.

I'll have to burn these shoes.

I now had a ratty green couch between me and the psychotic
bearded guy with the club. It did not feel very reassuring.

"The Flare came for you? You were the successful
candidate? You helped them bloody procreate?"

"Whoa." Randall laughed. "You fucked that angel,
Carey? Nice."

"No! I . . . I don't know what they were there for. They
lured us into the tunnels and there were gears and kids
jumping into them and . . . shit. I just wanted to save my
friends. And I did. And now I just want to nuke the bastard
that killed the ones I couldn't save. That's all we want. Just
let us help."

Tub seemed to deflate.

He muttered one long, soft string of obscenity as he
hobbled toward the beer TV.

He reached his hand in. There was a loud snap.

The fucking mousetrap.

I steeled myself for a rebar enema.

Tub didn't even blink. He pulled his hand out, removed

the trap, tossed it on the ground, and came out with an entire six-pack. He hobbled back over to me, and I skittered around to the other side of the couch, ready to bolt. He just sighed and settled heavily into it. He sunk nearly to the ground. Frame must be busted.

"If we weren't so shorthanded already, I'd shank you both in the gentleman's area and leave you to sing the *Orfeo* for bobs on a Brixton corner," he said, cracking open the first beer.

"I don't know what that is, but it sounds awful," I said.

On the one hand, I was wary that this whole couch gag was an elaborate trap to slip a length of filthy rebar up my ass. On the other hand, I'm pretty sure that was the last of the beer.

"Sit, boyo," Tub said, sounding tired.

Randall vaulted over the back of the couch and landed hard on the cushions. Something snapped in the frame. I sunk beside him. We stared quietly at the fire for a few minutes. Finally Tub held a beer out to Randall, then to me, and started what I guessed was a very familiar speech.

"Something lives beneath London. Right under our feet. Thriving, fucking, eating, and killing our kids as we go get the bloody paper and sip our bloody tea. The Faceless are the most common. They pass for people, but they got this aura that makes you forget to pay attention to them. They're grunts, pawns in the game. Plentiful and expendable."

He paused to look at Randall before continuing. Randall nodded.

Yes, yes—we're total dipshits, but some things we know.

"All right. If this is familiar territory, you get the abridged version: The Sludges, giant man-shaped things made of black acid. Make a noise like somebody stabbing a train crash, messes with your balance. The Husks also look like people, but they're not . . . what did you call the Faceless?"

"Unnoticeables."

"Right. They're not . . . noticeable . . . Jesus, that's stupid."

Me and Randall rolled our eyes, but not so much as he'd notice and take our beers away.

"But the Husks are just that: Shells. They're empty inside. Something got in them and hollowed out all the parts that mattered. The Husks make the Faceless. They spread their emptiness like a sexually transmitted void: semen, saliva, blood—"

Tub made like he was going to continue, but he must have seen me making a dumber-than-usual face.

"Didn't know that part?"

I shook my head.

"There may be other ways. Bodily fluids is all we've been able to confirm. With sex or saliva, you've got a few minutes to limit exposure before you're emptied out completely and wake up Faceless. But if they get their blood in you somehow, it's game over. Luckily, they seem to like sex best."

"Who doesn't?" Randall laughed, holding up his hand for a high five.

Tub growled at him.

Randall's hand went down slowly.

"Then we take a big step up the food chain and find the Flares," Tub continued. "Big balls of light that scream inside your head when you look at 'em. They make the Husks."

He checked with us again. I raised my beer, motioning for him to continue.

"Though it seems to be an accident."

"What?" Randall said.

Tub leaned forward and rubbed his bad leg. He spat on the floor and killed his beer before speaking.

"The Flares want to reduce people. They reach into your head and pick out the stuff that makes you . . . you. They yank at a few specific bits—memories, impulses, and tendencies that are like keystones to your personality. When it all comes tumbling down, they get some weird kind of energy from you. The ground shakes when it happens, so there must be a lot of it. Sometimes the process don't go right, and a body doesn't reduce all the way. You wind up with a Husk and a Sludge: the empty shell where a person used to be, and the living embodiment of all the garbage that was left over."

"And that's an accident?" Randall asked.

"Seems to be."

"That's bullshit," I said. "We've seen them call an angel just to make more of those things. They did some kind of ritual, and a ball of light came down and started lighting fires behind people's eyes. Making more Empty Ones. That's the procreation thing you were talking about, right? We've seen it. We were there."

Tub laughed bitterly. He tapped a little song on the concrete with his rebar cane. "The Husks worship the Flares like . . . hell, maybe you got us beat on that one term. They worship Flares like gods, or angels."

Randall sprouted a shit-eating grin.

Damn it, and I gave him credit for naming them.

"But they don't work together. The Husks may know how to call the Flares, but the bastards don't exactly take orders. The Flares aren't there to make more Husks. They're there to make more of themselves. They're procreating. Reproducing. That's what you helped make happen, son."

It felt like somebody'd kicked me in the balls. Not one of those good, meaty, *I-mean-it* kicks either. No, one of those sinister numbers that just grazes the sack, and leaves a nasty nauseous ache for hours.

"Shiiiiit," Randall provided, helpfully.

"They seem to need human involvement to procreate. I got a theory about that. I think, to make something as big and strange as a Flare, they don't need to get rid of stuff in your head like they do with the Husks. They need to change it altogether. And that's a problem. The Flares aren't like us. They're not builders—they don't produce anything. They only take things away from the universe. To make an actual change, they need a creative force. They need another human. Somebody with a compatible personality, that they can use like a guidebook while they're pecking away in there. That's what the ritual the Husks use is all about: putting the candidate—that's what we call people like you, son—through some shit that the host has been through already. Walking a few hard, bloody miles in each other's shoes. Forcing the candidate to have something in common with the host, then using the candidate's brain to twist the host into a Flare."

"I got a feeling like that, down in the tunnels in New York," I said. "It was hard to explain, but I knew there was somebody else nearby that I couldn't see, and they were using me against him."

"That's about the truth of it." Tub nodded. "But the angels don't give a cold damn about the Husks, or the Sludges, or the Faceless, or any of that. Far as they're concerned, they're just leftovers. Reducing people is like a nuclear reaction. The energy is the whole point, and all those monsters are just a bunch of toxic waste."

"So what are the angels? What do they want?"

Tub laughed. "That *is* what they want. We've seen references to them going back to the start of human history. They've always been around—solving people, stealing energy, moving it around—and they always *will* be. They're a part of the universe. They're like gravity, or the tide. They just . . . are."

Tub stopped speaking. He peered into the shadows of the second floor and, apparently not finding what he was looking for, turned back to us. "To be honest, the Flares aren't even the problem, though I'll spit in your eye if you ever tell Meryll I said that. They do their thing, and they take, what? Maybe a few hundred people a year? That's consistent, through most of history. The number never seems to swing much from century to century. They're like sharks. They're gonna kill, because they're designed to kill, and we'd be best just accepting that."

Something in me went cold. I had started to like Tub, to think of him like the drunken abusive father figure I never had. But he'd lost me at the shark analogy. *I won't ever accept that.*

"The real problem," he whispered, "is the Husks. A botched job that leaves behind a Husk and a Sludge is the exception, not the rule, so maybe only a handful get left behind in a century. But we can't kill them. So even though there aren't many, they've been building up over time. Our planet is a goddamned rubbish bin for monsters, and it's just about full up."

"Rubbish Bin for Monsters" would make a good band name, I thought. I figured I'd mention it to Randall later, though, because Tub apparently wasn't done yet.

"There's so many now that the Husks have started

THE EMPTY ONES 115

finding each other," he said. "The world wasn't always so connected. Every once in a while one would get made, and it would cause havoc in its area, and that was it. People would call them vampires, or demons, or whatever—and they'd just warn their kids not to go near them. That's Dracula's castle, boy. That forest is haunted. That's just the way it is, and you can't do anything about it, so stay away."

Tub drew a big circle in the dirt with his cane. He crisscrossed it with long, straight lines.

"But then the Husks started moving. Boats, trains, airplanes, cars. They found each other, and they started talking. And they did what every screwed up lonely little mistake does when it finds out it's not alone. They built themselves a religion. They made up a reason for their existence. And then they got down to spreading the gospel. Making more Flares. Seeding the Faceless. They know they're an accident. They accept that. But they think that means this world and everything on it is an accident, too. The Flares exist to solve mistakes, and the Husks want the whole world solved."

I took a drink, because that seemed like a fine thing to do after hearing that news.

"We heard about what happened in New York," Tub said.

Randall raised an eyebrow.

"Maybe not about what happened to you two personally, but we heard about the disappearances. A few dozen kids, at most. What's happening here? Isn't anything like that. Thousands are disappearing *by the week*. You tangled with one Husk and his gang of Faceless. We have trouble counting how many *armies* have amassed here. You boys went through a nasty street fight. This is The Great War."

I stayed quiet. I figured Tub had earned himself a pretty dramatic pause.

"Man," Randall finally said. "You Brits seriously just will not shut up about World War II."

Tub stared at him, then remembered he should be slapping him in the back of the head. So he did that.

"Ow, shit!" Randall hopped up and ran to the other side of the fire. "I'm just joking. God damn."

"That's the problem," Meryll said, from somewhere above and behind us. "You're always joking, and you're rarely funny."

Yes, she's okay!

Yes, she insulted Randall!

Holy shit, how is she okay?

TEN

Long straights, cruise control, droning music, blasting through flat beige landscapes that never seemed to move no matter how fast we went. Highway hypnosis. I was thinking about home. About West LA and what I missed: Japanese food. Frozen yogurt. Zankou Chicken.

Maybe I was just hungry.

But there was also my apartment. Melissa, my stupid roommate who always left dishes on the floor.

On the floor, Melissa? Really?

My couch and my TV. Binge-watching *Kids in the Hall* and practicing all of the voices. I missed getting on stage—even the small, dimly lit ones in the basements of comic book shops. And making the audience laugh—even if the audience was a dozen dorks just killing time until some guy who shades *Batman* took the stage.

I missed the beach. We'd been bombing around the butt crack of the Southwest long enough that you'd think I'd be sick of sun and sand. But it's not the same. The sand here is too coarse. It doesn't run between your knuckles like silk when you pick it up. It's not a bunch of stones polished by time and oceans. It's not sand. It's just dirt. The sun doesn't penetrate into you, warming your organs first and spreading outward. It stops at your skin. It leaves you feeling burnt and fluish. It's not sun. It's just fucking hot.

And, oh man, the people in these towns. Holy crap. Like every car is an IROC. One time I saw a guy with *two* mullets. I don't even know *how*.

I miss people that don't look like they're one zipper away from wearing your skin as a coat.

But you know what I really, really miss? I miss safety. I miss locking the door to my apartment, changing into my Hulk Hogan pajama bottoms and my Wayne's World sweatshirt, sitting cross-legged on the couch and playing stupid phone games, and never, not once, thinking a fucking tar monster was going to kick in my door and turn me into a blood Slurpee. Or that the faces in the audience I can't quite make out aren't just sitting in shadows. Or that some hollow-eyed pretty boy is going to eat my soul and turn me into some Stepford-core cultist.

I should not have to worry about this crap.

I *wouldn't* have to worry about this crap, if not for Kaitlyn.

I love her, God bless her, but when she said we had to run, and I said, "I'll come with you," I really wanted her to be like, "No, no, you totally can't. You're too precious. Stay here and live your awesome life while I embark on a thrilling but dangerous adventure, stopping by occasionally to have margaritas and laugh about my shenanigans."

I didn't want to go. I liked my life. I *hate* adventure.

But she started crying. That little Kaitlyn cry that's more like tiny hiccups. She thanked me, then she helped me pack. What was I supposed to do? She was my girl. If she needed me, I had to go.

That's how friendships work . . . right?

Right?

So yeah, I had a lot on my mind. I wasn't paying attention. It was just past sunset. You could see light over the horizon, but it wasn't making it down here. It was black on the ground, and black on the road, so when something black loomed up in front of the Jetta, I didn't even see it in time. Carey jerked the wheel, but that just made us hit it sideways. It gave a little on impact, like punching a brick of Jell-O, then rebounded just enough to send the car flipping down the road.

Cut.

Scene missing.

Guitars are twanging. An angry man rants about guns and butter.

My eyes open, but one won't focus. My head is full, my vision red. I've been upside down for a few minutes. My fingers move slow, and because I'm still hanging from the seat belt, there's so much tension on it that the buckle won't release.

All this talk of blood and iron / it's the cause of all my shaking.

One speaker is blown. The song is even tinnier than usual. Carey's not in the seat next to me. I wonder if he was wearing his seat belt.

I laugh a little.

I would be goddamned amazed if he was.

It hurts too much to turn my head. I can check on Kaitlyn once I get myself down. I grab the steering wheel and haul some of my weight off it. I click the release button. I fall.

The fatherland's no place to cry for / it makes me want to run out shouting.

I land on my neck. Should have planned better. After I finish whimpering, I turn to crawl out the passenger side window and hit my nose. It isn't broken. Huh. I assumed everything just shattered, in a car crash. That's how the movies make it look. It feels silly, unlocking the door, pulling on the handle, and exiting my upside-down car as if I meant to flip it and now I just have to go run errands. The metal grinds on the pavement.

I hear some talk of guns and butter / that's something we can do without.

I move onto my side and drag myself around to the back window. I see Kaitlyn still inside. At least, I think that's Kaitlyn. There's too much blood to see her face.

If men are only blood and iron / Oh doctor doctor, what's in my shirt?

I grab the handle and open her door. I purposefully don't check to see if she's breathing. I don't need to know that yet. I *can't* know that yet. I lift her weight as best I can with one arm, and release her seat belt. I loop my hands under her arms and drag her clear of the wreckage. I don't know why I'm doing this. Do cars explode when they're flipped upside down, or is that just in *Grand Theft Auto*?

I'm too foggy. I can't think straight. I give myself a mission: Drag Kaitlyn's skinny ass to safety, then pass out and probably die. But first things first.

The car stereo fades as we reach the shoulder. I keep moving until there's a big rock behind me. Big rocks are good. Solid, dependable rocks. They'll know what to do. I pull Kaitlyn up to the boulder and prop her up against it. It's still sun-warm, emanating heat like a radiator. When I'm sure she'll stay upright, I collapse next to her. That's when I make my first big mistake. I look back toward the car. Past it, into the dark behind it. And I see that the night is moving.

I've never encountered any of those tar guys that Kaitlyn and Carey talk about. Apparently I very nearly *was* one, but I didn't think to take a selfie at the time, so I've never actually seen them until now. It's nighttime in the desert, and they're pure black and pretty far away, but even so I can tell that the things are built like André the Giant. Roughly human shaped, but too tall, too thick. Large heads, massively disproportionate hands and feet—with something glinting in their faces. They are quiet. No sound when they move. And they are apparently social creatures.

Because I see now that there are thousands of them. Maybe tens of thousands.

I thought there were only a few, at first. That the shadows rippling like a disturbed pond in the distance were just my eyes playing tricks on me. But no. There were so many of the things. Bunched together tightly, and moving as one unit. One unit that extended as far back as my eyes could see. And, I got the sense, even farther.

Luckily, they aren't moving toward us. Or at least they weren't, before Carey stumbled out from behind the Jetta, threw a tire at one, and called it "cancerous diarrhea."

The tar man splits off from the main group and plods slowly toward Carey, who is just standing there on the far side of the highway, past the overturned Jetta and the shower of off-white plastic it left embedded in the asphalt. A few more seem to take notice of the first tar man and follow him. Half a dozen are coming Carey's way now, and the asshole, is backing up toward *me*.

"Don't you bring that shit over here," I yell at him.

"Hey, you're alive," he says. "Cool. Help me kill these things."

I make six faces at him at once. I can't decide which of the many valid questions I have about his plan are the most dire.

"What?" I decide. Then, "Why? H-how?"

"If I can get enough of them over here by the car, they'll catch the rest on fire when I blow it up."

"How the hell are you going to do that?"

"I . . . shit. I guess I just figured I'd throw my lighter at it. You think that'll work?"

"I think that's only in video games and action movies," I say, conveniently not mentioning that I'd had the same thought. If only briefly, and while concussed.

"Well . . ." Carey says, "that stinks. Because I've already pissed these things off."

I try to get my feet under me, but they aren't cooperating. I try to shove and drag Kaitlyn around the edge of the boulder, but she just flops over and bleeds quietly into the sand.

"I can't move her," I say. Then more urgently, "Carey, I can't move her!"

Carey thinks for a second. Looks like it hurts. Then he feints left, but bolts right around the nearest tar man. Once he's past it, he loops back toward the Jetta. He starts banging on the door panels, hooting and hollering.

"Over here," he yells. "Come take a bite of this asshole sandwich."

The tar men turn, and begin lumbering in his direction. Carey disappears out of sight behind the car, leading an impromptu parade of monsters away from me and my unconscious best friend.

All of them but one.

Maybe it's just closer to us than Carey, or maybe it has tar where its ears should be, or maybe it just thinks cute, bloody girls make a better snack than crusty old punks. I don't know why, but it doesn't turn and follow Carey. It's fixated on us. On Kaitlyn.

It doesn't have eyes. It has two brass gears roughly where its eyes should be. No mouth. No nose. No skin. No face. Just a thick fluid like crude oil, flowing in slow motion. One hand is stretched toward us, though it's still fifty feet away and moving slowly. Thick fingers that nearly flow together into an indistinguishable mitt. A piece flows down its thumb, seems about ready to drip off, then retreats. It runs down the thing's arm instead, and rejoins its body. It leaves no prints behind, no puddles. It's about forty feet away.

I can move my legs, but I can't get any strength in them. I prop myself up on my knees, wrap my arms around Kaitlyn's feet, and throw all of my weight into it.

She moves an inch. That's a generous guess.

I should've gone jogging with her. At least once. She asked so many times. She was always saying stuff like, "Hey, let's go for a run instead of rewatching RoboCop for the one hundredth time," or "Let's go hiking instead of drinking margaritas on your roof," or "Let's go to the gym instead of the hot dog stand," but no—Jackie digs wieners. Jackie's gonna die for her love of goddamned wieners.

I have moved her maybe four inches.

The tar man is now thirty feet away.

It's moving so slowly, like watching a fat guy swim. That's the worst part. I could mosey, and still outrun the stupid thing, but my legs just will not respond. They get the message. They twitch and stretch, like they understand what I want, but the lazy bastards give up when it actually comes time to follow through.

I pull. I heave. I throw everything I have into it.

Jesus Christ, Kaitlyn, you cannot weigh this much. I am looking at you, and it is physically impossible. Unless your ass is made out of dwarf stars, you cannot weigh this much!

I've moved her, like, six inches. The tar man has advanced another ten feet.

I am going to die in slow motion.

Then something that looks like a giant bat flaps out of the darkness behind the tar man and wraps itself around the thing's head. It's covered in patches and duct tape. It has spikes on its shoulders. It's Carey's jacket. He's somehow gotten behind the tar man and thrown his coat over its head. It seems to be contemplating whether or not it cares about this new development.

Carey takes advantage of the distraction. He runs around in front of the tar man, grabs the part of his jacket that's still over the thing's face, feels around for something in there, and appears to find it, latch on, and yank backwards with all of his strength. There's a sound like duct tape being peeled from the roll, and Carey falls on his ass, holding his jacket in both hands. He looks up at the tar man.

Nothing happens.

At all.

The thing is frozen in place.

Carey shakes his jacket out, and two shiny brass gears thunk into the dust. He looks back at me and gives me a big shithead smile. He is just never going to shut up about this, I can tell already.

"What, no hand jobs for the hero?" he's going to say later, when we get out of this. *If* we get out of this. And once again I'm going to tell him that he looks like he just escaped from the punk rock internment camp and smells like a homeless basketball team.

Oh, but that's all moot. Because here comes another tar man, drawn by all the commotion. I haven't stopped shoving, pulling, twisting, and otherwise uselessly manipulating Kaitlyn's stupidly heavy body. We're maybe a full foot away from where we started, and I'm done. I'm out of energy. I'm hurt and dizzy. Waves of nausea ripple out from my stomach and crash against the backs of my eyes. I'm sweating, and even though the desert still has plenty of lingering warmth, I'm also shivering.

Carey steps around the frozen tar man toward the approaching one, and he pulls out his lighter.

He's just about to throw it when I tell him, "Don't waste it! Look around!" I point to his left.

More tar men have broken off and are pouring in from the side. Carey looks to his right, and sees more of the same. They work more like fluid than animals. Enough start moving one way, and the floodgates open. They all come pouring in.

Carey rapidly displays two looks that I've never seen on his face before. The first is utter and total defeat. The second is something I'd call "thinking," if I didn't know him better.

He bolts for the Jetta. It's unnecessary. He could have walked over there. There are dozens of tar men, in a huge, rough circle now, slowly closing in on our boulder from every direction. But they're in no hurry. Carey rips off his T-shirt—it's black with a yellow hand displaying a sort of reverse peace-sign, the letters SLF across the top—and twists it up real tight. He flips open the gas cap to the Jetta and shoves most of the shirt in there. Then he pulls it out, now soaked in gas. He flips it around and puts the dry end back into the tank, then gets out his lighter. He flicks the flint and it catches on the first try. Carey turns to sprint back toward me and Kaitlyn. Just as he reaches us, he dives, lands on his stomach, rolls, and quickly wraps himself around our bodies, shielding us from the blast.

Which does not come.

I'm staring past his armpit, watching a flaming T-shirt hang from my wrecked car.

"So uh . . ."—I finally break the silence—"is this cuddle time or . . . ?"

Carey carefully unfolds himself and stares back at the Jetta. The flames have traced themselves up the shirt and into the tank. They're starting to spread across the rear of the car, but it doesn't look like it's going to explode. It just looks like it's going to burn for a while.

"I thought that was going to be way cooler," he says.

"Nice atmosphere, though," I say, trying to sound all calm and flippant.

That's me. That's firmly within my funny-girl character to say. It would not be within my funny-girl character to scratch Carey's ugly face and scream and cry and beg the encroaching horde not to melt me and my best friend. That's what I want to do, but it just doesn't seem like "me."

We watch the fire burn for a minute.

"Can you move?" he finally says.

"I don't know," I answer, and I try my legs.

They're responding now, just a little. I might be able to hobble away, but . . .

"I'm not leaving Kaitlyn," I say.

It surprises me, too.

Is this loyalty, or are you just performing for an audience? Would you sit here and die with her if you were alone, with nobody to judge?

I don't have any answers for myself.

Carey loops one of his arms under Kaitlyn's and drags her to her feet. He motions for me to follow. My legs are overcooked spaghetti, but they get me upright. I put an arm around Kaitlyn's other side, but it's just a gesture. I can't take much, if any, of her weight. I'm leaning against her for balance as much as I am holding her. We start to make our way around the boulder, out of the flickering orange light, and into the darkness of the desert. But it's like I thought— we're in the middle of a much larger crowd of tar men. A few dozen paces away there's a river of black acid, peppered with dully shining brass.

But the boulder is lopsided. It's lower to the ground on the back end. We get Kaitlyn rolled up there, though "we" is being pretty generous. Really, I stand and rest my hand on her hip while Carey, shirtless, all ropy muscle and scars and shitty tattoos, wrestles her off the ground. He pulls me up after her, and together we drag her up as far as the slope would allow. It's not very far, maybe ten feet off the ground. One of those tar men could probably just reach up here and grab us. Anybody could walk right up that little slope and eat our screaming faces.

But they don't.

The tar men that had been closing in on us back on the highway follow our path around the boulder, then just keep going. They merge into the mass of tar men on the far side and shamble away.

"What just happened?" I ask Carey.

"I don't know," he says. "I don't think they were after us."

"What are they doing, then?"

"It looks like they're . . . migrating."

I ask if we shouldn't make some sort of tourniquet for Kaitlyn's head. Carey says that's a great idea, and waits for me to take off my shirt—he already lost his while performing "acts of stunning heroism." I tell him I'm not wearing a bra—I don't generally need to; I'm not exactly packing heat—and he says he doesn't mind. I finally convince him to give me his jacket. I make sure there's no tar remnants in it that will burn my flesh off when I slide into it. But it's clean.

Well, that's a relative term. I mean, it's still *Carey's*. But it won't melt my skin. Probably. At least not right away.

Carey tears my *Adventure Time* shirt into strips and ties them around Kaitlyn's forehead, neck, and upper arm. They're soaked through with blood in seconds.

We watch the tar men flow like a glacier toward the horizon. We watch the car burn itself out until it's just a steel skeleton. Like some huge, bizarre turtle died and was picked clean by gigantic vultures. We watch the sky turn from black to clear and blazing blue.

We watch Kaitlyn bleed out onto the rock. It flows down the slope and pools on the ground. We watch the blood stop, and wonder if it's coagulating, or if she's just run out.

ELEVEN

Meryll had her own stash, and she was eight beers deep already. I was eight beers more in love with her. She could drink like a fucking longshoreman, and it was literally the hottest thing I had ever seen. All I wanted to do was hold her and feed her beer until we both grew old and died from liver disease, together, in each other's arms.

Shit, I'm getting all sappy here. Head in the game, Carey.

Tub was still talking. I couldn't even process it anymore. There was too much already. Randall had done the smart thing and fallen asleep an hour ago. He was drooling onto his own shoulder.

Here's what I gathered before my attention span hit empty: The angels don't give a shit about humanity. They show up at random, collapse some poor bastard into his own chest cavity, then skip off into space to the planet of celestial assholes, or wherever it is they go. It's the Empty Ones who have forced structure on them. They're some sorta number freaks, like my drunk-ass mom who actually bought lottery tickets using the numbers on the backs of those little slips of paper in fortune cookies. The Empty Ones have developed all sorts of rituals to manipulate the angels. Ceremonies that can summon the bastards to Earth, or even force them to solve specific people. But then there's the big one: Every thirty-six years they conduct a ritual to try to birth a new angel. The problem is, for each angel, there are only thirty-six candidates in all of humanity who qualify for the "honor," and only one will make the cut.

"You can see this reflected in mythology," Tub was saying. "Jews called them the Nistarim and believed they were the thirty-six saints whose existence justifies humanity to God blah blah fart Bob's-your-uncle Mary Poppins."

That's where I tuned out.

But one of those candidates is born with a mutation. An extra digit on their left hand or foot. Most times, this mutant doesn't do a damn thing except maybe die horribly, crushed between some sacrificial gears or melted by a tar man. But if they figure it out in time—if they know what they're doing when the Empty Ones and the Unnoticeables and the tar men come for them—the mutation has the power to fight back.

They almost never figure it out in time.

Tub couldn't even shut up long enough for me to make a move on Meryll. She seemed to be mostly fine now. Her voice was still a little raspy, and there was a massive red handprint across her neck. But, let's be honest: I've fucked girls with worse wounds.

She should be dead, though. Do you think that makes her more or less game to screw around?

"Early Christianity often depicted saints and other holy entities as possessing a sixth finger, or extra toe," Tub had said. "You can even see it in some depictions of Jesus on the cross such as yadda yadda pip-pip cheerio I'm a fucking beer hog."

Seriously, the guy grabbed the last six-pack out of the broken television, gave me and Randall one measly beer each, then sat down and drank all of the rest. I mean, yeah, I would've done the same thing if I were him—but I was starting to lose my buzz. You try processing a mountain of crazy guru-yogi crap on the cusp of an early hangover. If you're going to destroy a man's entire understanding of the world, you give him the lion's share of the six-pack. Maybe even chip in for a half rack. Damn.

Something else I picked up before Tub's voice turned into background noise: The mutations all get a kind of Superman gig—stronger, faster, heightened senses, better reflexes—but as they kill angels, they start to take on some of their powers. No idea how much of this to believe, but Tub swore that, way back in the day, one of them could melt people by looking at them. Another knew what was going to happen ten seconds before the event. One of them could even control the tar men. Bet that was a nasty surprise for the Empty Ones. Would've loved to have seen that happen with Gus—his stupid donkey mug going all slack as his cronies turn on him. As they put their acid hands on his skin and melt his gangly frame into a dickhead milkshake. Push their fingers into his eyes, shove their fists down his throat, and burn him from the inside out, like he did to Thing 2 back at our place in NYC. I'd love to see his spine cracked and—

"You all right?" Meryll was looking at me funny.

"Yeah," I said, shaking myself out of the fantasy.

"You looked pretty cheesed off just then."

"It's nothing," I said.

"Nothing, hell—you were punching the air a little bit. You were turning red."

"What are you all worked up about?" Tub said, draining the rest of the last beer and tossing it into the barrel fire. "I was just getting into pre-Germanic myth cycles. . . ."

"Jesus Christ," I moaned.

"Well, no," Tub said thoughtfully. "That's a tenuous link at best, although there is something to the mutation and the messiah figure in many reli—"

"Stop it!" I stood up and kicked a piece of cinder block. That was dumb. I felt my toes fold up through my flimsy canvas Chucks. "I don't give a shit about cycling myths or pre-Germans. There's only two things I want from you, and you can't give me either."

Tub stared at me. He grumbled deep in his throat and spat on the floor. "What's that?" he finally said.

"I want a goddamned beer, and I want to kill Gus so bad my dick is hard."

"Gross." Meryll laughed.

"Well, I—"

"Yeah, I know," I said, holding up my hands. "You can't kill 'em. We hit that fucker with a train and he practically skipped away. I got it."

"That's . . . not quite right," Tub said.

I felt my heart turn over like an engine.

"It's true enough that *you and I* can't take out a Husk," Tub continued. "We're just people. But a mutation can do all sorts of things. . . ."

"Great, let's just go out and get our hands on one of *them*." I rolled my eyes and went for the broken TV set where they hid the beer. I'd already raided it twice and came up empty, but I guess I'm an optimist.

I patted around blindly inside the hollowed-out innards of the old TV. A little tube here, a spiky bit toward the back. Some cables with something hard beneath them. I felt a little deeper. I pushed them aside. Round. Metal. Slippery with dust.

Oh God, oh God please . . .

I brought my hand out and my heart sank. It was a can of something, all right. A red label, with white lettering that said PARTY SEVEN. But it was way too big to be beer.

"We don't have to go anywhere," Tub said from the couch behind me.

I turned back toward him and saw Meryll. She'd taken off one of her combat boots. Her bare foot was pointing at me. She wiggled her toes.

All six of them.

"You look surprised," she said. She smiled, proud and a little cruel.

"I'll be honest," Tub said. "I thought you'd figured it out ages ago."

"He's a bit slow," Meryll said.

Tub sighed and started thumping the barrel fire with his rebar cane. It flared to life with a sound like a shopping cart falling down an elevator shaft.

Randall jumped awake, snapping off a long string of drool that spiraled across the room and landed on Meryll's foot.

She sneered down at it, then wiped it off with her sock.

I don't even have to compete. The poor bastard is losing the game all by himself.

"Tell you what," Tub said, settling back into the busted couch, now that he'd gotten the fire going again. "You crack open that beer and we'll go over it all again. I'll use real small words this time."

I looked down at my hand. DRAUGHT BITTER, it said in smaller letters toward the bottom. You could've stuffed a baby in that massive can.

We might have a way to kill Gus, Randall had spit all over the foot of the girl we both liked, and I just found a fucking monument to alcohol. Maybe things were going to be all right after all.

"It's a pain in the ass, is what it is," Meryll said.

She took the god-sized beer can with both hands and took a long sip, then passed it to Tub.

"Gotta buy two pairs of boots in different sizes," she continued, stretching her toes out to stare unhappily at the extra one. "Gotta add an extra piggy to the song. But I guess if it means I get to nuke those bloody Flares, it's a fair trade."

"No," Tub said, "the deformity itself doesn't do anything. You're not poking at them with your bloody extra toe. It's just a sign of something bigger going on inside you."

"I got s—" I started, but Randall cut me off.

"I think it's kinda hot," he said. Meryll blushed and gave him a crooked smile.

Damn it! I was going to say "I got something bigger that could go inside you." She would've loved that.

Tub tapped his cane against the fire barrel and gave Randall a look that could kill a man from two states away. Randall didn't notice. We were halfway through the ogre of beers, and his face was flushed, his eyes unfocused.

"Seems like you really hate the angels," he said, and Meryll winced.

"Sorry, Flares. You hate the Flares," he corrected.

"Yeah, of course. What are you, best friends with 'em?" She passed him the minikeg, but he just shuffled it right off to me.

Aw, shit. I know that move. He only turns down booze when he's hoping to get lucky. Trying to avoid whiskey dick. Well, whiskey and my dick are best friends, sucker.

I chugged from the can, distantly hoping the girl would be impressed by the sheer volume of alcohol I could consume. They never were. But a man can always try.

"No," Randall said, and laughed, even though it wasn't goddamned funny. "I mean, it seems personal with you."

"It is," Meryll said.

And nothing else.

She hopped off the edge of the couch, stuffed her bare foot into her boot, and headed for the ladder to the second floor.

"I'm tired," she called over her shoulder, and started climbing. "I'll see you tomorrow."

Hahahahaha—eat it, Randall!

"Crap," he said. "What did I do?"

"Sometimes there's crossover with who the Flares go after," Tub said. "They like bloodlines. Something in the genes. They often revisit the same family. Usually over generations. But, Meryll—a Flare came for her nan one day. They were close. The old lady took care of Meryll while her parents were working. It came for her while she was cooking. Meryll walked right in on her being solved. Saw the Flare, saw her nan crumple up like paper, fold into herself screaming, and then just stop being."

"Shit," Randall said.

"Shit," I agreed.

"They found Meryll hours later, still sitting on the kitchen floor. Shell-shocked. She didn't talk for days, and when she did, when she told them happened, well . . ."

"Well, what?" Randall asked.

"What do you think?" Tub growled. "It sounds nuts,

doesn't it? Her nan was gone. No body, no signs of struggle or violence. And Meryll with her crazy story—they figured, best-case scenario, the old lady had bugged out and Meryll was some kinda pathological liar. Worst-case scenario, something bad had happened and it broke Meryll's mind. Either way, it was the institution for her."

"And you brought it up while hitting on her." I laughed.

Both Tub and Randall glared at me.

Oh, what, I'm the asshole here?

"I got her out of the asylum, once we figured out what she was. Boys keep an eye on admittance papers. People start babbling about sludge giants and immortals and balls of light, we take an interest. When we saw the medical records, the extra toe, we knew. Busted her out the next week, and she's been with us ever since. Five years, it's been. I trained her up, and we've killed two of the Flares already. Well, she killed 'em. I mostly stood around and watched. Maybe clapped afterward, if it was a good show."

"Holy shit," Randall said, motioning for the beer back now that his prospects had dried up. "She's really killed those things?"

"Yeah, and I figure she's not finished yet. This bloke you've come all this way after . . . what was his name?"

"Gus," I said. It spat out of me like a curse.

"Maybe there's a way we can help each other. We've got to make a move soon. We don't know what all this buildup is about—the Sludges in the tunnels, the kids going missing by the drove. But we can't just sit here and wait for them to do whatever it is they're going to do. If you got history with a Husk, we might could use that. Have you lads draw him out, and either we take him, or he takes you and we tail him. See where this is all coming from."

"Wow," Randall said, "you didn't sugarcoat that at all. You want to use us as bait, maybe even hand us over to the psycho that killed our friends?"

"That's about it," Tub said.

"Are you fucking insane?" I asked.

"Probably," he conceded. "You boys didn't strike me as the cowardly type. If you're not up for it—"

"Obviously we're up for it," I said. "We just want it on the record that you're crazy as a shithouse rat."

Tub laughed, thick and laced with coughing. It sounded like somebody trying to push-start a tugboat.

"Dick!" he yelled.

Me and Randall giggled reflexively.

"Dicky boy, get over here!" He drummed on the fire barrel again and woke the gaggle of punks sleeping on the chairs and couches behind us.

"What, man?" Dick said.

He was a tall kid. Wide shoulders and long, skinny arms that hung down halfway to his knees. Looked like a malnourished ape. Had a Nebraska face—square forehead, close-set eyes, big lips . . . I don't know, you can just tell when somebody's from the Midwest. They always look incomplete without a tractor.

"You and yours have been tailing Husks in the south end, yeah?"

"Yeah," Dick answered. He rubbed at his eyes, puffed out his cheeks, shook his head. I knew that dance. Trying to shake off a buzz that was right in the middle of melting into a hangover. "Husks? Yeah. I think . . ."

"Up, Dicky boy!" Tub cried, swinging his length of rebar into the ground at Dick's feet. He jumped and nearly fell over.

"I'm up! I'm up!" Dick pleaded.

"Husks. South end. Yeah? One of 'em was in a band, you said."

"Right," Dick's brain was finally starting to catch up to him. "In a band. The uh . . . The Talentless. Good name. Playing at the Marquee tomorrow. I hear they're fucking crazy live. Strip naked and cut themselves and shit. Sounds cool."

The Talentless. Gus's band.

Tub was watching me. He saw the name register. Saw my face draw tight.

"Well," he said, "looks like we're going fishing tomorrow."

TWELVE

The boy is pretty, I'll give him that. A bit too limp for me, but I see what the girls like in him. He's got eyes like pond water, murky and deep, just a bit of glittering green in among the brown. Skin the color of creamy coffee. Cheekbones you could cut yourself on. He's tall, and fit, and stylish—wearing a pristine white blazer with thick shoulder pads, no shirt, dark purple slacks, pink loafers with no socks. His hair is dark and thick, like a shampoo commercial. Lots of hairspray. Real, real pretty.

If you're into pretty boys.

I like my men rough. Well, not *too* rough—but there's nothing like a handsome bloke who looks like he's been on the wrong end of a fight or two. I just can't get behind the flawless, magazine-pretty boys that are all the rage these days. They don't look like men to me. But this one is a man. I can see that through those tight gemstone slacks. He made sure everybody could see it.

Looks like the boy's saving a salami for later.

I wonder if that's just a pair of socks or something. I'm

curious, so I slide through his personality like an oiled cobra and comb through his data. I'm lost in a sea of irrelevance. First dates and one night stands. Primping. Prepping. High fives and crying girls. These are his memories, and the vast majority of them revolve, in one way or another, around sex. Thinking about sex. Bragging about sex. Having sex. Avoiding the repercussions of sex.

I slide into a memory that stands out from the rest. It glows hot and bright blue. A keystone. A bit of it plays out: He's fifteen. His cousins are laughing and pointing at the bulge in his tight, bright-red shorts. He's embarrassed, cringing away from them, but he doesn't see the girl behind him. He bumps into her. In one smooth motion, she reaches out and yanks his shorts down.

The girls gasp.

They're not laughing anymore.

That's the first time he realizes that what he has down there isn't normal. It's a weapon, of sorts. Power.

Huge chunks of his persona branch out from this moment. His confidence comes from his cock. Nothing else. He knows he's not smart, or funny, or kind. He learns to take advantage. He knows he intimidates the other boys—and the girls, too. But that's okay. They're curious. They come to him. Some of them love it. Some just think it hurts. He likes either way just fine.

Weapons are supposed to hurt.

It's the smell of his cousin's perfume: obnoxiously girl. Slathered on from a magazine. And a shade of red, textured like polyester. Bright, with a white stripe through it.

Those two symbols will collapse all the branches that come after that memory, simplifying them back to just the one moment behind the shed, at a Labor Day barbeque with his giggling cousins.

Huh. I guess he wasn't stuffing after all. Good for him.

I've solved a few people recently. Took an old lady just down the street from here this afternoon. I'm all good on energy. I don't need to solve this boy. I just want to practice. I want to see what I can make from his pretty but vacant little body.

I look into his code and try to track the simplifications. See if I can figure out what I'll be left with if I take away certain portions of his life.

I think if I solve the paths that branch out from the barbecue, and also that time he stood naked, coked out of his mind on the beach watching the sunrise, and that other time his mother bought him a Rocket Pop from a cart on the promenade, I can turn him into . . .

Haha. Oh, shit.

That can't be right. But what if it is . . . ?

I have to know.

I pull out the perfume, the shade of red, the feel of wet sand, the body-buzz of a good coke high just starting to fade, the texture of cheap wood pressed against the tongue, and a stabbing, frozen headache. I weave them together. I have a solution.

I show him the secret moments that have dictated so much of his life, and I laugh as he starts coughing. Blood from his nostrils, eyes, ears. His legs collapse, too weak to hold him. He drops to his knees and tries to grab at his crotch, but his arms are withering now, too. All of his muscle mass is retreating, migrating elsewhere. His skin goes pale, parts of it already atrophying. His face is gaunt and skeletal.

But his cock. His cock is the size of a boa constrictor, and growing.

I am losing it. I can't stop laughing.

His purple slacks explode, and it flops onto the ground. It twitches, and starts moving. It's prehensile!

Oh lord, this is too much. I haven't laughed like this in ages.

Then the fucking thing grows spikes, and I pee myself a little.

THIRTEEN

2013. Highway 57 Mexico. Jackie.

The pickup truck looked like it wasn't going to stop. It slowed down to a crawl, then began daintily maneuvering around the shattered plastic and spilled oil. Like it was just going to mosey right on by the horrific wreck of my Jetta, still smoldering on the side of the highway. The driver is an old Mexican guy with a face like cracked mud—sun-damaged, deep lines networked together tightly over a perpetual squint. He didn't even pause to gawk. Eyes on the road, hand working the wheel. Like he sees this kind of thing all the time.

He sure looked surprised when I came sprinting out of the desert and leapt on his hood, though.

The driver slammed on his brakes and I slid off onto the asphalt, still cool from the chilly desert night. I landed on my back, the wind knocked out of me. I rolled once or twice, bumping my bony elbows painfully, and lay there, working my mouth like a fish out of water. The driver opened his door slowly and scanned the horizon for a long time before stepping out. I was looking right at his feet, visible just beneath the open door. He was wearing cowboy boots with little points on the toe, like elf shoes.

He said something to me in Spanish.

"Donde," I said, still trying to catch my breath.

He leaned closer.

"Donde esta," I panted, *"la biblioteca."*

It was the only Spanish I could remember.

His crumpled-paper face pulled into itself.

"You want the . . . library?" he asked, his English slow, clear, and careful.

"Hola!" Carey yelled from beside the boulder, dragging a limp wad of roughly Kaitlyn-shaped flesh toward us.

She was, like, Marilyn Manson white. Sort of blue. She looked deflated. No wonder, since she must have lost a bucket of blood on those rocks over the last few hours. Carey insisted that it looked worse than it was. He was sure she'd be fine. But I cut my wrist open scooping ice cream once and—

You're going to ask, aren't you?

Fine. I used to wait tables. Every girl in LA has, at one point. Restaurants use these gigantic Costco-sized tubs of ice cream. The less popular flavors sit in the freezer for so long that, by the time they get low and you have to reach way down in them to scoop, the leftover ice cream higher up on the sides has iced over. Nobody likes tutti frutti. Some of that ice is razor sharp. Boom, slashed wrist. I spilled maybe a fifth of what Kaitlyn had left on that boulder, and I passed out. Had to get a transfusion at the hospital. I'm still paying off those fucking medical bills.

The point is, I know how much blood you have to lose to be "not okay." And Kaitlyn lost way, way more than that. I was trying not to think about it, but it wasn't easy, after watching Carey manhandle her maybe-corpse across the highway. He eyeballed the driver, and, after a minute of careful consideration, he slowly and loudly said, "LADY . . . NEED . . . RIDE."

The old Mexican guy stared at the pair of them warily.

"*SENORITA*," Carey tried again, "Uh . . . *ME GUSTA*. . . . RIDE. EL RIDE-O."

Then polished it all off with a big smile and a thumbs-up.

The old guy closed his eyes and breathed in half the desert.

"Fuck you gringos," he said, finally. "That girl better not die in my truck."

The old Mexican guy said his name was Gerardo, and I laughed.

"'Rico Suave,'" I explained. He just glared at me.

I shouldn't be cracking jokes in the passenger seat when my best friend is probably lying dead in the bed of the truck, but I can't help it. It's automatic. I wasn't even really paying attention, just letting my mouth operate on cruise control. I was wrapped up in my head, thinking about what the hell we were going to do.

I said hospital. *Obviously* I said hospital. Gerardo said hospital, too, because that's what sane people say in this situation. But Carey said no. I slapped him right in his busted mouth, but he was insistent.

"She doesn't need a hospital," he said. "I've seen plenty of shit like this before, and you just gotta trust me. A hospital would be bad."

I went to slap him again, but he caught my wrist and said, "I don't trust doctors, you know. Bunch of soulless bastards. They're totally *empty inside*."

Carey shot a meaningful look at Gerardo, who clearly didn't give a shit what we said, because he had already decided that we were all escaped mental patients.

Would the Unnoticeables really come for her in a hospital? In public like that? Even worse, would Marco come himself? We must be close enough by now—just a short drive for him. . . .

A series of still images flashed through my brain: Marco's limbs bent at wrong angles, flailing as he danced amid the monsters in a crowded chapel.

These are things you do not think about, Jackie.

I decided to drop the issue, at least until we got to a phone. My cell was busted, spider-cracks across the whole screen. I couldn't find Kaitlyn's. Carey and Gerardo said they didn't have cell phones—didn't believe in them—then issued those little nods of approval that old guys give each other when they're being totally fucking unreasonable.

The highway was empty, had been all night. Gerardo's faded blue-and-white Chevy was the only vehicle we'd seen in hours of waiting. He was going to take us to civilization, and I would find a damn phone, and God help Carey's crusty ass if he tried to get between me and it.

We hit a nasty pothole, and the suspension on the pickup could have generously been described as "a rusty memory." I checked the back, and saw Carey sitting cross-legged in the bed of the truck, holding Kaitlyn's head on his lap.

Maybe I'm hysterical. In shock, or PTSD'd, or something.

She didn't look so bad anymore. Ragged and beat-up, sure, but at least her skin wasn't the color of old eggshells. Carey saw me looking through the open half-window at the rear of the cab.

"She's breathing," he said, sounding relieved.

Holy crap. Was she not, at some point?

I started to say something, but the truck swayed wildly and seemed about to tip over, which I knew from experience meant we were making a gentle turn. I turned around. We were pulling up to a squat concrete bunker, the kind of place where one would buy stale chips after the apocalypse. Dingy walls stained black with exhaust fumes. Old-timey gas pumps straight out of a Rockwell painting that somebody had dropped in the sewer—pockmarked with rust, parts held together with bailing wire. A pile of busted crates holding nothing decomposed beside the door, which was a fancy wooden thing clearly pilfered from a much nicer abandoned ruin. No windows. No pavement, just rutted dust clotted with oil. And spanning one entire wall of the building was a giant, seriously ancient, but otherwise impeccable Coca-Cola sign.

"What are you doing?" I asked Gerardo. "Why are we pulling in here? Dude, this is like, so obviously a trap laid by radioactive cannibals. We are not stopping here. My friend is fucking *hurt;* you need to get us to a hospital."

"But for that, we need gasoline. Besides, only the cartel lays traps out here. And they're not for tourists. Anyway, they don't eat them. Only chop off their arms and legs."

Comforting.

Then I saw something that shut me right up.

My brain wasn't running right. I'd been awake all night: first driving, wired to the gills on Red Bull; then fighting, hiding, and huddling on top of a rock in the middle of the desert, kept awake by the cold and the residual adrenaline. Now I had nothing. The Red Bull had gored me and left me bleeding exhaustion. The adrenaline had bored through me, leaving shaky and nauseous trails through my guts. I was rapidly zombifying.

But even so, I had the presence of mind to spot those big wooden poles on the side of the highway shooting a wad of thick black wires into the gas station.

They had a telephone.

I was jogging for the station before the truck even stopped. I grabbed the handle of the inappropriately lovely door—a cast iron number, twisting around itself in intricate flowery patterns—and thumbed the tab.

I braced myself for mutants.

Half-broken fluorescents cast a sick greenish light over a few sad racks of snack food. There was a massive chest freezer with what looked like bullet holes in the side and a dirty white counter with an old, broken-looking cash register on top of it and an old, broken-looking attendant behind it. She put down her novel—a trashy romance, judging by the half-naked pirate on the front—looked me in the eyes for a second, then looked back down at her book and pointed to a bright red Coca-Cola machine humming quietly in the corner.

"Telephone," I said.

No response.

"Telephone," I said, louder.

No response.

"Telephono?" I tried, cringing at myself.

Maybe Carey was rubbing off on me. Probably not in the way that he'd like.

Still no response. The door clattered behind me and the empty soda cans tied to the back of it with fishing line sounded an alert chime.

Gerardo squinted into the corpse-light of the fluorescents.

"How do you say telephone in Spanish?" I asked him.

"Telefono," he answered.

Holy shit, I was right.

"Then why isn't this lady telling me where one is?" I huffed.

"Because you didn't say 'please,'" the woman answered. "Telephone is for customers only."

"We're filling up out there," Gerardo said.

"You have to buy something from in here."

Gerardo scanned the store like a pioneer surveying the prairie horizon. He finally settled on the chest freezer. He hauled open the lid, rummaged around, and came back up with some kind of ice cream cone. Had a spaceman on the side of it, surrounded by a bunch of bright letters and cartoon explosions. He slowly walked a circuit of the rest of the store's meager selection. He paused at the Coke machine, stared at it like it had just asked to marry his daughter, then thought better of it, and finally moseyed back up to the counter. He set down his ice cream.

The old woman sighed and lifted a heavy beige telephone from beneath the counter. I grabbed the receiver and stared down at the base. There were no buttons. Just a big round thing with holes in it. I'd seen such things in cartoons and old sitcoms, but never in real life.

"How do I . . . ?" I said, miming the poking of buttons.

Gerardo and the attendant shared a complicated look that probably said a lot of things about race, culture, youth, and many other ills of the world. Then he reached over and hooked a bony finger through one of the holes.

"What number do you—" The clatter of the cans cut him off.

"Carey, God damn it, if you try to stop me from calling for help I will kick you in the balls so hard you'll know what they taste like."

A laugh.

"Trust me," said a girl with an English accent, "he probably already knows."

I turned. She was young. Seventeen. Eighteen, maybe. Pretty, if a little chubby. Big lips, big eyes made bigger with liberal use of mascara. Her hair was cut into a severe bob and dyed bright orange. She wore a miniskirt over torn fishnets, combat boots so old the leather was cracking, and a too-tight T-shirt from a band whose logo had gotten so faded over too many washes it was impossible to read. Each wrist was weighed down with a few dozen bracelets.

"Hi there." She gave us a little wave. "I'm Meryll."

I returned her tiny wave by reflex. During the drive, I'd started subconsciously thinking we were the last people alive in the world. The attendant didn't count. She was, if anything, a part of the store. She was landscape. It shouldn't have thrown me quite so much, that another customer would walk into the station just then. But I couldn't figure out how to make my mouth make words. There was a knot in my stomach. I was holding my breath.

The girl walked over to Gerardo, casual as could be, like they were good friends just seeing each other for the first time in years. She put a hand on his arm, and he grunted disapprovingly.

"You're an interesting one," she said. Her tone was ominous. Lust, or hunger—some sort of veiled threat I couldn't figure out.

The door clattered again. Carey entered, tunelessly yelling lyrics to himself. " 'Sex and drugs and rock and roll, is all my brain and body need—' "

He stopped when he saw the girl. His face went slack, then white, then twisted up in rage.

"Carey!" the girl chirped. She bounced up and down on her heels. "About bloody time."

Everything happened too fast. Sorting through it afterward, I think Gerardo screamed first. Then Carey grabbed the dusty gumball machine sitting beside the door and sent a home run into Meryll's skull. The attendant was saying "no no no no" over and over again in one unending breath. I just stood there like an idiot, and put my hands up to my face. I am no good in these adrenaline situations. My body doesn't go into a fight-or-flight response; it decides that emergencies are the perfect time to carefully debate all the options before making any rash decisions, then leaves me standing around gaping like a blow-up doll. The attendant, still repeating her panicked mantra, started rummaging beneath the counter for something. Gerardo kept screaming. The gumball machine shattered on Meryll's face, and she took a knee. Gumballs and glass exploded in every direction like a confectionary big bang, rattling and bouncing across the concrete floor. Carey reared back to swing again, but slipped on the gumballs he had just freed from their dusty prison—that's hubris for you. He was lying on his back grimacing, flailing around on the gumballs like a spastic turtle. I laughed—I couldn't help it. It came out like a nervous hiccup. Gerardo was still screaming. He had to run out of breath at some point, right? The attendant found what she was looking for under the counter, and came up with a fucking machete. I would've been less freaked out if she'd hauled out a flamethrower. There were dark stains on the blade that I sure hoped were rust. She pointed it at Carey, still droning "no." Meryll was slowly getting to her feet again. I cringed, anticipating her nasty new faceholes. I had seen quite enough blood over the last night to last a lifetime, or at least until the next Tarantino flick. But there was nothing—she was clean. Undamaged. She said "wow," and giggled a bit. Gerardo was screaming and screaming and screaming. Jesus. Say what you will about my "paralyzed fish"–style response to emergencies, but at least I don't scream like a—

Mother of fuck.

I looked over at Gerardo for the first time since this all started. Nobody had been paying any attention to him. His face had caved in on itself like sunbaked mud, big black holes where his eyes should be. The skin on his nose hugged the cartilage like Saran wrap. His lips peeled back up above the gums, also receding, showing long, yellow teeth. His clothes, a close-fitting button-up and tight cowboy jeans, were practically hanging off his frame. A tangle of flesh-colored snakes hung from each shirt cuff—his fingers. They already stretched to reach the ground, and were still growing. Sprawling out behind him. Touching, grasping, seizing on nothing. They bent in impossible ways. Dozens of knuckles, one every inch or so, cracked and popped as the fingers writhed senselessly on the filthy concrete.

"God damn it," Carey spat. "Get on your knees and fight me like a girl."

Meryll laughed. "I missed you, mate. Seriously, I did."

Carey feigned floundering, then came up quick, a flash in his hand. Meryll stared down at the three-inch shard of glass sticking out of her belly and sighed. "You got old, Carey," she said, "and boring."

"No," the attendant said, and slapped the flat side of the machete on the countertop. "No no no! You go! You both go!"

Meryll flashed her a winning smile and said, "No worries.

I'm going right now. Looks like he might want to hang out for a bit, though."

She inclined her head toward Gerardo, now basically just cracked skin wrapped around a screaming skeleton, and ten writhing digits, ranging in length from three to twenty feet.

The attendant followed Meryll's gesture, seeing what Gerardo had become for the first time.

"Chinga tu madre," she whispered, and the machete dropped from her fingers. It clattered on the weathered laminate.

One of Gerardo's probing fingers had found its way to my shoe. I stared down at it, still paralyzed. My own fingers were in my mouth now. I don't know why—I think I was trying to crawl into myself to get away from this. What looked like it had once been Gerardo's thumb tapped at the rubber soles of my Pumas. It writhed up onto the canvas, past the laces, and up to my bare ankle. It touched my flesh, and I squeaked. The thumb jolted alert. It raised up like a cobra, oscillated about, then slowly settled, pointing toward my calf. It shot out, too fast to see, and wrapped itself around me. The knuckles crackled like Bubble Wrap as it tightened. Pain shot up my leg. My skin bulged and turned purple where it squeezed. The thumb yanked, and I lost my footing. I fell onto a mat of hard, round gumballs and glass. Another yank.

The other fingers had gotten the message. They were all turning to face me. I'm sure I'm anthropomorphizing here—they were just a bunch of fucking fingers, after all—but I swear they looked . . . curious. Curious, and hungry.

Yank. Yank.

I tried to grab onto something, but the gumballs beneath me were rolling. I may as well have been on ice.

What, were they going to eat me? H-how?

"Finger food," I said, out loud, and laughed hysterically.

I looked to Carey for help, and saw he wasn't paying the slightest bit of attention. Meryll was carefully picking her way around him, toward the door. He lunged for her ankle and she danced away.

"Sorry about all this," Meryll said, "but I heard about your little friend and that Flare in LA. I really don't need the competition. Not right now. Ta!"

She paused in the doorway to shake her butt tauntingly, then left. Cans clattered, there was a blaze of natural light from the desert outside, and she was gone.

Another pull. The other fingers were moving now, feeling their way toward me. A wave of crackling, like static. I looked into Gerardo's face, thinking I could plead with him, but there was nobody home. He was still screaming, or trying to. But I guess his vocal cords had withered now, too, because all that came out was a high-pitched hiss. His teeth clacked against one another automatically, like those little windup toys. I couldn't even see his eyes, just the sunken holes where they used to be. His skin had drawn so tight that I could trace every ligament in his jaw. Most of him had just melted away, flowed down to these crawling, tapping finger snakes. While I watched, one of them split at the tip. The split flowed down the length of the finger, and then there were two worms undulating there. Another pulled the same trick. And another, until I stopped counting.

"The machete," I called toward the counter.

I could only see the underside of the counter from where I lay on the floor. Particleboard, dried gum, cobwebs. I hoped the attendant was still on the other side.

"Give me the machete!" I yelled again.

A face, round and wrinkled like a plum left out in the sun, poked itself over the counter and stared down at me.

"Please," I said, my voice strangely level. "Hand me the machete."

The woman's eyes roved down my leg, saw the thumb wrapped around my calf like a boa constrictor, and froze. Her face slowly withdrew.

"No!" I demanded. "The machete! You need to give me the machete!"

Another pull. The nest of fingers was just a few inches away now. They were tapping the concrete, feeling around and shoving the gumballs away. Lunging blindly. Searching for me.

A long, slow scrape. Then another. I looked up just in time to dodge the falling machete. The woman had tipped it over the edge of the counter bladefirst. It nicked the concrete where it hit, and skipped off my forehead.

I wasn't sure whether I wanted to kiss the old woman, or punch her in the neck.

I didn't have time to consider it. I grabbed the black rubber handle and swung. The machete snapped through the meat of the finger more than cut it. Its edge had gone dull. What I thought was blood, I could see now was just rust. It looked a century old, but was probably just a cheap piece of shit the attendant had picked up a few years ago. A small chip of metal flew off the blade where it bit through to the concrete. The writhing mass of fingers reared back, tensed, then angrily scrabbled at the air. They darted out more desperately, now. The nails scratched at the concrete. They caught on the imperfections there and snapped off, leaving bloody slug-tracks where they traveled. I scooted back on my butt and pressed myself up against the counter as hard as I could.

I tapped the secret psychic powers I was always so sure I had—the Force, my hidden X-man mutation, the Harry Potter wizardry left tragically untutored—and phased through the wall behind me.

Well, I *tried*.

Nothing happened.

Damn it all, Jackie, nothing ever happens. You have to entertain the possibility that you might not be an undiscovered superhero. That you might fucking die right here in a gas station in Mexico, strangled by a thousand spastic fingers.

Carey hadn't gotten his footing yet. He was slipping on the gumballs, too angry to take the time to find traction. And, besides, he wasn't heading for me. He wasn't even looking at me. He was trying to get to the door. He was trying to go after Meryll. He was trying to leave me to die.

I gripped the handle of the machete so tightly I could feel that one of the screws wasn't flush. It bit into my palm.

You have to move.

I stood into a crouch, my head still just beneath the lip of the attendant's counter. I took a step. The fingers stabbed at nothing. One had knocked a bag of chips onto the floor and was angrily poking holes in it, smashing Doritos into the concrete. They should not be this fast. They shouldn't be this strong, either. It was like all of Gerardo's muscle had moved into these fingers. What was left of his body stood there, looking like a POW from hell, every joint and bone poking out of his own skin, which was pulled so tightly it split in places. The chattering of his teeth had grown weaker. So had his screaming: just a breathy rasp now, directed at nothing and no one.

But the fingers . . . they bulged like hot dogs in the microwave. They were flush with blood, veins standing out thick and ropy as they pressed all around themselves, feeling for me.

All but a few.

Some of the shorter fingers—thinner, and with fewer knuckles—were pretty much still. Their tips were unnaturally thick. They bulged out at the ends like fleshy lollipops. Their pads were pressed into the floor, and they quivered slightly now and then, but otherwise didn't move.

I took a step.

The shorter, fatter fingers pulsed. The longer ones, thousands of them, swung toward me as one.

Oh, shit.

I thought back to Kevin Bacon in *Tremors*. What did he do to kill the worms? All I could remember was his butt in those tight cowboy jeans and that old Chinese guy saying "Graboids."

No, wait—they used a tractor, and dynamite!

Well that's fucking helpful, Jackie. Do you have either of those things?

I didn't have a plan. I probably wouldn't come up with a good one in the next few seconds. So I did the only thing I could think to do, and I ran. It was a mistake. I made it two steps before a dozen long fingers seized my legs so tightly that I instantly lost feeling. I thought the thumb alone was crazy strong—it had sunk into my leg like razor wire. But, together, the fingers were something else. They lifted me like I was nothing and whipped me into the chest freezer so hard that it tipped backward and nearly fell over. All the breath went out of me. I saw little sparkles, fading.

The other fingers were coming now. Some inched like worms, some hopped, others slithered. I looked down, and was amazed to see myself still holding the machete. In all those action movies, that's the first thing to go in times like this—the weapon flies off into the distance, leaving our hero unarmed. Builds drama. But I was holding onto that sucker with a vise grip. My whole hand had gone white with the effort of it.

I swung the blade down and cut through half of the fingers wrapped around my legs. The others recoiled instantly. They waved and pounded at the ground. I swung again at the one closest to me, but only clipped it a bit. Still, the others writhed and grasped in pain.

They didn't just get the blood and the muscle. They got the nerves, too.

I looked at the short fingers, which were feeling the ground for my vibrations. The others had thrown me closer to them. If I was quick I could—

I didn't think.

I jumped, lunging as wildly as I could—not away from, but directly *at* Gerardo's screaming husk, and the squat feelers at its feet. I brought the machete down right across their tips, and managed to cut clean through a few of them before the blade shattered against the concrete.

The whole mass pulsed, then flopped on the ground and writhed slowly. They were still alive, still moving, but senseless and in agony. I ran for the door.

I forgot about the gumballs. I forgot about my numb, bruised legs.

I ate shit into a shelving unit full of Japanese peanuts.

I crawled the rest of the way to the door. To my undying credit, I didn't even start crying until I had it shut behind me.

"Holy shit," Carey said, his back to me. "Look at her go!"

He nodded down the highway. I could just see a bent brown shape disappearing into the heat waves. The attendant.

"Lady sure can move, give her that," he said. And he laughed.

He fucking laughed.

"You left me to die!" I screamed.

I tried to stand, but it was all pins and needles.

"Did not," he said. "I saw you had the machete. Seems like you had the situation well in hand."

"Fuck you!"

"Did you get it?" Carey asked, and he turned around to face me. He wasn't smiling. His eyes were hard and empty. "Well in *hand*?" he said, again.

My legs were overloaded with sensation. All the fight had bled out of me and I could already feel the giddy, post-adrenaline exhaustion setting in. God help me, but I laughed.

Carey didn't.

"What the hell is your deal?" I asked, too tired—for now—to be angry, though I made a note to be fucking furious with him just as soon as I had the energy.

"She left her," Carey said, and pointed to the bed of the truck, where Kaitlyn still slept. "Why would she go through all that, and then just leave her?"

"Who was she?" I said. I sat with my back against the door and drummed my heels against the dust to get some feeling back into them.

"Just some chick I used to bang," Carey said.

"Bullshit! That's not 'some old girlfriend.' She turned that old Mexican guy into something out of *The Thing.*"

"You know what they say," Carey said. "Never stick your dick in crazy."

I rolled my eyes at him.

There would be a reckoning. The son of a bitch had a lot of questions to answer, and he would have to deliver them in between the ceaseless and rapid ball-kicks that I owed him. But for now, all I wanted to do was get the hell away from that gas station, curl into a ball, and sleep in a waterbed made of my own tears.

Carey helped me to the truck. The feeling in my legs was starting to come back, and I wasn't terribly happy about that. Thin bruises wrapped around my calves, already shifting from bright red to deep purple. He propped me up in the passenger seat and hopped into the driver's side. The old truck stuttered, stammered, and coughed to life. We eased out onto the highway.

"Shouldn't we like, cover Kaitlyn up or something? She'll get sunstroke back there, now that the sun is up."

"No, she won't," Carey said, with complete authority.

How the hell would he know that?

More questions. But right now I had more important things to do, like throw up out the window and cry until I hyperventilated.

FOURTEEN

2013. Tulancingo, Mexico. Kaitlyn.

I am floating in the ocean. There is no line between the ocean, the sky, and me. It's all liquid, all the same liquid, and it flows from my body into space. It sucks the heat from me and dispels it into the void. The ocean is deep. Limitless. There is no floor; it extends until words like distance and depth cease to have meaning. I cannot move.

Sleep paralysis, Kaitlyn, that's all it is. Just try to move something. Anything. A toe. A finger.

I am locked into place, floating and becoming the ocean, which becomes the sky. There are stars in the sky, so bright it's painful to look at them—but there's nothing else to look at, so I stare even as their images burn into my eyes. The water is not cold, I realize now. It is without temperature. The sky, the water—it's all a part of me. How could it sap my warmth? The only thing here that is outside of me, that is not of me, are the stars. It's the stars that are cold.

And with each degree of heat they steal, they burn brighter.

Everything. Put everything you have into it. You have to move.

It's just a malfunction in your brain causing these panicked dreams. Twitch. Please, just twitch.

Something moves beneath me, in the eternity of the ocean. It is impossibly, unfathomably distant, and it is impossibly, unfathomably large. The water does not ripple yet with its passing. Its presence is too far removed to have physical effects where I am, which is everywhere, but I know it's coming.

The thing beneath me is normally content to swim where the currents take it. But I did something. I did something that made it take notice of me. It turned to swim in my direction. The disruption in its wake obliterated galaxies in the ocean that is space; that is me. It's horrible to think such a thing could even notice me—how small I am, how brief I am. What could I be to this thing that swims through the universe?

Please please please move. There! My extra pinky. It's almost . . .

The stars flicker.

The heat is nearly gone from me. I can feel myself fading.

The stars flicker again, and then, one by one, they begin to go out.

Their frozen light sears me, stains my vision and bleeds my warmth, but it is light. And it is fading. They disappear. I am in the dark. There is nothing left here but the ocean and space and self.

And the thing beneath me.

My finger twitches.

I do not wake.

The giant beneath me surges. It is hurtling toward me with a speed that makes me nauseous to think of. I do not know if it is angry, or hungry, or if such things are beyond it. I can only feel its unceasing progress, gaining momentum by the second.

So faintly that I can barely register it, the water around me starts to move. It washes through my body. It ripples through space.

My head bounces painfully against the bed of the pickup truck.

I'm staring directly at the sun. I don't know how long I've been doing it, but when I look away I can still see the sun in the dead center of my vision. I can barely move—just enough to turn my head away and let gravity take over. I can see my own arm sprawled out next to me. My skin is burnt and bright red. I'm flushed with the fluish warmth of heatstroke. The truck hits another pothole and my skull rattles with the utter failure of its suspension. It smells like rust and sand. I can hear voices. A man and a woman.

". . . telling you the radio is broken and it's another two hours at least."

"I don't care! I'm not giving you road-head just to pass the time."

"So, what? Twenty questions?"

"Fine."

"Great. First question: Will you give me road-head?"

A slap, then laughing.

The dream has left a little bit of residual fear dancing around in my belly, but I'm so tired, and so warm. I should say something. Yell out for help or shade or water. You're not supposed to sleep when you have heatstroke, no matter how badly you want to.

Wait, no, that's . . . that's hypothermia. If there's a chance you could be hypothermic, you're not supposed to sleep no matter how tired you get, or how warm you feel. So it . . .

. . . it makes sense then. That . . .

You shouldn't
stay awake
with heatstroke. It's for my own . . .
good
sleep
good
. . .

I am wildly uncomfortable. I've tried sleeping on my side, on my stomach, on my back, and curled into a ball. This is the bed that serial killers sleep on in hell. There's a spring poking through the mattress in the middle, but that's also where it sags, so as soon as I start to drift off, my body relaxes and I roll into the spike trap.

But I'm so fucking tired and every part of me hurts. I don't want to wake up, even though I've been, like, twenty percent awake for hours.

Am I hungover? I can't remember. Too much of my brain is still sleeping.

I was supposed to do something. It was vital. I can almost remember it, but I'm really trying not to. Maybe if I spread my legs all the way across I can hook them on either side of the mattress and. . . .

Yeah, that's good. That'll do it. . . . Now I can get some . . .
Spike.

God damn this miserable fuck of a mattress. Where the hell even am I? This isn't my bed. My bed is a beautiful monster, a whole room filled with down and foam. It's like sleeping in whipped cream. This is like sleeping on an anthill.

I should just force it. Get up. There's something important I'm supposed to—

Oh, shit. The sun. I'm dying out here. Up. Up!

★ ★ ★

I awoke with a start, causing me to lose my tenuous grip on the mattress and slide down onto the butt spike.

"Ow, damn," I said, or tried to. My mouth was so dry it came out like a cat hacking up a wad of aluminum foil.

I glared back at the bed, and noticed there wasn't even a sheet. Just a dirty, bare mattress. There were dark stains all around the spring. I did not want to know what they were.

The floor didn't exactly look clean or inviting, but I figured that I'd rather get foot diseases than blood and butt diseases. I rolled off the bed, crashed into the floor, and focused on breathing until my body agreed to start working again.

"Like a swan," Jackie said. "Like watching a graceful, elegant swan go ice-skating. While drunk."

"Shut up," I tried to say, but it came out like somebody dragged a Dumpster over a gravel driveway.

Jackie sighed. Footsteps. A faucet turning on, then off again. More footsteps. Jackie held out a glass, and I drank from it. Only after I'd downed the entire thing did I realize it was the glass shell of a burned out candle. The water tasted like wax and dust. It was the best thing I've ever had in my life.

"Where?" I asked. I sounded like Clint Eastwood, but at least I was making human words.

"The shittiest motel room in the entire universe," Jackie said. She sat down in a grimy plastic lawn chair beside a TV older than my parents.

I looked around, and verified the truth of her statement: one room with two beds. Impossibly, I saw the tiger-pit that I had been sleeping on was the nicer of the two. The bathroom didn't have a door. The drapes were plastic. The carpet was deep brown, but I suspected it didn't start out that way. The place smelled like a locker room for a team of swamp monsters.

"Why?" I said. A little of my normal voice coming through, like a man going through reverse-puberty.

"We finally maxed out my dad's credit card," Jackie said. "We're operating on cash now, so the budget is tighter. I suggested we splurge on a space where the sheets wouldn't give us syphilis, but Carey figured that would cut into the beer money. He suggested a compromise, then brought us here, threw the sheets out the window, and went to get beer."

"Where is here?"

"I don't think it has a name. There's just a picture of a fat guy holding a flower on the sign. We are at the Fat Guy Flower Motel."

I started to snap, but realized I didn't have the energy for frustration yet.

"What city are we in?"

"Oh! Right. Tulancingo. Mexico. We made it, K! The city that never sleeps, because the vultures will think you're a corpse and try to eat you. The Big Difficult! The Bruised Apple! Drink it in."

"I remember driving. Did we crash?"

"Yeah, there was a . . ." Jackie trailed off.

"What?"

"I don't even know how to start. There was a Million Tar Man March. Carey's ex-girlfriend showed up, and she turns old farmhands into monsters. Everything went incredibly crazy, even by our standards. You should be dead, but you're totally fine."

I laughed bitterly. There was a lot to question there, but me being "totally fine" struck me as the weirdest statement.

"Fine? I feel a rotisserie chicken. Was I hallucinating, or did you guys leave me out in the sun to die?"

"You're fine," Jackie insisted. "You're not even sunburned."

I started to argue, but looked down at my arms and saw she was right. Light brown. Bit of a tan, but no burns. Not so much as a scratch from the wreck.

"How is that possible?"

"You tell me," Jackie said.

She wasn't herself. She was putting on a good show, but her delivery felt flat.

"What's going on, Jackie? Are you all right?"

"Am I . . ." Jackie laughed. "Am I fucking *all right*? Are you kidding me? My life in LA was shallow and meaningless. It was awesome. And you dragged me away from it. You pulled me into a goddamned nightmare and then you brought me to that nightmare's ghetto, pointed to the sewer, and told me to get some shut-eye. Fuck you, Kaitlyn. Fuck you for all of this. I am not okay. I am never going to be okay again. But you—you're perfectly fine! I watched you die, Kaitlyn. You bled to death on a rock in the desert, then we threw your corpse in the back of a truck and watched it bake in the sun."

"What? Jackie, I don't—"

"You don't have a scratch! Your face was practically gone. *You had no more blood.* Less than a day later and you're bitching like you've got nothing worse than a bad hangover. What the fuck even *are* you?"

"What the hell are you talking about? That can't be true," I said. "I don't . . . I don't remember anything."

"K, I don't even know if you're *you* anymore. Is something else in there? Did those things hollow you out? Because, I gotta say, if this is all some fucked-up prank before the shell that used to be my best friend throws me under a bus, I just wish you'd get it over with."

"I'm me, Jackie." I dragged myself up to lean against the

wall so I could look her in the eye. "It's me. Nothing's changed."

"*Everything has changed!*" she yelled, but she couldn't stop laughing. "Does this shithole look like nothing has changed? I don't want to be here, K. I don't want to do this."

What? I'm the one fighting unkillable psychopaths and acidic bigfoots. I'm the one apparently dying in a car wreck and being thrown in the back of a pickup truck to rot like garbage.

"Nobody asked you to," I said.

"Excuse me?"

"Nobody asked you to be here."

"I didn't have a choice."

"You volunteered to come. You practically insisted."

"No, you don't get to play that. You rescued me from that freaky church where I watched hell happen in front of me. I saw a guy pull off his own dick and eat it—*and then it grew back*. What was I supposed to say when you asked for help after that? 'Thanks for dragging me out of a Cronenberg film come to life, but kindly fuck off?' You didn't leave me any other options."

"And yet here you are now, bitching about it."

"FUCK YOUR MOTHER IN HALF WITH A—" Jackie seemed to collapse inward halfway through swearing at me.

She sighed. "Can we just go, Kaitlyn? I love you, but I hate this. We won, right? We got away from them—and sure, they came after us a few times. But we weren't really trying to hide. We're not even hiding now. We keep using my dad's card—I bet that's how they were tracking us. Let's just ditch it and go somewhere else, okay? How about New York? We've done the LA thing. Let's go be snobby about our fucking bagels and yell at tourists. We'll share a shitty apartment that will look like a mansion after this place. We'll get bunk beds and matching PJs and put socks on the door when one of us is getting laid. We got away before, right? In Barstow? You followed me out of that dried-up fart of a town. Follow me to New York, and let's pretend all this was a bad acid trip."

Jackie didn't cry often. She cried at the end of *All Dogs Go To Heaven*. And she cried about a fish tank once, when she got way too high and couldn't stand the thought of the fish living their lives in such a small space. She wasn't crying now, but I could tell she was right on the edge of it. This is how she was in Barstow, right before we left. She said the town would kill us. She couldn't stand the thought of us working at a Walmart all our lives and being buried in the same cemetery we used to bring boys to make out as teenagers. She couldn't go without me, she said. So I agreed. I agreed to pretty much anything when she got like this.

"No," I said.

Neither of us were expecting it.

"I can't, Jackie. Marco is still out there. After what he did to us, what he did to those other girls. I know he's going to do it again. And he won't stop coming for me. I can't live my life just waiting to see his face in a crowd. This has to end, and I know I can do it. I almost did it once before. It's fine, though. It's fine if you want to go. We'll get back to normal someday, I know it. I'll show up at your shitty Manhattan apartment with a pizza one day and we'll eat too much and make fun of reality TV like we used to. But I can't go yet. *You* can. You can just take off."

"Maybe I will," Jackie said, after a long, quiet moment. "Are you sure it's okay?"

It wasn't.

"It is."

"I'm just . . . I don't know what to do here. You and Carey

are out there lighting these dudes on fire and blowing up angels or whatever, and I'm in the back providing color commentary. So I'm going to leave. You have to promise not to hate me forever if I go, though. If you give me the cold shoulder after you're done saving the world, I'll tell everybody about the time I caught you jerking it to that Ginuwine video."

I leaned over to slap her, but leaning was a bad idea.

Jackie laughed. "I'm serious," she said. "I'll see you on the news all 'Girl saves universe from evil disco balls,' and then next up it'll be 'Savior's friend caught her flicking it to "Pony." ' They'll have to get Ginuwine on for some reactions, then we'll have a panel about what it means for R&B."

I laughed, too, even though it hurt my bones to do it.

When we stopped laughing, and I stopped dry-heaving from the exertion it took to laugh in the first place, Jackie left to get supplies. She had a feeling Carey wasn't picking up such frivolities as "food" or "water." The plan was for her to call her dad and ask him to wire her money. She'd say she was flying back, but she'd take a bus instead and split the difference in ticket price with Carey and me. That way we'd hopefully have enough shitty motel and shitty motel diner money to finish hunting Marco.

I smiled at Jackie when she stepped out, but my expression fell as soon as she closed the door. I felt like I should cry. I would have cried, normally—nice and alone, no one to judge me, just wrap myself up in a cozy blanket of self-pity and sob on the floor of this motel room that would need a shower to qualify as "concentration-camp grade." But it wouldn't come. I didn't feel numb, exactly. I could feel the response inside, but it was like it had to crawl through two acres of mud to get out, and by the time it did, it was too dirty and exhausted to do much of anything but sigh.

So I sighed.

A lot.

I should sleep. That bed was out of the question—it was by far the most uncomfortable feature of the room. But I bet I could prop myself up in the lawn chair, or just lie down on the floor and let the cockroaches snuggle me away to dreamland. It was the same thing as the crying: I was aware of the need for sleep somewhere far away, but it didn't seem like it was heading in my direction anytime soon. I struggled to my feet like Bambi, and went to refill my dusty candleholder.

On the bathroom counter, I found two moderately clean glasses sitting upside down beside the sink.

God damn it, Jackie.

It was for the best. Really, it was. She was right: I had been selfish, asking her to come with me. I needed comfort. I needed to bring a piece of home with me. I needed her color commentary, as she put it, to keep me from drowning myself in a toilet. But that's not a good enough reason to risk her life. I might actually take more comfort from her leaving. Knowing that she was safe somewhere, and I would have at least some small semblance of a life to come back to when all this was done.

It was something to look forward to. A light at the end of the tunnel.

Sometimes that light is a train.

Oh shut up, Kaitlyn.

I drank eight glasses of water. My stomach was so full that it sloshed when I walked. I flipped the mattress, and found that the underside was, impossibly, even more stained and disgusting, but there didn't appear to be any tiny knives poking out of it, so I considered it an upgrade. I lay down. I was laughing to myself about how miraculously, astoundingly uncomfortable it was when I heard keys in the door.

I don't know why, but I closed my eyes. It was a gut reaction—some variant of the "blanket over the head keeps monsters away" defense. If I was sleeping, surely nobody would come and talk to me, crush me with the psychic burden of human interaction.

Shuffling. Paper bags crumpling. The door slamming shut.

I jumped a little, but hoped the intruding presence wouldn't notice. Footsteps. A burp.

Silence.

Then, right next to my ear, at about crotch height, the sound of a zipper being undone.

My eyes flew open.

I scrambled backward, nearly falling off the bed, then held up a fist.

Carey was squatting awkwardly beside the mattress and holding the zipper of his jacket.

"What the hell are you doing?" I demanded.

"Ha! Knew you weren't sleeping," he said.

He smiled, pulled a can of Tecate from a paper bag on the floor, and held it out to me.

I nearly threw up just thinking about it. "God, no," I said.

"Come on—it'll put hair on your chest."

"I don't want hair on my chest."

"Sure you do! People'll call you 'hair-tits'; it'll be great."

But he wasn't even offering me the can anymore. He cracked it open and fell into the stained lawn chair by the TV. The legs bent crazily. It bobbed and weaved like a seasick boxer.

"Where's Jackie?" Carey asked.

"Gone," I answered.

"Good."

"Probably, yeah."

"I've had a lot of friends get mixed up in this shit. The ones that leave, live. The ones that don't usually last just long enough to curse you with their dying breath. I know it feels like somebody crapped in an open wound right now, but, really—it's good."

"I know, all right! Stop fucking talking about it and give me time to process. Jesus."

"Nah, that's not what you need. Your generation and your bullshit 'processing' and 'emotional awareness.' What you need is six beers, a good fuck, and a fistfight. And I can offer you two out of the three right now. You pick which."

"You seriously do not ever shut up, do you?"

Screw it, though. Why not? Like I have a reason to stay sober right now.

I motioned to Carey. He plucked a beer from the bag and tossed it to me. It was cold and wet with condensation. The temperature difference between my flushed skin and the can was so sharp that it stung just to hold it. I cracked it open, took one long pull, and it was gone.

"Holy shit!" Carey laughed. "I knew a kid who could do that once."

He tossed me another, and I took my time with this one.

"Is what Jackie said true?" I asked him.

"Absolutely not. Why, what'd she tell you? The shower thing? Girl needs to learn how to work a lock. I mean, talk about your overinflated sense of self, I was just—"

"About me. She said . . . she said we were in a bad wreck and it looked like maybe I wasn't going to make it. Maybe I . . . didn't make it?"

"Nope," Carey said, too quickly. "Shock is a hell of a thing. She was just confused. Your brain, it exaggerates when it comes to this traumatic stuff. Every time you remember something bad happening, your brain has to tell you a story about it. Like all good storytellers, that fish gets bigger and bigger every time. You took a little knock, is all."

"And this girl you guys ran into, this ex of yours?"

"Meryll. Shit. She told you about that, then. . . ."

"Yes."

I thought about elaborating on what, exactly, Jackie had told me, which wasn't much and didn't make a bit of sense. But Carey had quick, easy answers to questions I had barely thought to ask. Something was up.

"Look, Meryll is . . . I don't know what Meryll is. She used to be a hell of a chick, but that was a long time ago and another place. She somehow got mixed up in all this—don't gimme that look, I didn't bring her into it!"

I wasn't giving any look.

"She was at this game long before I was. Knew a lot more than me, and could *do* a lot more than me. Meryll could do crazy things. Things that didn't make sense. But she got too close to the angels, let too much of them into her. Now? I don't know what she's doing. I don't know what she is. I didn't even realize she was still alive. Not totally sure she *is*—she hasn't aged a day since then. I don't know what Jackie told you, but when she touched that Mexican at the gas station, he didn't get solved. He didn't disappear, or fold into himself, or turn into an Empty One or anything—his whole body just . . . *changed*. I've never seen anything like it."

I finally placed it—what was off about Carey. When he was just talking to you normally, there were all sorts of tangents and swears, lots of backtracking to elaborate on funny old stories or the quality of your ass. He was mostly bravado, lies, and perversion. Then there were times like this, when everything he said was tempered with reason. When it all made sense. When he was suddenly and perfectly lucid.

When he was lying.

FIFTEEN

1978. London, England. Carey.

"Do you bastards just grow gills eventually or what?" Randall said.

He was all hunched up under his coat—pure white with a pink fur collar. He'd taken it off the back of some rich lady's chair when she went to the can back at the bar. He looked like a fancy cat somebody had thrown into a river.

I couldn't blame him much for whining.

The rain was thick and nasty. Smelled like charcoal, and felt thicker than water. Like some sort of industrial gel. I wouldn't have minded it so much, but it was goddamned everywhere, and I couldn't keep it out of my beer. It was getting all watery, and the kind of beer I can afford is already about as watery as it can be.

At least the Marquee felt like home. Set into the bottom floor of a building so old it looked like they'd carved the club right into the brick, it was small, crowded, loud, and I could smell it from the street. There was a thick and chaotic line of punks sprawling down the sidewalk, drinking openly and eagerly. Most of them didn't seem to notice or care about the rain. Tub and Meryll weren't hiding under their coats like Randall, or pressed up against the brick wall trying, pointlessly, to shield their valuables from it, like me. Meryll's hair was plastered to her forehead, but her makeup didn't run. Girls are magical things that I do not understand.

Tub looked like he was born in this rain and he'd gladly die in it. He was leaning heavily against a signpost—he'd ditched his rebar cane behind a couple of garbage cans around the corner after Meryll had pointed out that they probably wouldn't let him in the venue with a ragged steel club. The punk kids were throwing odd looks in his direction. He was a few decades too old to be here, but he also looked half-crazy and all-ugly, so maybe he belonged after all.

From inside, I could hear guitars complaining and drums pounding nervously. The show would start soon. There were five bands on the bill, but only one we cared about: The Talentless, Gus's band.

"What if they're good?" Randall asked.

"No way," I answered. But part of me worried. It might be slightly harder to kill their lead singer if they actually rocked. "I think you need at least one soul between you for a decent punk band."

I took a sip from my can. Seemed like the water was mostly floating on top, so what I got tasted like a polluted river that somebody had spilled part of a beer in once, long ago. Tub saw me sneering down at my drink.

"We call that a Soho Shandy," he said.

Meryll laughed.

I didn't get it, so I flipped him off just in case he deserved it.

I scanned the line again. Drunks and junkies festooned with acne scars, cheaply dyed hair, and ragged clothes.

Some of them were already fighting, just to get practice before the main event.

Good people.

But then, clustered here and there like high school cliques, were kids with shoes that were just a little too clean. Jeans just a little too torn. Faces with no features.

"Only maybe a dozen Unnoticeables," I said.

"Yeah, but look at all the Empty Ones," Tub said.

"What? You can spot them?" Randall asked.

He'd been standing just a little too close to Meryll all night. She didn't seem to mind, and I hadn't yet spotted an opportunity to kick him into traffic.

"Of course. You can't? Look there, lad. The blonde." Tub nodded toward the back of the line.

She was gorgeous. Short white hair done up in random spikes, denim jacket lined with patches, and short shorts over black fishnets.

"What about her?" I bit.

"She's brought an umbrella to a fucking punk show," Meryll answered. Her voice went flat, a mockery of the Empty Ones' monotone speech: "Humans do not like being wet, isn't that right."

"There's that, true," Tub said. "But it's also in the eyes. She's not really looking at anything, is she? It's like they're painted on."

I looked, but didn't see it. She looked cold and empty, sure, but most pretty girls do. At least when they're interacting with me, anyway.

The line moved a few steps.

"Here we go," Randall said, excited for the chance to get somewhere dry.

He put a hand on Meryll's hip and steered her forward

just a little bit. She barely seemed to notice, but I did. I took it as an excuse to drink harder, and slammed the rest of my watery beer.

I skipped my empty can off the back of Randall's skull and we passed the time by wrestling in a puddle.

The inside of the Marquee was nasty, even by scuzzy punk club standards. I couldn't tell if the floor was carpeted, or if there was just a thick, soft layer of accumulated filth. The walls were the color of nicotine where they weren't scrawled over with crude profanities. The air didn't move at all. It congealed around you. Felt like you were breathing sweat-flavored gelatin. I'd already been elbowed twice, and a fat-faced girl had spat on my shoe and called me "a fucking yank wank."

I felt at peace for the first time in a long while.

I knew we weren't really here to see a band, drink some beers, and fuck in the bathrooms. We were here to kill—or, more likely, to die. But I could still feel that giddy excitement dancing around in my guts.

The stage was low, narrow, and overflowing with instruments. The first band got on it, and cast out a wave of distortion and screaming. The crowd surged as one, bouncing and jostling. Not enough room to dance, not enough room to fight, so you gotta do a little of both. Tub was standing stock-still, surveying the room. Meryll wasn't dancing, but she was returning the shoves eagerly enough. But me and Randall had the same idea: We hopped and hollered like assholes. There's only so much fun you can have before you're erased from the face of this planet. What's the point of being scared and grim all the time? If I gotta die in twenty minutes, I'm sure as shit going to spend that time doing something fun.

The other bands passed in a blur of noise, like a series of violent car crashes set to a beat. I wasn't sure where my beers came from—maybe Randall was getting them for me, or maybe I was just reflexively stealing them from lesser punks when the opportunity presented itself—but I drank them all the same. I jumped and I wiggled and I punched and I groped an ass or two and it was fantastic.

And then it was time.

The Talentless took the stage and the room went crazy, but in an orderly fashion. The crowd's screams sounded like background chatter in a movie. Believable, but only if you didn't pay attention to it. There was a guy a few feet to my left—"a guy" is about as specific as I can be; his features slipped out of focus when you looked too hard at 'em— hollering himself hoarse. But it was all the same refrain: "Woo! Fuck yeah! All right! Woo! Fuck yeah! All right!" A girl in the front row was screeching wordlessly, but the tone of it looped. Low- to high-pitched, little warble in the middle, deep breath, start again. I saw the blonde with the umbrella from outside. She lifted up her shirt to flash her tits and dance around. She pulled her shirt back down, waited a moment, then repeated the movement exactly.

I'm not complaining about it—I'm just saying it ain't human.

A few of the normals in the crowd were cheering too— mostly younger girls—but the rest looked a little unsettled. They knew something was off about the vibe, but they couldn't place it. Probably thought the coke was turning on them, or chalked it up to déjà vu.

Then he was there: Gus.

Slavic cheekbones. Hooded eyes. Long, greasy blond

hair and carefully nurtured stubble. Shirtless. Not exactly muscular, but so skinny he could pass for it. Faded black jeans pulled too low, so you could see his pubic bone. He stumbled on the stage, leaned heavily on the mic, pantomiming a dope high.

"What's the word, London?" he mumbled into the microphone and laughed to himself. The chick in front of me visibly swooned. Hand to the head, swaying on her feet.

What a dick.

"We're The Talentless," the guitar player yelled into his mic, "and this song's called 'Fuck Your TV.' "

Well, at least they're terrible. That's good. I won't have the early breakup of a decent band hanging over my head after I kill these sons of bitches.

I started pushing my way toward the stage, but Tub grabbed my arm with fingers like old wood and yanked me back. "The bloody hell d'you think you're doing?" he shout-whispered into my ear.

"I'm gonna go try to murder that band," I said, confused. "Isn't that the plan?"

"Right now?" Meryll was leaning into the conversation too, all of us yelling over the distortion in the quietest way we could manage.

"Why, you wanna listen to the rest of their set?" I said. "What's the problem?"

"How were you planning on doing it?" Tub asked.

"I was gonna feed the guitar player his guitar, strangle the drummer, then shove the mic stand up Gus's ass and parade him around like a dipshit-on-a-stick."

"What about the bass player?" Randall asked, all of us now huddled in a circle, scream-shouting in the most conspicuous way possible.

"I forgot about the bass player," I said.

"Everybody does," Randall said.

Meryll laughed.

"Look around, you bloody idiot." Tub nodded at the crowd. "There's a dozen Unnoticeables, three or four Empty Ones, and that's *not* counting Gus and the band. The last time you tried to take out so much as one of the bastards, you got half your friends killed."

Punch him in the neck. Bite his nose. Rockette-kick him in the dick.

I took a second to calm myself. "Don't fucking talk about that. You weren't there."

"I'm sorry, boyo," Tub said. "Truly, that was too far. But we can't take them here."

"So what—"

The music stopped. Scattered applause. Randall clapped sarcastically. I'm not sure how he did that, or what exactly it was that differentiated it from a normal clap, but he pulled it off. The swooning chick in front of us turned to glare at him.

"This one's called 'I'm a Punk and I'm OK,'" the guitar player announced, and the tuneless distortion resumed.

"These fuckers need to die based on their song titles alone," Randall said.

We all nodded agreement.

"But not now," Tub said. "We'll tail 'em after the show, find somewhere quiet where we can even the odds a bit. Then Meryll does her work."

I wasn't sure about that.

Meryll didn't look like she was, either.

★   ★   ★

The Talentless played twenty songs in thirty-five minutes. They played "Spit On My Love" (the swooning chick practically fainted when Gus pointed at her while singing the chorus), "Don't Listen to Daddy," and "I Drink Alcohol." It was like somebody gave an alien a drunken synopsis of punk rock and really emphasized that musical talent was not necessary or even welcome. A couple of the normal girls in the crowd screamed themselves ragged when the set ended. The Unnoticeables repeated their scripted cheers, and the rest of the crowd left shaking their heads—unsure about what they just saw, but sure they didn't like it.

The Talentless headed backstage, and we ducked out of the club to meet them in the alley. Faceless roadies loaded gear into a filthy white van with busted headlights, the body panels so dented they looked like crumpled tin foil. We were hiding in a crowd of punks milling about on the street. That directionless haze after a show, coming down off the adrenaline high, nobody sure of what comes next. Everybody debating whether or not they have enough money to go get properly drunk in the pubs, or if they should just stand here on the street and share a bottle.

Most share the bottle.

I slyly inserted myself into the drinking circle with the lines "Helluva show, right?" "What are we doing next?" and "Give me that bottle, motherfucker."

Tub and Meryll were keeping their eyes on Gus. Randall was keeping his eyes on Meryll's ass.

I hit the bottle so hard the guy next to me objected.

I practically threw it at him, and went to stand beside Randall.

I had a delicate subject in mind, and I wasn't sure about the best way to approach it.

I finally went with: "What's your fucking problem?"

"What?" He broke his hypno-gaze on Meryll's butt, and looked at me.

"You always do this shit. I like a chick, and you move in immediately."

"You like her?"

"Well, yeah—I've been trying to fuck her ever since I met her."

"You do that to literally every girl you see."

"Yeah, but with this one, I mean it."

"The hell was I supposed to know that?"

"I don't know, we're friends. You're supposed to pick up on my subtleties."

"You don't have any."

"Fine, but I'm into her. Now you know, so back off."

He gave it a moment's thought, then said, "Nah."

"Nah?"

"Nah, she doesn't seem into you. She seems into me."

"Well, of course she's not into me right now, but I fucking grow on people, all right?"

"Like mold."

I gave him a solid wanking motion.

"Listen," Randall said, and fixed me with his "I'm serious now" expression. "The way I figure it, I *could* back off, but she's still probably not going to have sex with you. Agreed?"

"Well . . . yeah."

I'm an optimist, but I'm not deluded. Besides, "probably" doesn't mean "definitely not."

"Or I could *not* back off," Randall continued, "and she will probably have sex with me. Agreed?"

"*Probably*," I stressed.

"So we do it your way, and nobody is having sex. We do

it my way, and at least I'm having sex. Probably her, too. That's a net positive."

"I . . ."

Shit. The man's logic is flawless.

"But I really *want* to screw her," I protested.

I knew it was useless.

"I know, man." He put his hand on my shoulder. "I want to win the lotto and buy a solid gold Buick, but that's just not the way the world works."

"Fine. You don't have to back off, but I'm not backing off either," I said.

"That's okay." Randall laughed. "I don't think that matters."

He sidled up alongside Meryll and Tub, who were parked at the far end of the punk circle. He touched her forearm to get her attention, and she smiled at him.

Randall's a pretty good guy. I mean, he's still a son of a bitch and I'm still not getting laid, but at least he puts forth the effort to make me feel better about it. That's what friends do.

Tub turned and motioned to me. I joined the huddle.

"There." He pointed.

Gus and the rest of The Talentless filed out of the back door into the alley. They were backlit by a bare lightbulb putting out roughly the wattage of a potato, but I could still tell him by his silhouette. Long, lean, moving like thick fluid in that heroin drift. He looked around. Satisfied that nobody important was watching, he let the junkie fugue drop away. He stood up unnaturally straight, head held at an odd angle to his neck. His arms went slack by his sides. Gus pointed back at the van and said something. The gesture was spider-quick. I didn't actually see him move. One second his arm was by his side, then it was held out, then by his side again. Like frames skipping in a movie. The roadies nodded at him, then one broke off to get in the van. It turned over with a sound like a sick bird singing. The headlights flashed, dimmed, then went out. The driver turned it over again. The headlights were even dimmer this time. He tried it one more time, and they didn't come on at all.

Dead.

Gus's silhouette clenched, twisting up into an angry crouch, fists balled, head twitching. Then he went slack again. He turned and began walking down the alley, away from us. The other Talentless followed him, leaving the unnoticeable roadies between us and them.

"Shit," I said.

"What?" Tub asked.

"The fucking van wouldn't start! Now we gotta get past the roadies, or we're gonna lose them."

"Well, yeah." Tub fixed me with a funny look. "I sabotaged the van during the show. How the hell were we going to follow a van? You don't look like you can run that fast."

"Plus, that'd be pretty conspicuous," Meryll agreed, "couple of skinny white Americans sprinting through traffic."

"So how do we get past the roadies?" I asked.

Everybody looked at me like I'd just choked on my own shoe.

"We beat the shit out of them," Randall finally answered.

Oh, right.

Plan A.

Tub had reclaimed his rebar cane after the show. He stumped up to the band, feigning frailty, then wailed on the first Unnoticeable that came to shoo him away. Me and Randall took that as our cue to charge, but Meryll was faster. She hit one with an uppercut so hard he did half a flip, then threw the other headfirst into a wall.

So goddamned hot.

Randall better appreciate boning her.

The whole fight took maybe thirty seconds, but Gus and The Talentless had already disappeared around the end of the block.

For the next twenty minutes we sprinted down blind alleyways and hid behind garbage cans. It didn't help that Gus and his bandmates weren't making a sound. Out of sight, they didn't bother feigning humanity. They all walked fast, at nearly a jog. Arms moving minimally, spines held stiff. At each corner they'd stop, all momentum ceasing abruptly. They would crane their heads—quick, neck-snapping motions—then pick a direction and lope away again.

By the time they stopped, me and Randall were exhausted. Tub was covered in the kind of sweat that doesn't come from just exertion. He was pale and shaking. With his limp, the pace had nearly killed him. Meryll wasn't even winded.

Gus had led us to some kind of industrial area—a zigzag of empty lanes and crumbling factories. The air tasted like rust. We were squatting behind a transformer at one end of a large courtyard between three buildings. A three-foot-high concrete ledge formed the perimeter. Big metal doors with flaking paint lined each side. It looked like trucks had loaded up here at some point, but the weeds growing through the asphalt told me that hadn't happened for a while. Gus and the Talentless were standing in a tight group at the far corner, staring at a closed loading bay. They hadn't moved for at least ten minutes.

What the hell were they doing? Is this where they slept? Did they sleep? Or did they just wander into an abandoned parking lot and stare at a wall until it was time to eat virgins and play lousy punk rock again?

"We're not gonna get a better shot than this," Randall said.

Tub popped his head up and did a quick survey.

"Looks like only one exit, back through us. Nowhere for them to run, nowhere for reinforcements to come in. Still leaves us with an escape route if things go sour."

He nodded at Meryll, and she was up and walking instantly. She hopped a bit as she did, loosening up. She cracked the knuckles of one hand, then the other.

She closed on the group quickly. "You boys lost?" she yelled.

Gus's arms shot out to his sides the second she made a sound. It looked like he was being drawn and quartered by invisible trains. His limbs strained so hard I could hear the joints pop and the muscles tear from a hundred feet away. They shook violently, then snapped through a series of wrong angles. The others followed suit. One guy—the bassist, I think—started looking up and just didn't stop. His neck bent all the way backward until he ended up looking at Meryll upside down over his own spine. The guitar player fell over sideways, thrashed on the ground, and started crawling around with his legs bent up like a grasshopper.

They were sleeping. And now they're waking up.

Even Meryll was pulled up short by the show. We all stood, frozen by the unexpected horror. Gus screamed, a long, high, juddering sound, like listening to a bottle rocket from the other side of an oscillating fan. He tested the scream again, stopped, grunted a few times. The other Talentless chattered meaninglessly, teeth clacking as their jaws worked. Slowly and with great effort, Gus seemed to take control of his movements. The limbs bent in more human directions, and his mechanical screeches started sounding more like a voice.

"Hk-hk-how—how are you guys doin'?" he finally said, his Iggy Pop drawl fading in and out.

"What the bloody hell was that?" Meryll said.

"It takes us a while," Gus said, his voice now flat and toneless like a strong wind through an empty field, "to remember how you move. So small and limited."

The rest of the Talentless had more or less put together their human costumes, except the bassist, whose left arm was helicoptering wildly around his head.

I laughed so hard I think I pulled something.

The rest of the situation was so alien and horrible, but here they were, finally looking more or less like a bunch of shitty punk rock posers, except for one guy who just couldn't get control of his own flailing arm. I think I'd done that once, while extremely high.

Gus's head adjusted quickly, spotting me.

"Hey, my man!" He grinned like a stoned donkey. "Didn't realize this chick was with you. What are you guys doing here?"

"W-we're here to kill you," Meryll said, trying to get her moxie back up.

Gus laughed, big and rolling.

"I don't think that's gonna work," he said, and gave her a shrug. "But you're welcome to try it."

A loud scratch, boots scuffing concrete, and her fist was halfway through his face.

She was so fucking fast.

Meryll didn't wait to see how the blow landed. She kicked

out the knees of the guitarist and used the momentum to hurl him into the drummer. I caught a glint of steel: brass knuckles reflecting light from the one dim streetlamp on the far side of the loading bay. She was a whirlwind. No hesitation, no awkward movements, no unnecessary effort. She was back to Gus now, nailing him with a goal-kicker crotch punt. He bent over, and she rocketed a knee up into his face that lifted him off the ground. She turned back to elbow the bassist. His head folded in on itself, but the rest of his body didn't follow. He latched onto her arm with both hands. She punched him in the kidneys, stomped on his foot, but he didn't seem to care. The drummer was back up now, and he wrapped himself around her legs. The guitarist followed suit, seizing her other arm, and they had her, mummified by a bunch of second-rate Stooges.

I got up to join the fight—like hell am I going to let Meryll think I'm a coward, hiding behind a metal box while she does all the heavy lifting. But Randall grabbed my arm. "What the hell are you doing?" he asked.

"What does it look like I'm doing?"

"It looks like you're going to kill yourself for a piece of ass," he said.

I went cold inside.

He's right, of course. I knew it even with the fight kicking around in my belly and that anger bubbling in the back of my throat. I couldn't take Gus alone, much less four of him. But fucking Randall—he should know that's not the point. We don't do this because we can win. We don't do this because nobody else will. We don't do this because it's the right thing to do, or it's the only thing we can do. We do it because: Fuck them. Fuck people who use their power to dick over whoever they can get away with dicking over. It doesn't matter if that guy's a high school teacher, or a Wall Street broker, or a cop, or a demon inside the shell of a store-brand Iggy Pop. You have to punch him in the face because he deserves to be punched in the fucking face. End of story.

I shoved Randall back, spat on the ground, and turned away. I didn't have words for him. But I could see it on his face—he already understood how he'd fucked up.

I walked toward Meryll and the Talentless. She was struggling, but she could barely budge the grip of the Empty Ones.

I was maybe a dozen paces away when Gus held up a hand for me to stop. "We will pull her limbs off, like a child plucking the legs off of an ant."

His human persona dropped. He stared at a point somewhere behind me, unwilling or unable to focus on me.

"Let her go," I said.

"Or what."

There was nothing to mark it as a question. Every word he spoke had the exact same weight and cadence.

"Or . . . I'll get blood all over your expensive leather pants," I said.

He laughed, joyless and mechanical. It stopped abruptly, halfway through an exhalation.

"She is weak, like a coma patient waking to atrophied limbs. But she is stronger than the rest of your kind. She should not be this strong. What is she."

"I'm the girl from Brixton who's gonna bash your bloody face in," she said.

"I see it in you."

"Who, me?" I said, having trouble following the flow of conversation.

"No, her. But you have it, too. There is an order to you, the both of you, that is so often lacking in people. People are a jumble. A mess. Apply order and you clean the mess. The mess disappears. But you and this girl . . . there is a thread within you that makes sense. It is small, hard to spot, but important. You are of use to the Mechanic. It can take what you are and make something out of it. You can help the machine. Like you did in New York."

"I didn't fucking help you," I said.

"Not willingly, but with our assistance the core of you helped birth a Tool of the Mechanic. That is vital work."

"The angel? I helped you make more of them?"

I didn't even care about the answer. But I didn't have any ideas for how to get out of this with my bones intact, and any time I could buy was more time for my stupid brain to come up with a good idea. No matter how unlikely that prospect was.

"Yes. And we thank you for that. We love you for that, always. It is why you are not a stain on the pavement right now. But this girl, she has the thread, too. And unlike you, hers still has potential. It can be used. If a thing can be used, it must be used. Otherwise there is no meaning to the thing. We will use her. If there is something left when we are done, you may have it. That is out of gratitude, for what you have done for the Mechanic."

"You're not taking her anywhere. Not as long as I'm sucking air."

I hoped Tub and Randall were using the time to do something clever, like gather stuff to throw at Gus. That's about as clever as I could hope from them.

"You will have no say in it," Gus said.

He stooped down, grabbed a hunk of loose asphalt, and lobbed it underhand at the shuttered metal door behind him. The sound bounced around the courtyard for a few seconds, then got swallowed by the silence of the big empty space. Then a single squeal, old metal on old metal. Others joined the chorus. The doors were rising. All of them, on every side.

Inside them was a thick darkness that boiled and churned. I caught the glint of brass, the one dim streetlamp reflecting light off of a thousand sets of gears.

SIXTEEN

2013. Tulancingo, Mexico. Marco.

"I guess I do it to feel like a man," the skinny thing says. It blinks hard, sets its jaw. It would fight another thing, if that thing said the skinny thing's eyes were watering.

"You *are* a man," this thing, wearing the shell of an actor called Marco says. It says this because it has been written down on a scrap of paper. The other things have insisted to this thing that this is the normal and expected way to behave. "Ain't nobody can take that away from you, *esse*."

This thing overpronounces the last word, to emphasize that it is part of a mutual culture with the skinny thing.

The skinny thing looks away from the cameras. It cannot face the other things in its current state. It is experiencing pride, or perhaps shame. It is hard for this thing to understand the trivial misfires that cause emotions in the other things.

A thing with an unkempt mustache and a trucker hat that says BLACK BEAR DINER—BEARY GOOD! motions for this thing to put its hand on the skinny thing's knee. This thing does so.

The skinny thing turns and opens its arms. This thing takes a moment to consider what the gesture means, before the thing with the scraggly mustache and ironic hat mimes an embrace. This thing embraces the skinny thing. The skinny thing trembles. This thing trembles, too. This thing does not want to appear strange.

When the cameras stop, this thing asks the skinny thing to accompany it back to the trailer. This thing says "Hey *hermano*," though this thing knows they are not brothers. "Let's have a rap sesh in my trailer. I got some big ideas for you. Big!"

This thing knows it is important to use pronouns. That was one of the first lessons this thing learned. The other things grow uneasy when this thing refers to them and itself as "things." It does not make sense. All are things. Matter is matter, and it merely comes in different forms. The other things are no more valuable than rocks, or dirt, or shit. This thing is different. It has seen the order of the universe, and has the strength to assist the eternal struggle against entropy. That makes this thing slightly more valuable than other things. This thing can therefore use the other things as it sees fit, because it is in the service of something greater.

The skinny thing looks uncertain. This thing realizes it has been staring at the skinny thing without blinking for some time. This thing blinks for the benefit of the skinny thing. The skinny thing does not appear entirely at ease. This thing gives the skinny thing two big thumbs-up, and a smile that it saw a thing at a coffee shop use once. At the time, the smile appeared to make the other things happy, so this thing stole it.

The smile proves its use yet again. The skinny thing

follows this thing back to its trailer.

This thing recognizes that the skinny thing has some appeal. It is not certain what that appeal is, but the other things respond to the skinny thing positively. It would further this thing's career, and therefore this thing's usefulness, if this thing were to mimic and incorporate that appeal. This thing must therefore study the skinny thing. It must interact.

It starts by asking the skinny thing questions.

It asks: "So, *hombre,* where do you see yourself in five years?"

The skinny thing says many words, but this thing knows that words are not important. It studies the skinny thing's mannerisms. The way it tilts its head and looks upward when it is considering how to express a difficult concept. The way its hands are always moving, tapping and drumming on the table. The way it smiles when it has said something stupid.

There is a very small part of this thing that responds to the skinny thing's appeal. Back when this thing was a disorderly mess like the other things—before the hand of the Mechanic burned all of this thing's garbage away and showed it what it was to be simple and useful and important—this thing would have been attracted to the skinny thing. This thing did not distinguish its partners by gender. This thing enjoyed that other things wanted it, and that was enough for it. This thing sees the want in the skinny thing, and the minuscule remnants of the mess that remain in this thing flutter and twitch.

This thing laughs when it seems appropriate to laugh. It furrows its brow and nods solemnly when it seems appropriate to furrow brows and nod solemnly. This thing is learning much, and practice is important. This thing is still young, and does not pass as well among the other things as it could. This thing must learn. But for now, this thing is doing excellently.

The skinny thing is in the midst of telling an important story. It is a story about the skinny thing's mother. The plight of the mother thing, the poor circumstances that the skinny thing hopes to raise the mother thing out of. The skinny thing starts to tear up. It notices this thing noticing.

"It's nothing, man," the skinny thing says, waving this thing's attention away. "I just got something in my eye."

This thing knows the other things like to help each other. It is important to help, to pass as a lesser thing.

This thing helps.

It reaches out and sticks its finger in the eye of the skinny thing.

This thing realizes it has moved too quickly. It is so hard, for this thing to act like it is trapped like the others. Bound by their limitations. They move so slowly, they bruise so easily, they die so quickly.

A mere accidental jab from this thing's pointer finger, and the skinny thing's eye has popped open. It is loosing fluid down the thing's cheekbones. The skinny thing is screaming and flapping its arms like an angry bird. This thing realizes it has made a mistake.

"Sorry, homey! My bad!" this thing says, and it gives the skinny thing the double thumbs-up that it once enjoyed so much.

The skinny thing is not appeased. It still screams.

This thing must not be discovered. The sounds must stop. This thing puts its hand in the mouth of the skinny thing. This thing's hand does not quite fit, so the skinny thing's cheeks and jaw split apart as this thing's fist forces its way in. But the sounds become muffled, and that is good.

The skinny thing is thrashing. It is trying to get away, to get this thing's fist out from the ruins of its face.

The skinny thing was once attracted to this thing. This thing believes it can use that attraction to correct the situation. This thing places its hand gently on the crotch of the skinny thing.

The skinny thing seems to respond to this gesture not with comfort, but increased fear. The thrashing intensifies.

This thing feels a twinge of rage, in the disgusting corners not swept entirely clean by the light of the Mechanic. The places where its humanity still hides, huddled and weak. Anger flares up within this thing, and this thing does not know how to respond to or control what scant emotions remain. This thing closes its hand against the skinny thing's genitals, crushing them. The skinny thing is no longer thrashing, but it twitches violently. Muffled moans come from the space beyond this thing's fist. This thing can feel their breath on its knuckles. This thing has made many mistakes in this interaction.

Mistakes must be fixed. A full reset is needed.

This thing drops the skinny thing's pulped genitals, grabs the top of the skinny thing's skull, and pulls. The head of the skinny thing splits in two at the jawbone. The skinny thing still lives, so this thing brings what remains of its head down onto the table until the skinny thing stops moving.

The entire inside of the trailer, including this thing's body and clothing, is covered in the gore of the skinny thing. The other things find their own gore unsettling. This thing will have to clean itself before going back out amongst the other things. This thing turns on the shower, as hot as the water will go. It recognizes pain as sensory input. As damage being done. But it does not understand why that input is more important than any other input. This thing regards pain in the same way that the lesser things regard sight, or touch. The water scalds this thing's skin, the red of the blood washing away to reveal the red of burns. That is fine. This thing heals.

This thing begins to sing.

This thing always sings in the shower. This thing recalls a time, before it was cleansed, when it was the star of a children's sitcom about teenagers in high school. There was an episode where the character this thing played sang in the showers after a football game. The scene got a laugh. The other things enjoy laughter. So this thing makes a point to repeat that scene every time it showers. It is good practice.

There is a noise from the room outside. Something has entered this thing's trailer. This thing has had a chance to clean itself, but not the room where the skinny thing was dismantled. The other things will likely find the cleanliness of this thing pleasing, but may still be distressed by the presence of gore in the room. This thing is unsure. This thing decides that it will pretend to be surprised, if the other things inquire as to the nature of the remains.

"Whoa, what?" this thing will say. "What happened here?"

This thing will then laugh in disbelief, to further put the other things at ease.

This thing turns off the shower and walks out the door. It remembers, too late, that the other things do not typically greet company while nude. This thing remembers, too late, that its burns are still visibly healing. The other things may be upset about this. This thing is not sure.

The other thing is not a lesser being. It is a girl thing that calls itself Meryll. This thing does not fully understand what the girl thing is, but the girl thing is not a mess like the other things. She, too, has been worked on by the Mechanic. Her internals are different, however. They have not been simplified and disposed of like this thing's were. They have only been rearranged. The mess within the girl thing is still present, but it has been repurposed in a way that exemplifies order and defies entropy. The girl thing has shown great power, and therefore great usefulness. Much greater than this own thing's power and usefulness. The girl thing is worth more than this thing. This thing defers to the girl thing.

This thing says: "Hey, *chica*, what's the haps?"

"Gross," the girl thing says. "Don't do that. Nobody's listening."

This thing lets the humanity slide from its frame. It is like relaxing a weak muscle that has been clenched too long, and is beginning to give out. "The practice is useful."

"Yeah?" the girl thing says. "What was the use in stripping naked and—I'm assuming you just ate a bunch of people? What the fuck happened here?"

"I was learning from a younger actor. He was teaching me much, until I made a mistake. It is better if people do not see your mistakes. They think you are stronger, and they like you more that way."

"You're just the belle of the ball, aren't you?"

This thing does not understand. It does not find usefulness in understanding, so it says nothing.

"I've been to see her," the girl thing says, after a while. It sits on a padded bench across from the blood-soaked table. It crosses its legs and picks at its nails as it talks. Despite its earlier protests, it is not disconcerted by the sight of the innards of other things. It is a thing that understands it is a thing, like this thing. The girl thing is simply better at pretending. This thing could learn from it.

"I found this bloody . . . anti-Christ, or whatever she is to you."

"The analogy is good," this thing confirms. It sits beside the girl thing. It pushes out its chest, like the girl thing. Then it crosses its legs at the knee and gazes at its own nails. "Kaitlyn has destroyed a tool of the Mechanic. She has brought chaos to a beautiful piece of order. Order is the closest analogy for God. Kaitlyn is disgusting, and I would like to piss in her heart."

"I don't see how she did all that," the girl thing says. It notices this thing copying it, and readjusts its posture. "There didn't seem to be much special about her. I found her and Carey in a little shop out in the desert. I twisted up a farmhand into something nasty for them."

"So they are dead?" This thing considers feeling disappointed that its hands had not split apart their flesh itself. But when this thing thinks about the blond thing— that trash on the floor of reality—it feels not just a twinge of hate, but something else. Only a remnant of a feeling, but that remnant quivers and crawls. This thing grabs its thumb, and yanks it backwards. It uses the fragment of exposed bone to scratch a bloody smiley face in the flesh of its own leg. This distracts.

"Eh," the girl thing says. "Maybe. Carey was looking a bit rougher than the last time I saw him, but he was always a wily one. And if the girl killed one of your precious Flares, she's apparently got some tricks I didn't see."

"If they are not dead?"

"Well, that's why we have you, don't we?"

"I am not certain of the plan. I do not know if it is useful to use me as bait. I am strong. I am valuable. If I was not strong or valuable, I understand why you would risk me and why you would not care if I were to die. But I am strong. I am famous and can use my influence to further order. I could ask a woman to come with me and she would. She would not consider what happens after, because I am known to her. That gives me value."

"Are you . . ." The girl thing gives this thing a look that this thing doesn't understand. "Are you afraid of her?"

This thing considers the possibility. It does not know how to respond. It decides to use a gesture it remembers from its sitcom. It shrugs, and gives a certain kind of smile that is meant to signal coyness and uncertainty. "Don't ask me, I'm just a jock!" it says, just like it used to on the television show.

The girl thing laughs so hard that she snorts.

SEVENTEEN

1978. London, England. Carey.

The darkness moved.

Luckily, tar men are slow—they hadn't even made it out of the loading bays yet—so there was enough time for us to haul ass out of the courtyard before they could melt us down to sludge. But there was not enough time to wrestle Meryll out of the grip of roughly half a dozen inhuman dickheads before we got to safety.

Think, Carey. Think!

I threw a rock at Gus's head. It drew blood, but he didn't so much as flinch.

Well, that didn't help.

I threw another rock.

It still didn't help. "I'm out of ideas," I said.

I turned to Tub. He was the wise old wizard to me and Randall's drunken hobbits. He was the tactician, the strategist. The wisdom of years was on his side.

"Fucked if I know," he said. Then he turned and started hobble-running away.

"What the hell, man?" I yelled after him.

He passed right by Randall without pause. Randall was frozen. He wanted to run, but he was waiting on me.

On me. It was all on me. It was all hanging on my ingenuity.

And I was out of rocks.

I glared the hell out of Gus and the rest of The Talentless on the off-chance that I had Superman heat-vision this whole time and just hadn't wanted it bad enough until right now.

No dice.

Something grabbed my arm. I thrust my elbow back, then spun around to crack whatever it was in the face, if it had one. But it was just Randall.

"Come on," he said. He pulled on my jacket.

"Fuck you," I said. "We can't leave her."

"You tried, all right? Nobody's going to say you didn't try. But we have to go." His eyes were mostly white. They kept darting back, toward Tub and the only exit from the courtyard. His voice cracked.

He's afraid? Randall—who once asked a cop if his nightstick smelled funny from all the time it spent shoved up his own ass— is scared?

Shit. Maybe I should be, too.

The tar men were everywhere. There wasn't enough light in the overgrown lot to see them individually. You could catch hints of brass here and there, but otherwise it was just a big, black wave of molasses, slowly consuming everything it touched. I couldn't even see Meryll, Gus, and the Talentless anymore. They'd been enveloped by the tide of monsters. I struggled in Randall's grip. I shook him free.

Maybe if I crack open my lighter and empty the fluid out on that patch of dried grass, I can form a sort of torch to—

Impact. Pop. Fuzz.

Muffled voices echoing inside my head.

Faded lights, and the implication of movement.

Must have drank too much.

Where am I?

It smells like piss and fish. That doesn't narrow it down any— half of London smells like piss and fish.

God, my head. What was I, mixing grain alcohol with jet fuel? Jesus. I thought I was beyond this.

They say alcoholics don't get hangovers, because they're drunk too often.

When is that shit going to kick in for me?

Those muffled voices again, like they're coming from the other side of a waterfall. Made of pudding.

Shit, whatever bed I passed out on really sucks. It feels like hard, wet pavement. This pillow is like a rock.

I opened my eyes.

I was laying on hard, wet pavement. My head was on a rock.

Way to pick 'em, Carey.

The voices were a little clearer. I lifted my head and the world shifted unpleasantly. Randall and Tub were talking.

". . . think the cripple's gonna carry him? That's your burden, boyo. Shoulder it."

"So what, you're just gonna leave us?"

"If you can't beat those bastards in a footrace, you deserve what you get."

"Christ," I said, and tried to spit out whatever disgusting thing was in my mouth.

It was my tongue.

"Here we go," Tub said, then turned and started limping away, leaning heavily on his rebar cane.

"Why'd you let me pass out in a fucking quarry?" I asked Randall, and sat up, which turned out to be a terrible decision.

"Listen, I know you're pissed but . . ." Randall was sweating. He kept checking behind him.

"Nah, just get me—"

Meryll.

It came back to me.

"You motherfu—"

"What was I gonna do, let you dive into a pool of tar men? You weren't thinking."

"Thinking ain't what we do, and you know it!" I stood up quickly and aimed a kick at his crotch, but I missed by about a yard and fell down. I threw up for a minute, then decided that if I just kind of scooted toward him on my butt, I could kick upward into his dick just fine.

"Hey! Stop!" Randall jumped away as I crab-walked toward his genitals. "Stop! Tub said she's fine! She's fine!"

"The hell she is! Five Empty Ones and a tsunami of tar men—what kind of fucked up definition of 'fine' are you working off of?"

"I don't know, man. Tub said something about it all going down pretty much like he thought, and that now we just have to find a ride to catch up with them."

"What? He knows where they're going?"

"He does. It's going to be all right—Tub's got some kind of plan."

"He better," I said, offering my hand to Randall so he could help me up.

He smiled and took it.

I kicked him in the crotch as hard as I could.

Randall walked funny all the way up Oxford Street. We'd caught up with Tub, and had been trying to flag down cabs for twenty minutes, but, strangely, nobody wanted to stop for an old hobo wielding a nasty piece of rebar; one bleeding, crusty, punk rocker; and one asshole in a stupid shirt walking like he had spikes on his testicles.

"I swear on your mother's grave, old man, if we get there and she's already butchered, I'm going to—"

"You'll do fuck-all, son," Tub said. "I could take you on my worst day, half drunk and with one leg—which is good, because that's precisely what I've got."

I eyeballed his cane. There were dark brown stains all across the tip. I wouldn't have put money on them being rust.

"Relax," he said, and waved the rebar at a passing car. It didn't slow. He took a swing at the car as it passed.

"How the hell am I supposed to relax? They got Meryll!"

"Well, yes." Tub tapped over to the wall of a shuttered newsstand and leaned heavily. He was still sweating, even though it was freezing out here. "Did you think she was gonna jump in there and *slap* the Husks to death?"

"I . . ."

Yes, that is exactly what I pictured. Meryll delivering huge, reeling, superpowered backhands to Gus's stupid horse face until it inexplicably exploded.

"Ha!" Tub slapped his own leg, then winced. "You told me yourself you boys hit one with a train. What's a strong right cross gonna do?"

"You said we could kill them!"

"We can, but not like that. The only way I've seen a Husk go down is when they get caught up in the blast from a dying Flare."

"An angel?" Randall wrangled up like a cowboy that had just rode twenty hard miles, bareback, on a metal horse. "You can kill it?"

"*She* can," Tub said, "and has. Twice already. But she's gotta get taken first. The Husks—they use people like Meryll to summon Flares. Well, the Husks *think* she's like them, anyway. But she's got a surprise in store. They take her and do their little ritual, the Flare shows up, then boom: Anybody standing within the blast, including Husks, gets turned into a bloody puddle."

"There's got to be a better way to do that than just letting Gus grab her off the street," I said. "What if he'd just killed her?"

"Well, this isn't Plan A, obviously," Tub said. "We were hoping to tail them back to the ranges, do this on our terms. But one takes what one is given."

"We? She was in on this?" I asked.

Randall waved at a cab. The driver slowed down, waited for Randall to jog up, then drove away. He flipped a backward peace sign out the window.

Tub laughed.

"You try to stop the girl when it comes to killing Flares. Hates the damn things like a Welshman hates the English. Or the Scots. Or other Welsh, for that matter."

"Wait," I said, mentally scrolling backward. "What's 'the ranges?' You know where they're going?"

"Most likely," Tub said. He sneered as yet another cab drove by us. I looked closer, and noticed the cabbie looked familiar.

The motherfucker was circling the block, just taunting us. That's . . . almost great. You really gotta respect that degree of spite.

"The bloody Faceless are everywhere," Tub continued. "You've seen 'em in the tunnels, in the clubs, in the streets. It'd be impossible to tell which of their hidey-holes Gus crawls off to, normally. But now that he's got Meryll, well, he'll be needing a ritual site. The Purfleet rifle ranges. Used to be an army range, just outside of London proper. Now it's just a swamp. Gotta be there. Boffins have found remains dating back to the Middle Ages at Purfleet. Sacrifices, by the looks of things. Mutilated and . . ."

"The fuck is a boffin?" Randall interrupted.

"A researcher, or an academic," Tub answered. "Smart folks. Though maybe not as smart as they think. See, they believe Purfleet was a druid site."

"And you know better?"

"Druids weren't much into human sacrifice, by all accounts," Tub said, "and most of the corpses they recovered were deformed in some way. Extra fingers. Sixth toes. . . ."

I put it together. Though I sure as hell didn't like the implication.

"We've got to get there," I said.

"We're bloody well trying, aren't we?" Tub said.

Randall sighed.

"What?" I asked.

"We're gonna have to do a Sit 'n Spin, aren't we?"

I smiled.

"Yes, Randall," I said, "and after that sucker punch earlier, guess who's doing the sitting?"

The Sit 'n Spin goes like this: You find a car going slow, but not too slow. Ideally it's rainy or foggy out, so they can't see too well and there's less chance of them stopping in time. London was apparently made for the maneuver. When the car gets close, somebody jumps in front, tries to go ass-first into the windshield.

Three reasons you want to go ass-first:

You're less likely to break your more important bones.

You're less likely to break the windshield.

It's funny.

That's the Sit. The driver gets out, either to check and see if you're okay, or just to yell at you for being a dipshit, then your friend clocks 'em from behind and you take the car for a nice Spin.

It's brilliant.

Well, it's brilliant in its simplicity.

Well, at least it's simple.

You gotta give me that.

It was the same cabbie, coming back for another taunt. I almost felt bad for the guy—he had The Sonics in the cassette player and two packs of Camels and a warm can of beer in the glove box. In a different scenario, I think I could have called him "friend." But this was an emergency, so we left him by the side of the road with a bleeding head and yet another reason to hate Americans.

For some reason, Randall got to drive. He always gets to drive.

He insists it's because he knows how to drive, but I don't get what that has to do with anything.

From inside the cab, London was a blur of damp stone and watery halos of light. Tub snapped out directions and Randall barely made the turns. Eventually, the honks, screamed profanity, and streetlights grew fewer and farther between, until we were barreling straight through the black night, our dim headlights cutting out little triangles of road directly in front of us.

"Stop!" Tub said, and Randall slammed on the brakes. I crashed into the dashboard, and felt Tub do the same to the seat behind me.

"What?" Randall said.

"We're here," Tub answered, rubbing his bruised face.

I looked out the window at nothing. It was dark, sure—but even in the pitch-black, you could tell there wasn't anything around for miles. You could just feel the emptiness. A scraggly tree here and there, picked out by what faded starlight made it through the soggy blanket of clouds.

"There's nothing here," Randall said. "In fact, I'm not sure there's ever *been* anything here. I think we left the damn universe. You're sure this is the spot?"

"It is," Tub said, stepping out of the cab. His hip crackled like Chinese fireworks.

Me and Randall got out after him. The open air smelled like a basement. Not one of those nice ones from the magazines with shag carpeting and a pool table, either. One of those shady, forgotten, cobwebbed "I'm certain there's something under the stairs that's gonna reach out and grab my ankle" kind of basements.

"This place sucks," I said.

I'm always so much more eloquent in my head.

Tub grunted approval. He pointed at something with his cane. I gave it a minute, and little lights picked themselves out of the darkness. Either small, or impossibly distant.

"There's no road out that way, is there?" Randall said, but he already knew the answer.

I do not recommend walking through a swamp in a pair of Chuck Taylors. If you absolutely have to, though, I highly recommend taping up the tears in the sole first. If you can't do that, I at least recommend wearing socks.

I was following zero of my own recommendations.

"How you doing?" Randall said, somewhere out in the black.

"Fine," I snapped. "I'm just over here foot-fucking a mound of rotten pudding. How about you?"

Randall laughed.

Tub hushed us.

I could hear it now. I thought the low chattering was birds at first. But as we grew closer to the noise, I could start to pick out an occasional voice in the static.

Happy yelling.

An angry bark.

A sharp, short burst of laughter, abruptly silenced.

We crested a small, soft mound of something. I tripped on a less-soft mound of something else, and fell onto a series of hard somethings. I crawled past them and reached the top of Mount Whatever. There were two silhouettes ahead of me, outlined against the background light.

If they weren't Tub and Randall, what was I going to do? Fight them in the pitch-black? Run? I couldn't even fall down properly. I sidled up alongside them, elbowed one in the ribs, and half waited for death.

"Ow," said a voice. Luckily it was Randall's.

I started to say something, but he shook his head. The fact that I could see the gesture at all told me something had changed. I looked below us and saw blobs of fire, suspended in the air, surrounded by hollow, ghoulish faces. A series of barrel fires, people clustering around them. Their faces registered as normal, if you weren't paying attention. If you tried to pay attention, you were rewarded with what felt like the start of a migraine, and a blurry smear of nonfeatures.

The Unnoticeables were having a party.

They were milling around in tightly clustered groups, all along a shallow depression between two hills. At the far end, they had a crude stage set up: a bunch of sawhorses holding up some plywood. I've seen dozens of those at shitty outdoor shows upstate. They generally fall over when the band gets too drunk and forgets that they're playing on a set of Lincoln Logs. In the darkened areas, where the light from the barrel fires couldn't reach, the shadows churned. Tar men.

It was too dark to even guess at how many.

A couple hundred Unnoticeables. God knows how many tar men. And at the far end of them, Gus and Meryll, standing alone on that rickety stage.

Meryll was lashed to a branch halfway up a massive old tree at the back end of the stage. Gus had his back to me, but I could tell it was him. You know how you can instantly pick out somebody you love from a crowd, even if you're not really looking? Turns out I can do the same thing with somebody I hate.

It was too dark, and they were too far away to make out details, but by the way Meryll slumped against that tree— like a boxer who's spent the last ten rounds losing—she was in rough shape. Gus had something in his hands. Long, curved, and off-white. Bone? He reached out to Meryll with whatever it was, and ran it down her face.

I could hear her scream like she was next to me.

The crowd cheered.

"Was this in your fucking plan?" Randall asked Tub.

He didn't answer, just ground his teeth.

Gus yelled something to the crowd, but I couldn't hear it over the hooting and catcalls from the Unnoticeables. I got the sense that it was a question, and the crowd responded in the affirmative. He turned back and cut Meryll again with the bone. She just shook this time, still in shock from the last swipe, unable to get the breath to scream.

The question wasn't whether or not we were going down there. We were going down there. The question was: How many of those assholes could we take down before they kill us?

Then I thought of a better question: What around here is flammable?

EIGHTEEN

2013. Tulancingo, Mexico. Marco.

". . . it's about family, *esse*," this thing says. "It's about love, y'know? Love from right here."

This thing thumps the skinny boy's chest. It is a gesture meant to indicate the heart. It is stupid, to think that emotion comes from a pump located behind the rib cage. Emotion comes from human instincts failing to keep pace with evolution. Humans have fear because, long ago, fear kept them alert for predators. Now they fear abstract concepts—failure, embarrassment, being alone—because they think there are no more predators.

They are wrong, of course.

This thing has been talking, even while it reflects on glorified muscles and evolutionary failures. It finds convincing social interaction difficult, but it has long ago memorized this speech. It has used some variation on it at several charity events, one award show, and thirteen dates.

". . . and you can't let what's in here,"—this thing points to the skinny boy's head—"get in the way of all you got in *here*." The chest again.

There are tears in the boy's eyes. He nods. He leans in. This thing scrambles to analyze the cue—is it an attack? This thing could tear the skinny boy apart in seconds. Hook the thumbs into the eyeholes, apply outward pressure to the ocular cavities, and rend the skull in twain—

A hug.

The skinny boy is attempting emotional solidarity through an embrace. After a moment, this thing returns the gesture, because it would be frowned upon to pull the boy's head apart now.

The director yells cut. Its obnoxious trucker hat is soaked. Its sparse, ironic mustache is dripping with sweat. It is apparently a very hot day in Tulancingo. This thing must practice how to appear bothered by temperature. None of them notice the absence of distress now, but one day they might, and then this thing will have to eliminate them before they can disperse that information.

This thing stands. There is motion all around it. Now that they are freed from the obligation of "the scene," there is real work to do. This thing is looking at nothing in particular. It is just waiting for the other things to complete their functions. This thing is not looking, but it sees anyway.

The prey moves amongst the crowd. It realizes it has been seen. It flees. This thing pursues.

This thing has forgotten that it must appear artificially slow, bounded by the physical constraints of a human's worthless, dysfunctional body. This thing hears the gasps from the assembled gawkers as it rushes through them at speeds they consider unnatural. This thing knocks aside two men, one woman, and a small child to get free of the crowd. It has momentarily lost its prey.

This thing scrambles up a drainage pipe to a roof. There

are screams from below. They fall behind as this thing runs. It jumps to another rooftop. It squats atop a chimney. It tilts its head and listens.

It hears footsteps more rapid than others. Running.

This thing leaps. It drops three stories. It lands on an overweight man, because the overweight provide superior cushioning. This thing would not be harmed by the fall, but the force of the landing may have caused this thing to stumble, losing precious seconds. It is better for this thing to use the fat man as an impact cushion, so that it may be up and running more quickly.

The impact cushion barks out its own blood on the pavement.

The rapid footsteps are not rapid enough. This thing is gaining.

It skids around a corner, sees a car blocking the alleyway, and jumps atop the roof. There are a series of obstacles littering the path between this thing and its prey. There are animals. There are crates. There are garbage containers. There are people. This thing needs maximum traction and maneuverability. This thing drops to all fours and converts its movement to a quick, scuttling lope. It weaves through the obstacles, and the people scream—is that all they know how to do? Every time this thing does something perfectly logical, the humans scream. It is a useless gesture.

The prey is cornered. It is only a low fence. Eight feet high, at most. This thing could be over it in seconds, but the prey is handicapped by its own shell. It is scrambling for purchase. Its hands are looped through the links, but its shoes are too broad and have no traction.

This thing considers laughing, to show its disdain.

The prey is old. Not ancient, but it appears much older

than it is. It has not taken even minimal care of the disposable flesh that it occupies. Its face is blanketed by wrinkles, tanned, covered with innumerable small scars. Its hair is cut short and receding. It is so skinny that this thing can see its ribs through the hole-ridden T-shirt. Though it is hot, the prey is wearing a jacket. The same jacket it always wears: Black leather with worn metal spikes on the shoulders.

The humans call this thing "Carey."

This thing feels fury welling up inside of it. This thing hates that sensation. It should be beyond even these thin vestiges of emotion. But certain extraordinary circumstances still provoke the response.

The thing called Carey interfered with this thing's mission. It prevented the candidate from ascending. It destroyed something beautiful. It helped kill an angel.

This thing is too angry to even consider torturing its prey. Humans enjoy living, and despite extraordinary difficulties, will attempt to continue doing it. Their lives are ruled by sensations: Pleasure. Angst. Anger. Lust. Torture allows the humans several more hours of life, blissfully full of sensation. It is an honor this thing will not bestow upon the thing called Carey. This thing will dig its fingers into the chest of its prey and it will hurl its organs on the pavement, then it will squish them beneath its feet and dance in the gore.

That seems the appropriate response.

The thing called Carey seems to guess at this thing's intent. It holds its hands up in a fighting stance.

This thing smiles and is on its prey before the other thing can even register the movement. It cracks the prey in the nose with its forehead. The other thing staggers. This thing kicks its legs out from under it. It falls. This thing brings its fist down on the prey's chest. Then its genitals. Then its neck. Then its face. Again and again. The prey is convulsing and twitching from the blows. It tries to breathe, but every gasp is hammered out of it before the lungs can fill. The prey spews blood, but this thing clasps its hand over the prey's mouth. The blood pools in its mouth, and the prey begins to choke. This thing laces its fingers in the spaces between the ribs. It will latch on, and pull the entire rib cage from the body in one swift movement. Then it will—

A sensation. This thing takes a moment to register it. Pleasure? Cold?

Pain.

Something has struck this thing in the back of the head. This thing stands, and turns around, prepared to eviscerate the distraction.

This thing sees the candidate. The one who devoured the angel. The one humans call "Kaitlyn." It is holding a bottle. It has apparently just thrown one at this thing, and is prepared to throw another.

This thing feels a sensation.

It thinks. It tries to categorize the feeling, but it is having difficulty.

At last, it comes: Fear.

It is consuming. It is controlling. This thing does not often experience that sensation. It is not good at controlling it. It has no practice. This thing is surprised to hear that it is screaming. This thing does not recall telling its legs to move, so it is also very surprised to learn that it is running.

NINETEEN

Carey and Randall are trying to sing "Sugarlight," but they're too pissed to even stand, much less enunciate. It's coming out as a series of gargled howls. They don't seem perturbed by that fact. The louder one yells, the louder the other yells.

It's just past midnight, and they're lying on a couple of lounge chairs beside a bright blue pool. The underwater lights cast undulating shadows on the walls of the slick little mansion behind them. I figured they must have hopped the fence, and are just hoping nobody's home. Can't imagine anyone inviting them into a place like this.

They're wrong about the place being empty, though: Lights are coming on inside. Somebody slides the patio door open. A young black kid with a shaved head. He's in a pair of Mickey Mouse boxers and nothing else. He looks pissed, but not surprised. Carey and Randall see him now, and they start yelling greetings. The black kid says something low and unhappy, but they're too oblivious to catch his tone. They holler back at him, all blissful ignorance. Carey holds out a beer and says something. The black kid smiles. He takes it, cracks it open, and downs the whole thing in a matter of seconds. I hear the ensuing belch all way up here on the hill. Carey and Randall applaud. They hold out another, the black kid takes it and sits down. He nurses this one. Soon all three are yammering a bit too loudly. The patio door opens again, and this time a pretty blonde steps out in an oversized T-shirt. The guys fall silent. She glares at each in turn, then pulls up a deck chair. She sits down, crosses her legs, and holds out her hand. They all cheer as Randall passes her a beer.

It took me forever and a day to find the two of them after they left London. I went to New York first. I trawled the Manhattan punk clubs for months with no luck. Some kids remembered Carey (not fondly), but they all said he took off for England a while back. So I stopped following the guys, and I started following trouble instead.

There were rumors of Unnoticeables all over the place—Baltimore, Detroit, Chicago—but LA came up the most often. I hopped a series of trains, bummed a few dozen rides from assholes expecting road-head. A few got aggressive. I broke some bones. One had a gun. I didn't mean to, but I did something to him, that thing I swore wouldn't happen again. I saw a little piece of his insides, and I changed it. Then the rest of him changed. His jaw fell off. His upper teeth wouldn't stop growing. They plowed down into his stomach and grew right through his skin until they pierced his back, pinning him to the driver's seat. I bolted, leaving him there to pull at his own canines.

When I got to LA, I started hitting up the seediest clubs I could find. Carey and Randall were regulars at every single one.

I'd followed them back to this house after the X show. I guess they were staying here legitimately after all. Certainly a step up from the Rape Office.

How the fuck do they deserve this? After everything we've been through—everything they put me through—they're the ones that get a happy ending in a Barbie Dreamhouse? To hell with that.

I could jump down there and beat them all to death without much fuss. Maybe I could do that thing again, change them all into something else.

Or maybe I could just go down and say hi. They'd yell and holler like they did at the black kid and the pretty girl. They'd hand me a beer and we'd all get right and properly pissed.

Right?

I remember the way Carey looked at me, when we last saw each other. That horror in his eyes.

No. We're not drinking buddies anymore.

I could take their fairy-tale ending away. I could do it right now. I'm so much stronger than I was, and I was always pretty strong. It would be over in a matter of seconds.

But tonight, down there, they're not thinking of anything. Of the Husks, or the Faceless, or what happened to me. They're not remembering the blood and the loss. They're just friends around a pool, drinking too much and bugging the neighbors. They don't deserve this happiness. I deserve it. But I can't have it, so I at least deserve to watch.

TWENTY

I don't know what the hell I was thinking.

Sure, girl, just whip a bottle at Marco. You broke his neck and he didn't so much as blink, but the recycling will totally kill him. Empty bottles of Fanta are like silver bullets to his werewolf.

The glass exploded across the back of Marco's head. It didn't even draw blood. He stood up slow, then turned around so fast I couldn't even see the movement. He silently appraised me with those black doll eyes.

I was more or less just waiting for him to kill me. I still felt like shredded crap from the car wreck. My knees were boiled rubber. I had a blinding, dry headache—like my sinuses were packed to bursting with sand. I was freezing, even though it was a hundred goddamned degrees out. I could no more fight than I could do a standing backflip. I thought about running, and nearly passed out—even thinking burned too much energy.

Marco took a step.

Backwards.

Something feral took over his face. His lips peeled back over his teeth. He hunched low and hissed. Then he leapt ten feet, straight up, over the chain-link fence behind him. He ran down the length of the alleyway, his fading screams high pitched and feminine.

What. The. Fuck?

There's no reason for Marco to run away from me, unless. . . . Oh, God.

There's something worse than Marco behind me.

I turned slowly.

Fear danced across the little hairs on my neck.

Almost there. Slowly now. Slowly . . .

Behind me, I saw . . .

Nothing.

At least, nothing that wasn't there before. There was an old couple huddling in an alcove, but they'd been hiding there since Marco first scuttled past. A small wire pen with two chickens. An upended garbage can.

Carey coughed. It was wet and thick. I know jack about medicine, but I know that cough wasn't good.

I managed to walk to him without collapsing. His mouth was full of blood, so I turned him on his side and he threw up an unhealthy amount of it. His breathing was better, but it still sounded like somebody working an accordion underwater.

"Call for help!" I yelled to the elderly couple, but now that Marco was gone, they were swiftly backing away.

I looked around for something—a conveniently idling ambulance would be lovely—but unless one of those chickens possessed magical healing powers, I was shit out of luck.

I wasn't up to dragging Carey anywhere. I could go find a phone, but what if Marco came back? Was it safe to leave him here, even for a minute?

A shuffling noise behind me. I grabbed what remained of the broken Fanta bottle and tried to look threatening.

"Jesus pogoing Christ," Jackie said. "What the hell happened?"

"I thought you left!" I wanted to stand, run to her, give her a big hug, but instead I sat down cross-legged on the pavement and tried not to faint.

"Like I'd ditch you? Seriously? You know me and my dramatics. Sometimes a girl just needs to make a gesture."

"It was Marco," I said. "Carey told me he was just coming down to the set to scout it out. See if Marco was alone, or if there were more Empty Ones, or what. He wouldn't take no for an answer. I followed him, but I guess Marco saw and—"

"I'll call an ambulance," Jackie said. Then stared at her phone. "What's uh . . . what's Mexican for 9-1-1?"

I laughed, despite everything.

"No, seriously," she protested. "It's a different number, right? Is it?"

"It's 066 in Hidalgo," said a girl's voice.

Young. Raspy. British accent.

"Thanks," I started to say. Then I saw Jackie's face. Stark white.

"You're resourceful, darling, I'll give you that. I was sure the old farmer would get his fingers in you, one way or another. You scared off Marco, eh?"

"You're the one, aren't you? Carey's ex. The chick who turns people into monsters," I said. I tightened my grip on the Fanta bottle. My mighty sword. My mighty, grape-flavored sword.

Jackie nodded.

"I didn't know anything could scare the Husks," Meryll

said. "I mean, aside from me. Is that what you are? Something like me?"

"I don't know," I answered. "What the fuck are you?"

Meryll just smiled.

"Are you going to kill us?" Jackie asked, her back still to the girl. Like, if she didn't turn around, didn't see her with her own eyes, she wasn't yet real.

"You, personally? I don't even know if I can," Meryll said. "Besides, that sounds boring. No, I've come to invite you to a party. A grand old bash. They threw one just like it for me, years ago. But this one's yours."

"And if we don't go? If we just leave?" Jackie's voice trembled.

"I'd be very disappointed." Meryll laughed. "It's important that you come voluntarily. But if you don't— well, I'll just find you again. I'll send Marco for you. And if you've broken him . . . well, I know plenty of other Husks that listen to me like I'm the bloody messiah." She twisted her skirt, smoothed her Misfits T-shirt back down over it. "I'll have them pay you lots of friendly visits. Leave more disasters like Boris Karloff here"—she gestured to Carey—"bleeding out in filthy alleyways. Until one day you decide you *want* to volunteer. Up to you. The chase might be fun, for a few."

"I'm done running," I said.

Jackie caught my eyes. Her whole body shook like a resonating fork. But she set her jaw and nodded. "Where do we go?"

TWENTY-ONE

With every new gash on Meryll's body, the Unnoticeables clapped, stamped their feet, whistled, and howled. Gus was hamming it up on stage like a pretentious asshole. He presented the bone to the crowd, made a big show of sharpening it, then cut her and took an exaggerated bow.

Jerk-off.

"What the hell are we gonna do about this?" I asked Carey.

He didn't answer. I turned to look at him, but it was too dark to see. I patted the ground around where I thought he was. Came up empty.

"Where'd Carey go?" I asked Tub.

"What am I, his nanny? Shut up. I'm thinking."

Doesn't seem like that's your strong suit.

I thought about saying it out loud, but there was no point in antagonizing the guy right now.

Then I thought about it again.

"Doesn't seem like that's your strong suit," I said.

He grunted.

Another ribbon of red flowed down Meryll's arm. Cheering. Hooting. Honking.

Honking?

A pair of lights jumped the hill to our left. One shattered and went out when the wheels hit the ground, but that was fine—I could still make out the car by the light of the flames.

It was the cab we'd jacked and driven here. And the whole front end of it was on fire.

I started laughing. It was beyond idiotic, torching our only ride out of here. Suppose we actually rescued Meryll? What then? We're stuck hoofing it through miles of empty marsh with a hundred Unnoticeables behind us?

But you've gotta give it to Carey: as a distraction, it was very distracting.

I figured he would be sneaking around behind Gus right now, hoping to cut Meryll free while they were still dealing with the flaming wreckage hurtling toward the crowd. Then the flaming wreckage veered sharply to the right, steering toward the nearest huddle of Unnoticeables.

You give Carey way too much credit.

He was driving the car. He lit the fucking thing on fire first, then he got inside, started it up, jumped a hill, and was driving it straight into a crowd of monsters.

It's like the asshole has never even heard of "Step 2."

TWENTY-TWO

1978. Purfleet Rifle Ranges, England. Carey.

"HAVE LOVE," I screamed out the open window, "OH BABY, WILL TRAVEL!"

Man, this is how you have to listen to The Sonics: on a shitty car radio, the volume turned up way beyond what the speakers can handle. Every little pop and hiss rattling the rearview mirror. You need to hear the cracks in Roslie's voice when he screams; those cracks are *goddamned important*.

I drummed my fists on the steering wheel, hit that post-chorus "WOOP," then veered into a cluster of faceless assholes.

I didn't have enough time to really focus on them so I could make out their features before I hit them, but I bet they looked surprised.

The curtain of flames parted slightly right where the hood peaked, forming a kind of targeting sight. I lined it up with the crude stage and gunned it. Just before I hit, I pulled the door latch and fell out, only mildly aflame. I was still rolling from the impact, so I figured that would probably put out the fire.

All told, this was going way better than I expected.

The cab hit a small mound of dirt just in front of the stage, and went a little airborne. The grill caught Gus right in the crotch with a couple tons of flaming steel, plowed straight through the rest of the cheap plywood, and went ghost-riding off into the darkened marsh. The flames grew more and more distant, until they were no bigger than a campfire. With no more stage to support her, Meryll hung limply from her wrists. Her head was down. Her eyes were closed. Her shirt was torn and soaked with blood.

I really hoped Meryll wasn't dead, because then she would've missed how completely cool that was.

TWENTY-THREE

1978. Purfleet Rifle Ranges, England. Randall.

Tub and I were surfing the wake of destruction. Small fires dotted the high spots, where the grass was still dry enough to burn. Crushed, burning, or crushed *and* burning Unnoticeables moaned and rolled on the ground in agony. Somewhere off in the shadows, I could feel, more than see movement. Something big and slow. Tidal.

Carey had gotten the attention of the tar men.

We reached the stage before the crowd could recover and close in on us. We could maybe even have slipped out into the dark and gotten away, if Carey hadn't destroyed our getaway vehicle in the most beautifully stupid fashion imaginable.

We'll just have to improvise, like always. Too bad we're so terrible at it.

Carey was holding Meryll's legs, trying to lift her up and over the branch she was hanging from. His hair was singed, parts of his jacket were melted, and clumps of muddy grass were embedded in his shoulder spikes, but he seemed mostly okay. Meryll sure didn't. Looked like she'd dove headfirst into a pool of blood. Her hair stuck to her face. Her skin was pale, even for an English chick.

"How's Mary?" I said, jogging up behind Carey and helping him hoist.

"Meryll, asshole," he said.

I know, man. Jesus, of course I know.

"Whatever," I said. "Is she dead, or what?"

"I don't know," Carey said.

One more big push and we had her hands up and over the end of the branch. Tub broke her fall, and laid her head on the ground. He put his ear to her mouth. Held his hand on her neck and pulled up her eyelids.

"Barely," he said. "I don't think she's going to—"

He stopped, looked at her funny. He pawed at her neck, then held her wrist.

He shook his head.

A big emptiness hit me in the guts. Then a spark caught, and lit into fury. I ground my teeth so hard I tasted enamel. I wanted to wade out there and personally strangle every single faceless fuckhead I could wrap my hands around.

Instead, I said, "No use crying over spilled milk. We need to get the hell out of here while we still can."

Carey glared at me, but he didn't say anything.

He didn't really have the chance.

The world behind us exploded. As bright as a lightning strike. I turned and stared into the ball of light hovering there. I saw something twist inside of it. I heard something that sounded like the beach—if the beach could scream.

I grabbed Carey's shoulder and pulled him toward the path that the car had cleared. The Unnoticeables were still reeling, so if there were no tar men lurking out there in the dark, we could . . .

There were two fires out in the marsh now. One larger, and more distant than the other. . . . the car. One closer, and moving toward us.

Gus.

TWENTY-FOUR

2013. Federal Highway 132D, Mexico. Kaitlyn.

A pack of Unnoticeables stood guard around an old Volvo idling at the end of the alley. Meryll had Jackie drag Carey to the car, but she wasn't managing it very well. I took his feet. He was trying to say something, but he couldn't get the breath. He left a smear of red across the filthy asphalt. One of the Unnoticeables—I couldn't master Carey's trick for pushing past the blur and making out their features—opened the back door. Jackie shoved past him and hefted Carey in after her. I tucked his feet in, and huddled up next to him. Meryll took the passenger seat and made Jackie drive. The car ride was awkward, to say the least. Meryll refused to even talk to me, instead directing a stream of innocuous questions at Jackie.

"You're from LA, right?" Meryll would say, staring down at her chipped black nail polish.

And Jackie would fire right back with, "Yeah, why? You thinking about breaking into the biz? You'd play a mean psycho bitch."

She did her best to keep up the banter, but every once in

a while Meryll would hit her with a curve. "I can see where he touched you, after the birthday party. You've only been able to make friends with girls ever since."

Jackie didn't have a clever response for that.

We left Tulancingo behind and hit a long, straight stretch of empty highway. Sand, shrubs, and the moon. Hours passed. Meryll plugged in a series of battered cassette tapes, all plunky guitars and distortion and off-key yelling. Carey would have liked it, if he'd been conscious. Desert gave way to forest. Too dark to see, but you could feel the shift in the air, see the edges of it crowding the road. Meryll told Jackie to turn. A dirt road, divided into two tracks by waist-high weeds. The Volvo bottomed out at every bump. Carey groaned.

After miles of creaks and sways, we pulled into a clearing. Meryll reached over and twisted the keys. The engine died, but the headlights stayed on: cookie cutters defining a pair of sharp circles, two patches of dense forest picked out of the darkness.

Meryll and Jackie got out and started toward the tree line.

"Hey!" I hollered after them. "I can't lift Carey alone."

Jackie turned back.

Meryll stared at her. "What's your problem?" she asked.

"What about Carey?" Jackie said.

"I'll send some of the beasties for him. He'll definitely want to see this. Well, see it again, anyway."

She grabbed Jackie's arm and shoved her toward the forest.

What was I supposed to do? Wait here? Just sort of bundle in with Carey and wait for "the beasties," whatever those are?

"Hey," I yelled after them, "I don't know what to do here!"

No response.

The jungle sounded like a city street early in the morning. Distant honks, horns, chattering. All from unseen creatures out there in the dark.

I didn't have a flashlight. I couldn't even see the path they'd taken, if they'd taken one.

I shook Carey's shoulder as much as I dared. He wheezed and rolled over onto his side.

Well, at least he won't choke to death on his own vomit. That's probably an ever-present threat to his lifestyle.

Somewhere far away, I heard an excited yell. Definitely human, or at least something trying to pass for it.

I patted Carey down, hoping he maybe had a weapon hidden somewhere on him.

No such luck. All I found was a battered and faded Zippo with a cartoon bumblebee on it. I took it. Maybe if Meryll stood still for long enough, I could singe her shirt before she killed me.

Sight stopped at the edge of the headlights. Nothing but deep, unbroken black—the kind you forget exists, living in the city. No diffuse glow from distant streets, unseen factories, and passing cars. Just the two neatly delineated circles of light, and then a big, wet, blind expanse of jungle beyond. I headed off after Meryll and Jackie, sweeping my feet in front of me first to make sure I didn't trip over a root or kick an alligator in the face or something.

When I reached the tree line, I opened the lighter and flicked it on. The tiny flame was so pathetic against the massiveness of the surrounding dark that I actually felt bad for it. I crouched down and held it closer to the ground. I could only see a foot in front of me, but it would have to do.

I crab-walked as fast as I could down a thin jungle path. I call it a path because the plants were slightly more trampled in the center than they were to either side of me. Whoever made it had only started coming here recently. After a while, I could see that the jungle around me wasn't entirely dark. There were little glints of light between the trees, off in the distance.

Fireflies, maybe?

I kept focused on the patch of grass and broken branches directly below me. It was my whole world.

This must be how a dachshund feels.

I checked the fireflies again. Tried to see if maybe my eyes had adjusted enough that I could see something by their light.

Shit!

I wasn't paying attention. I held the lighter at the wrong angle and burned my hand. I dropped it on the ground somewhere, and it went out. I patted around. Branch. Wet thing. Slimy round thing. Moving thing.

Oh god.

Small, cool rectangle.

I picked up the lighter and felt around for the flint.

I looked out into the jungle again. No fireflies.

. . . weird?

I struck the flint. It sparked but didn't light.

The fireflies came back for an instant, then blinked out again.

I flicked the lighter. Spark.

Fireflies, then gone.

I flicked it again and the flame caught. The fireflies stayed with me this time.

Are they like, responding to the light? Do they think I'm a giant, stupid firefly just stumbling through the jungle or . . .

No.

They're not fireflies. They're just reflections, catching the light from the Zippo. They are thousands of reflections of my own meager flame, coming from thousands of brass gears floating out there in the darkness.

The tar men.

I am swimming in an ocean of them.

I froze in place. My first instinct was to run, but where, and how? I'd run blindly into a tar man, or else I'd trip and break my neck, or I'd get lost in the jungle, then run into a tar man, then trip and break my neck. Stupidly, I thought about putting out the Zippo so they couldn't see me.

They don't have eyes. Can they even see?

If they could, I was a lighthouse out here. They had already seen me a long time ago. I watched the glints, hovering in the darkness. They were all pointed in my direction, but not moving toward it.

There was nothing to do but press forward, and hope this path led to somewhere other than an embarrassing and untimely death. I willed one of my feet to move. After it refused with every ounce of resistance that a foot can muster, it eventually complied. I bent low. I watched the twelve-inch patch of light. I crab-walked through a sea of monsters.

When the jungle broke, it was like stumbling out of the desert and onto the Vegas strip. There was a great big bonfire dancing at the far end of a clearing. A series of spotlights pointing at the sky were dotted all around it in a massive circle. They were hooked up to a generator, dutifully thwacking away somewhere unseen. Wherever the light touched, I could see people.

It didn't take a genius to guess what came next.

I focused on their faces. I suddenly thought of a hundred things more important than looking at them. I focused again, and was met with a scratchy migraine blur.

Unnoticeables, a crowd of them. They were all intent on something up by the distant fire.

There were no spotlights up there. The figures they were watching were just silhouettes before the flames.

I didn't come this far to turn back now, and I got the feeling the tar men wouldn't be so passive if I did. I had been invited to this shindig. Might as well put on my cocktail dress and make an entrance.

"Hey, assholes," I yelled.

A few dozen featureless faces swiveled in my direction.

"I come in peace. Take me to your leader."

I laughed at myself. Nobody else was going to, and it was either laugh, or tear my own hair out and never stop screaming.

Three of the figures broke off and rushed at me. I pocketed the Zippo, then held my hands up. Two of them grabbed my arms and twisted them painfully behind me, while a third put something sharp against my back. He dug the blade into my skin, and I moved forward involuntarily. They marched me through the crowd, weaving from spotlight to spotlight until we were close enough to the conflagration to navigate by firelight. I could hear it now—this wood must not be great for burning. It was snapping and popping like Chinese fireworks, shooting out errant sparks in random directions. There were two silhouettes by the fire, both small and female. One of them didn't seem to care that tiny comets rocketed from the bonfire and bounced off of her face. The other silhouette flinched and cursed at every pop. I recognized Jackie by her voice. The other figure, I had to assume, was Meryll. Another silhouette joined them, this one tall, muscular, and male.

"It is here," Marco said. "The thing from the chapel."

"Well, no shit," Meryll said. "I'm holding her bloody hand right now, aren't I?"

"No," Marco said. "The other thing. The profane thing. The arrogant little bitch of a thing that destroyed a Tool of the Mechanic."

"This isn't her?" Meryll asked, sizing up Jackie.

Marco gave a poor simulation of a laugh. It came out like a bark. "That thing is garbage," he answered.

"Hey, buddy," Jackie said, "you're B-list at best, yourself."

"Do not take offense," Marco said. "All humans are garbage. We are here to clean."

"I don't see her," Meryll said, though I was only maybe ten feet from her now. I could see her clear as day, thanks to the massive and barely controlled bonfire.

"There." Marco pointed.

"Where?" Meryll asked.

"There." Marco pointed.

"Where?" Meryll asked.

"There." Marco pointed.

"Whe—"

"What is this, a vaudeville bit? You gonna do this all night?" I said, losing patience.

Yeah, you're super eager for them to chuck you in that fire, right, Kaitlyn? Better be sure to hurry that right along.

"It is the one speaking," Marco said, those black eyes of his reflecting nothing. Not even the erratic light from the flames.

"Nobody said anything," Meryll said. "Are you fucking with me? Is that a thing you freaks can do now? Play pranks?"

"You cannot see her," Marco observed. He stepped forward, and was on me before I could even react. He grabbed my arm and jerked it downward. I fell to my knees.

"Bloody hell!" Meryll laughed. "You just disappeared! That was fantastic. Do it again."

Marco let go of my arm, and Meryll clapped. "And you're back!"

"I do not understand," Marco noted.

"I get it," Meryll said, "she's like me, but different. She took down a Flare, so now she can do things. I got to see a little bit of the code behind the universe, and learned how to manipulate it. I guess she gets to be invisible to things like me. Wow, seems like you got the short end of the stick on that one, honey."

"Tell her I'm here now," I said, "so she can let Jackie go."

"It asks you to release the other thing," Marco said.

His hand spasmed open and shut like a dying spider. It flew out from his body and struck me across the face. The whole world flashed red, and I was on my side, cheek in the cool dirt. Marco was punching the ground beside me so quickly that his arms blurred. He frothed at the mouth and screamed. Then, like somebody had hit his reset button, he was back upright, standing calm and expressionless. His hands were ragged, bloody mittens.

Meryll giggled. "He does that sometimes," she said. "What little bit of humanity is left in the Husks surfaces now and again. They just don't know how to handle it. I think he might be a bit cross with you."

I tried to talk, but my mouth was numb. The sky swam and the stars bulged. I felt like vomiting.

Is this a concussion? Do you feel it that quickly?

"Well, as novel as all this is," Meryll continued, "it doesn't really change anything. Let's get on with the show."

Marco grabbed my hair and pulled me to my feet. I thought about hitting him in the neck—knowing full well that it would do nothing but make me feel better—but I couldn't move my arms very well. They felt mired in the air. Lifting them was like trying to punch underwater.

Marco leaned in close to my face and went through a rapid series of expressions—his mouth twisting in agony, his eyebrows raised in surprise, his cheeks pulled in— before finally settling on his trademark smirk.

"We're gonna have us one heck of a fiesta, girl!" he bubbled.

Meryll pointed to the husk of a stripped tree, ten feet high, just beside the fire.

What does the tree mean? I'm so dizzy. I'm supposed to be doing something, but I forget what it was.

"Fiesta means party *en espanol*!" Marco explained, needlessly.

"Leave me alone for a minute," I tried to say, but it came out slurred and incomprehensible. Something cold latched onto my wrist. I looked down and saw a hand, but couldn't fathom it. Another joined it on my arm. It felt like my head was on backwards. I tried to understand and failed miserably.

Hey, look at all these hands I got now!

More hands on the other arm. Now they were dragging me somewhere, which was good, because walking seemed hard. The new hands pulled me up against the withered old tree, and then bound my own hands behind it. This served to keep me upright.

Smart. Otherwise I would absolutely fall down.

A spasm in my gut told me this situation was bad. I looked around, but it was like trying to hold a conversation with a native after briefly glancing at a phrasebook: the framework of understanding was there, but there were too many specifics that just wouldn't fall into place.

Marco rummaged through a duffel bag on the ground by my feet. He grabbed hold of something and held it above his head. Everybody cheered.

That must be a great thing, whatever it is.

He turned and showed it to me. A brown length of metal. Cheap rubber handle in a camouflage print. Took me a minute to place what it was: an old machete. The bulk of the shaft was covered in rust, but a narrow strip along the blade's edge shone like starlight.

Awful pretty.

Something in Jackie's face worried me.

Marco leaned in and held the tip of the machete against my hip bone.

Jackie was screaming.

It was like a magic show. I was on the edge of my seat.

What on earth would he do next?

He pushed the tip of the blade into my skin. It gave way. Clarity hit me like a pissed-off heavyweight.

TWENTY-FIVE

1978. Purfleet Rifle Ranges. Meryll.

Carey was standing over me. That's not accurate. He was standing 38.6 inches to the left of the leftmost part of my body, which, due to the awkward way I was sprawled, was my superfluous pinky-toe. I twitched it. It didn't hurt. That was not news. It had not hurt in ages, not since I took the first Flare.

Angel.

Tool.

That's what they call themselves: Tools of the Mechanic. I say I "took a Flare," but what I mean is that I "took one down." But I see there is more accuracy in that statement than I intend. At the time, I had unconsciously exploited the inherent weakness in the Tools of the Mechanic. Their vessels in our world are based on human thought patterns. They need a template with which to interact with this dimension, and ours is the most suitable for occupation.

Where the hell is all of this information coming from?

Ah. The light. A ball of luminosity hovering in the air between Randall and Tub. Sharp and distant things shift within that light. I did not understand them at first, but I see now. They are abstracts. Fractals. Shapes representing dense strings of information. It is trying to network.

With me.

Why me?

Oh, I get it. I've taken down a few Flares—Tools—but they did not suddenly cease to exist. Energy cannot be created or destroyed, only manipulated. I dissipated much of the Tool's energy aimlessly in a blast that burned away the nearby Husks, Faceless, Sludges, and anything else influenced by their touch. But I had also unwittingly taken some of their energy into me. The energy meshed with my own, and now I am compatible with the other Tools—to some degree.

Oh, fuck. I'm part Flare.

I should be scared, or disgusted, or at least angry, but it's like there's just an empty closet where I used to keep those things.

I see Tub. His jaw is set. His fingers are clutched white against the length of rebar he uses for a cane. I see Randall. His eye twitches. He's up on the balls of his feet. He is about to do something very stupid. I see Carey. He's Carey. He's always about to do something stupid.

I'm up and moving before either of them can start.

I push off the plywood. It bends beneath me. It is wet with my blood. I feel my body protest. It wants to die, but that's just biology. I shunt some proteins around and fire up a few hormone factories, and its complaints begin to quiet. The Tool of the Mechanic is still networking with me, exchanging information at a rate beyond understanding. I see stars collapse and planets spin out of orbit. I see a shape like a triangle that folds onto itself, and inside there is a series of tunnels like tentacles that weave in and out of the borders. I hear the sound of cosmic gears, grinding to a halt. It is a sound that hurts me deeply but implacably, like seeing an ex-boyfriend laugh at another girl's jokes. It is something that I feel I must stop, at all costs. Life, love, loyalty—what use are they if the gears stop turning?

This isn't me. This shit isn't me. This is the Flare. I don't give a damn about exoplanets and dimensional drift; I just want a warm place to sleep at night, food in my belly, and drugs on the weekend. I want a boy with strong hands and soft eyes who'll listen to me without giving me advice, like he knows so much more than me. I want somebody to punch my dad in the mouth and buy me the new Misfits record. I don't want to funnel the excess energies from fleeting life forms and use it for the greater preservation of an interdimensional ecosystem. I don't even know what the fuck that means. Get. Out. Of. My. Head.

The information flow stops. My brain feels like it went skinny-dipping in the Atlantic. In January. But I'm me again. Well, mostly me. Sorta me. Everything is so cold and clear, but it's already warming up, and the details are fading. I know—I don't know how I know, I just know—that I have a few minutes of this left. A few precious minutes of thinking like a Flare, before it all melts away.

I see Tub, and know he's thinking about ducking out while the boys start a fight. I see Carey and it's like there's a shadow image of him, from ten seconds into the future. He's running forward, trying to land an ill-advised dropkick on Gus, who, for the record, is still on fire. I see Randall about to knock Carey unconscious and attempt to drag both him and me out of here while a Husk and a hundred Faceless try to tear us all to pieces.

I see Gus, and know that he's going to catch Carey's feet. Hold him close and burn him up. I see Tub, and know he'll get away. But there's something else there—something eating at him. He'll put a gun in his mouth by the summer, but I can't see why. I see Randall, and, oh god—how stupid is this? He totally likes me!—but he won't make it ten steps carrying both Carey and me.

Me.

I see me.

I see a thousand of me, branching off in as many directions. One runs into the crowd of Faceless and gets raped to death. One flees toward Gus, his burning scarecrow frame dancing giddily up the hillside after it. One just sits here and stares as everybody around her dies.

But this one, she does all right. I decide to follow her.

I hop down from the makeshift stage, my feet sinking into the bog. It's the easiest thing in the world to just follow in her footsteps. It's like one of those little dance routines they paint on the floor in gymnasiums. Left foot here, pivot—a Faceless careens past me; it was coming up behind me, going for a tackle. Right foot here, half a step back, left foot here, right on the Faceless's groin. Now a few more steps, these a bit quicker, and duck low. I'm crawling in the space beneath the stage. There's yelling from above. The plywood above me booms. It bows and cracks, but doesn't give way. Then some lighter, more hollow sounding thumps—footsteps, approaching. Another boom, and another. The plywood finally breaks, and Tub comes crashing through it. His face is a bloody mask. I see my future self, like my own ghost, pause and listen to him breathe for a second. Tub stirs, and says something to her. She nods and moves on.

From that, I can tell he's alive, so I figure there's no need to check like she did. Suddenly she blurs, a dozen different paths with subtly different movements branching away from her.

Shit.

I can feel the foresight fading already. I feel limited. The pressure of reality pushing all against my body, like being at the bottom of the ocean. There's no time. I pick the centermost girl and follow her up through the stage, pulling myself over the jagged lip of the busted plywood. Its edges look like Weetabix. The splinters grab my leggings and pull long rips in the fabric. Future girl rolls to the side, so I do too. A second later, a black hand, the skin split and still smoking, claws at the spot where I climbed up.

Gus looks like a stop-motion skeleton. He was always skinny, but there's barely any muscle or fat left on his frame. What flesh is there is barely hanging on, just wisps of black ash sloughing off as he moves. His face is gone. His eyes have boiled away. His lips are peeled back, revealing teeth you can see all the way back to the roots.

Jesus Christ, we have so much teeth hidden by the gums. He looks like he has fucking fangs.

I'm distracted. I'm not following the ghost girl quickly enough. She's already moved so far ahead that her afterimages are starting to fade. I move before it's too late. She slides right between Gus's legs. He grabs for her, but misses. The exposed bones of his fingertips sink into the wood. Ghost girl doesn't turn to attack him, like I figured she would. Instead, she breaks into a dead run toward the Flare. She doesn't even pause. She just dives right into it.

I've taken down a Flare before. I know this is how it happens—I burn them out from the inside—but I'm always pretty fucked up afterward. The first time I was out for days. The last time I was out all night. I can't afford that now. I gotta help the boys.

The foresight is giving out. I saw it all so clearly at first, but now I can't remember how this all turns out. But I was sure this was the right path, at first.

Yeah, but you also screwed up down there, beneath the stage. You did like you always do, and you didn't follow directions. Is this still the right way?

Do you have any better ideas?

I jump at the Flare, and it all happens like it did before. Feels like crashing through thin ice into cold pudding. I can hear music, but it's not music. It's static. But it's not static. It's screaming. But it's not human. It's bright—so bright I can't see. But in the blind spots, there are things moving. Shapes that hurt to look at. I remember they meant something before—information?—but about what, I can't recall.

I know what to do next. I tap into the old fury.

I remember Nan and her terrible cooking. She'd burn the toast, every time. I ate it that way for so long that any other way tastes weird to this day. I remember her dancing, alone in the backyard, while she hung up the laundry. I remember the light. The chimes. I remember the floorboards shaking, and the smell when she disappeared. Like pine trees.

There it is. Anger so bright the light around me dims in response. It starts in my back. It tingles. Spreads out through my chest, flows into my feet. I don't think I actually have a body here, inside the Flare, but I imagine myself pulling my boots up and stomping holes in this motherfucker. I imagine the light freezing and shattering, my feet crashing through into reality. And as I imagine it, it happens.

Beyond the cracks, it's dark. But not black. Things are moving out there. A shadow flits by, then something falls. I kick again, and the cracks expand. I kick again, and the world comes back in a supernova.

The Faceless nearest the blast just vanish. The ones farther away wither first, like watching fruit rot in time-lapse. Maybe two hundred feet out, and they just burn. The shock wave picks up Gus and sweeps him off into the trees. His hands are pulled from around Carey's throat. Carey's body rag-dolls onto the ground, landing right next to Randall's. Neither of them move. The explosion doesn't touch them for some reason, but whatever Gus did to them while I was gone apparently wasn't a party.

The ghost Meryll is gone. The foresight went with her.

I have no fucking idea what to do.

I decide on collapsing into a broken little pile.

It doesn't seem to matter much. The Faceless who weren't caught in the blast are running. They scream as they wrestle through the muck and scrabble up the hillsides. The tar men are moving away, too, but glacially and in silence. The only thing moving toward us is this ridiculous stick figure thing, coming up from the woods. It climbs the stage with difficulty, then crawls over to Carey and Randall, still lying unconscious.

It only has one arm left, and big hunks of its torso are gone. But the face is coming back. It has an eye, some skin, lips.

"Hey man," it says to Carey, all junkie casual. "I'm real sorry about all this. After all you did for the cause back in NYC, you'll be remembered as a saint! But you gotta die before you become a saint, man."

Gus wraps his single bony black hand around Carey's throat, and begins to squeeze.

I never understood what Gus was, exactly. I mean, I knew the name for things like him—he was a Husk—but all I really knew about them was that they had to die. Now it was like I could see him. Really see him. It was sad, what he was. He was just parts. Just garbage. The remainder of an equation that couldn't be neatly solved. He was supposed to just disappear when the Flares solved him, but there was junk in his code, and now there are only little bits of him left. He's trying to make sense of himself, trying to figure out why he wasn't just dispersed like he was supposed to be. The only thing he can figure is that he was meant for some greater purpose, because he just can't fathom that he's an accident. He's old leftovers, forgotten in the fridge. He worships the Flares, because he doesn't know they don't give a shit about him. They'd flush him away, if they even cared enough to bother in the first place.

All these little pieces. They make the whole make sense.

I don't have much strength left in me. Burning out a Flare takes a lot. But I have enough to stand. Carey's turning blue. Gus's one arm is shaking from the effort of choking him. I lean close to the burnt space where his ear should be, and I whisper.

Light pours out from inside of his skull. He screeches like a barn owl. There's a burst of colors I've never seen before. The stage shakes so hard that half of it falls off the sawhorses. And Gus is gone.

He was just a remainder. And now I've solved him.

That's something even the Flares couldn't do.

TWENTY-SIX

1978. Purfleet Rifle Ranges, England. Carey.

Fuck, I'm blind. I'll have to get a cane and a dog. I don't even like dogs, always looking at you with all that love and adoration. It's too much goddamned pressure, living up to a dog's expectations. Can't hear much, either. Feels like the first few minutes after a really good show, your ears stuffed so full of guitars you gotta yell right in the face of the dude next to you to be heard.

My face feels like I put it on inside out this morning. After dropping it in the dirt. And stepping on it a few dozen times.

Couldn't see much of anything, but there was a pretty decent shape in front of me. Had some nice lines on it. Kinda wanna fuck that shape, whatever it is. Luckily it turned out to be Meryll, and not Randall . . . again.

That's a long story we'll get into never.

"Whaaabbagush?" I said.

"He's dead," she answered. "Gus is dead."

Holy shit, she understood me. She really is my soulmate.

"Whoo! Ahnooitfursht—" I rolled on my side and spat

out a solid pint of stale blood and some chunky bits I really hoped were just teeth.

"I knew it," I said, this time more legibly. "First time I saw you, I said you were a fucking genius."

She stared at me. Through me. Like she was looking at something a mile behind me. It made my balls pull up a little.

"Hey. Hey! We won, right?" I said.

"Yeah," she finally said, and the start of a smile broke through the mask. "Yeah, I guess we did."

I smiled back—well, probably two-thirds of a smile at best, now.

Pop.

Her eyeball exploded.

Warmth and wet sprayed my face.

Meryll fell to her knees, then over on her side. She didn't move.

Tub stood behind her, holding a fucking ridiculous-looking pistol. It looked like something a Confederate would use on a Yankee. That kind of gun doesn't kill people. It sits in a museum. It has a little plaque with a bunch of boring facts under it and it bores the shit out of fourth graders on field trips. It doesn't kill pretty young girls with fists like hammers.

She's fucking invincible. She heals. She gets up.

She wasn't getting up.

"Wh—" I wanted to ask a million questions, but none of them would come out.

I felt like I was gonna throw up.

"You can't let her take too many," Tub said.

He sounded tired.

"They take a Flare," he continued, practically collapsing onto his cane, "and a little bit of it gets inside them. It starts to eat away. It changes them. They take two Flares, and maybe they start acting weird. They take three, four— maybe they're not entirely human anymore. They take five, six, and you'll never stop them. They're not Husks. They make you dream of Husks. They're so much worse. You gotta do it right now. Right after they take a Flare, when they're at their weakest."

"Motherfucker," was the first and last word that came to me. The rest could be said with punches.

But when I stood up, the world bucked like a stalling motorcycle. I took a knee.

Tub took a step back. "You think I wanted to? I raised that girl like my own. I put the food on her table, and the beer in her belly. I kept the perverts at The Office off her when she passed out. I brought her tea and stew when she was sick. But a man does what a man has to do, boyo. You're in this fight now, and it can't be half-assed, because you best believe your full ass is in the fire. You *stay* in the fight, and maybe someday you'll have to make this decision, too. When a thing like Meryll starts doing things a human being can't, when they start getting that thousand-yard stare, you must put something of significance through their left eye. Do it, or they will do something much worse to you and everyone you love later."

I grabbed his knee and pulled, but he just swatted me away like I was an excited dog jumping all over him after he got home.

"Why?" I asked. "Why not kill her after she took the first angel, then? Why bother playing house at all? Why pull the trigger now?"

My punches were on the fritz, so I guess we had to go with the last resort: talking.

"Because she was useful, son. Things like her—they're the only ones that can kill the Flares. Not to mention the Husks. They're worth the risk."

"They're . . . fucking *worth* it? Messing with her head, toying with her life, and then taking it—just to put out a few fancy lights and kill some immortal hipster dipshit?"

Tub stabbed his rebar cane into the plywood. Then he did it again. And again. He screamed something—not words. Then he took a minute and made some words instead.

"You . . . you'll see. You stay in this world, and you'll see. The Flares will take everything from you. Everything. And when that happens, you'll do anything it takes just to kill a few of the bastards. Some little girl's life? No matter who she is, that's a trade worth making. It always was. It always will be."

"It . . . always was?" said Meryll.

Holy hell.

Meryll.

She's alive.

She should not be alive.

Tub went white. Well, he was Welsh. He went *more* white. Transparent.

"You've done this before?" Meryll's voice was even and measured. Her hands were still. The twitching hole full of gore in place of her eye was the only thing on her that quivered.

"Of course," Tub said, and he laughed a little bit. A laugh you'd give when your car wouldn't start, so you had to take bus, then it started pissing down rain once you got to the stop. Then the bus blew right by you, spraying you in filthy street water as it went. That kind of laugh. "I wonder if it's me that's off, or the number . . ."

"The number?" Meryll asked.

"The caliber of the bullet. Well, I guess it's more of a ball. .36. It's a significant number. It always worked on the other girls. It's gotta be me. I didn't care enough."

"What the hell are you talking about?" I said.

"It's how you kill things like this," he said, and the look he gave Meryll was sad, angry, and scared all at once. Like she was a beloved family pet that had gone rabid. "The weapon's gotta be significant, sure, but the person using it has to *care*. They have to love the mutation. It's the same way she kills the Flares. The bloody lights take all those gooey sentimental bits away when they turn you. You have to give some of it back—anger, sadness, love, something *human*—to destroy them. A thing like her, once she takes enough Flares, the same rules start to apply. Ah hell, it's my fault, I know it. I've just done this too many times. I'm burnt out. I don't care enough to kill them anymore . . ."

"How many?" Meryll said. "How many other girls before me?"

"Who cares?" Tub said, and spun faster than I'd ever seen him move. His rebar cane whistled through the air, but that's all it did.

Meryll stood a mere inch beyond the strike. She had barely moved. Just enough.

She stepped forward, like she was moving up a place in line at the post office, and touched Tub's hand. A spasm went through him. He dropped the cane. His spine bent so far backward it snapped. A sound like Chinese firecrackers. His face was looking straight at me, but upside down. His eyes rolled back in his head. He opened his mouth and a thin black liquid trickled out from the side. Light—pure and without color—poured from his eyes.

But he didn't disappear.

He just bent even further, completely in half. The back of his head rested against the backs of his heels. A bouquet of bones sprouted from his stomach, spraying blood. The bones snaked upward in a dozen directions, before articulating and bending downward like spider's limbs. They continued growing until they dug into the wood. The rest of Tub's body grew progressively more limp as the bones expanded, until he was just a sack of soggy flesh. The bone legs hit solid ground, and took the weight of his body into the air. Tub hefted up and swayed there, below the bone-spider, just a wad of pendulous weight hanging like a human ball sack.

He opened his mouth and screamed.

I peed. So much.

TWENTY-SEVEN

1978. London, England. Meryll.

What did I do? Oh Jesus god damn what the hell did I just do?

I only touched his hand. I didn't mean—

How could I have even—

This isn't happening.

Tub shot me, and I'm dying right now. I'm hallucinating as the blood leaks out of my brain.

The thing that used to be Tub scuttled toward Carey, its thin, bloody bone legs clacking across the plywood. The limp wad of skin that used to be Tub's body quivered with the movement. Somehow, he was still able to scream, a high, terrified, and unceasing wail. He would scream until he was out of breath, take in just enough air, and start screaming again. Carey rolled backwards out of the way of the charge, but not quickly enough. One of the bone spears stabbed through the back of his jacket, pinning him to the plywood stage.

I didn't mean to do that to Tub. I just wanted to knock his teeth in a little bit, maybe castrate him—nothing like this. But when I touched him, it was like with Gus: He just made sense to me. He didn't want to hurt those girls—the others like me; that was true. But he did it anyway. He got good at it. He spent a lot of time learning how to play them, how to twist their emotions, how to act the father figure while still convincing them they were lonely. By the end, they'd do anything for him. I would have done anything for him. I *did* do anything for him. And Tub was ready to throw me away. He set out the traps, pulled the girls in, sucked them dry—and then he killed them.

Like a spider.

That was the last thing I thought when I touched him, just before he started changing.

I finally realized that I was just standing there, mouth open, staring uselessly as Tub squatted over Carey and drooled something black from his mouth. It dripped onto Carey's shoulder and started sizzling through the leather of his jacket. He twisted away from it and managed to get the arm out of the sleeve, but the other was still stuck to the stage.

He was going to die, because of me.

Maybe if I touched Tub again, and I thought of how he was supposed to be—his gray beard, his round chin, his ribs sticking out of his sweater—I could undo this.

I ran forward and grabbed the nearest bone-leg. It was slick with gore and warm to the touch. There was something running down the underside of it. It flexed when the leg moved. Tendons, I guess. I tightened my grip and I thought of the Tub I knew. I tried to put all the anger and betrayal out of my mind. Just Tub and those terrible eggs he made on Sunday. Just Tub and his weirdo jazz records. Just Tub and his smell, like cherries and tobacco.

The bone slid out of my hands, cutting through my palms. It was sharpened at the tips. Then it raised up and lashed out, cutting a deep gash through my arm. I fell. I screamed. I looked around for help, and caught Randall's eye. I wished I hadn't.

That stupid sense of relief I had when the foresight hit me—"he likes me!"—that was gone.

He looked at me like I was a pile of sentient dog shit that had just knocked on his door, trying to sell him magazine subscriptions.

Fine. I'll save your friend's ass on my own then, jerk.

The Tub-spider had its front two legs raised, poised to stab down through Carey's back. Most of its weight was shifted rearward, balancing precariously on a piece of plywood on the end of a sawhorse. I kicked a boot out and caught one of the spider's legs, throwing it off balance just enough to get its attention. It started to turn toward me, but there were no joints left in Tub's actual body. The legs had to rotate that limp bag of face all the way around just to see what had hit it. It took a few seconds, and that was all I needed. I hopped up and stomped down, right on the edge of the plywood. It bounced and jumped off the sawhorse. Both of us went tumbling into the dark, cold mud beneath the stage.

There were little sparks flitting around in the black. Dizzy. I must have hit my head on a rock or something on the way down. I jumped back up and reached for the stage, but it was like being in the ocean at night: I couldn't figure out which way was up. I kicked off of a lump and fell on my side. Bog in my mouth. Tasted like shitty Scotch. My hands just sunk when I tried to push myself up. I could hear the Tub-spider scrabbling around behind me. Something scraped against my boot and made my foot feel wet. Blood, probably.

A thin crack of weak light from above. No time for second

thoughts. I jumped for it. My palms slapped wood. Something was pulling on my boot. I pulled back. But I had no traction. I was sliding, back into the dark with that thing.

That thing I made.

Then there was Carey. I'd never been so glad to see his goofy face, all wrong angles and bumps. He was on all fours, shrugging back into the sleeve of his shredded jacket. He looked up and saw me. I smiled. I held out my hand.

He didn't take it.

I reached out for him—

I'm right here, jackass. Be a gentleman and help a lady up.

He threw himself backwards and crab-walked frantically out of my reach.

None of that old, thinly veiled teenage-boy lust left in his eyes. Before, he'd always looked like he wanted to toss me on the ground and fuck me, every single second we'd been together. It had gotten kinda creepy, to be honest. But it was better than this.

Now he looked at me like I was a leper.

From below, the spider pulled. From above, there was no help. I slid backwards. My fingertips pulled up splinters from the wood. Then they lost their grip entirely, and I went backwards into the pit.

Shit. Shit! You rotten-ass coward, what the hell are you doing?

Meryll was counting on me, and I couldn't even put out a hand. It wasn't a conscious decision, I swear. I wasn't even thinking about what she did to Tub, and the possibility of her turning me into, like, a testicle-scorpion or something with her touch. I just got up, and then she was there trying to grab me—a mysterious hand reaching out to grope my face—so I backed away. If I'd had time, I would have saved her.

I would save her.

It's not too late.

I crawled to the edge of the hole that Meryll and the bone-spider had fallen in. Couldn't see a damn thing.

Wait, no—movement!

Shit! Movement!

I ducked just as a jagged length of bone speared the place where my head had been. I laid on my belly and tried to shuffle backwards. I didn't get far before the legs started appearing. Slick red shafts of bone coming up from the darkness, moving with that slow spider grace. They spread out to every side of the hole and hefted. Tub's withered body eased into view, his mouth still screaming, his eyes rolled back in his head, looking at nothing.

Shit. Shit. Shitshitshit—

I sang a little song to myself, and every lyric was "shit."

The spider spread its legs wider and lowered its body, getting ready to pounce.

I pushed off the stage and tried to run, but I tripped over something.

A rusty brown length of rebar, with a round bit of concrete at one end.

Tub's cane.

"Hey, Tub," I said, gripping the shaft in both hands. "I got something of significance for ya."

I dove straight into the hole, right below the bulk of the spider. I thrust the cane out in front of me as I fell, and it sunk deep into Tub's withered, hanging face.

I hit bog with a sound like squeezing an empty mustard bottle. I awkwardly shifted around on my back and looked up through the stage. I could only see the spider above me as a silhouette, barely distinguishable from the cloudy night. It twitched and spasmed, made that sound like somebody trying to scream after getting the wind knocked out of them. Then something that felt like a wet garbage bag full of ham hocks fell on me.

I gagged and swore and pushed Tub's mangled body off me. I retched into the muck for a bit, then felt around for Meryll.

If she was hurt, we'd get her help. If she was dead, we'd get her a proper burial. If she was fine, we'd make out.

But she was none of those things. She was just gone.

"Hey," a voice called from above. I could see the outline of Randall's dipshit face peering down after me. "Are you spider food, or what?"

TWENTY-EIGHT

2013. 1.7 Miles Off of Unnamed Rd., Puebla, Mexico. Kaitlyn.

I've never been in one of those sensory deprivation tanks, but this is how I picture it: not cold, not warm. Aware that you're floating, but unaware of the water you're floating in. My sense of self is blurred—the surface of my skin feels indistinct. At once it's here—so close—and there—so far. I'm spread thin, diluted by the water. Above me, the night sky is full of stars. An impossible number of stars. There's nowhere on Earth you can see this many. There's more light than dark. But it isn't pretty or romantic. There's something up there that scares me.

The ocean is still. No waves, no sound. I move my hand—at least, I think I move my hand—but even that causes no ripples.

I know what comes next. I've had this dream before. Something stirs in the dark waters beneath me. Hundreds of feet, thousands of feet—thousands of miles?—below. The stillness begins to give. The water swells around me. All around me, as though something the size of the ocean itself is coming up.

I know this ocean goes on forever.

Whatever lies beneath must go on forever, too.

And it sees me. It's coming for me.

I wait an eternity. The thing in the water is so far away, but it moves fast. Time crawls, but then you look back on how much of it has passed, and it seems like an instant.

The waters around me break. They slosh steadily at first, then grow chaotic and violent. My diluted body is tossed around, folded on itself, spread apart, and whipped into a frenzy. I used to get scared at this point. I knew the thing from below was close now, that it was almost here. But I'm not scared anymore. Or, rather, I'm more scared of the stillness. Of it continuing how it is, forever, and my body slowly merging with the ocean until there's nothing left of me. Most of all, I'm scared of living another minute under those cold, cold stars.

Whatever is coming up from beneath me, at least it's not the stars. In fact, as it gets closer, something strange seems to happen. The stars twinkle. Their light was always steady and unbroken, but now they flicker. Some even go out. The waters are rising all around me now, lifting into the air. Physics dictates that they should be pushed out of the way as whatever this massive thing is emerges. But there's too much of it. It's too late, and there's nowhere for the water to go. Together, the water and I are flung toward the sky. As we lift into the air, the stars drift apart. No, not drifting. They're moving away from me, like a school of fish separating around a shark. They're afraid of the thing in the water, but they're also afraid of the water. I *am* the water, though. And now, I understand, so is the thing.

We break through the sky.

We are in another place. A place that is not this place, as

impossible as that is to understand. Just thinking about it
makes my brain hurt, but if I don't think about it, it makes
perfect sense. This place that is not a place is nothing like the
place that I know. The angles don't work. Time doesn't flow.
I try to move, only to find that I've already moved; I stop
moving, only to find that I'm just starting the movements.
This is a place made of places. A billon places stacked on one
another, woven through each other and fused together to
make a new place. A shape like a pyramid that is also a
sphere. And all throughout this place there is light. Writhing
tubes of cold starlight that snake through the other places,
burning wherever they touch. There is no central hub where
they meet, just an endlessly dense network of tentacles,
twitching like living lightning. They grip the edges of the
pyramid-sphere and they pull, twist the shape until it buckles
and turns inside out. Now it's a sphere that is also a pyramid,
and the other places shake. Some of them disappear entirely,
only to be replaced by new places. But the light survives.

It sees me now. The tentacles stretch in my direction.
They whip and writhe, grope and lash, and are almost on
me. I try to shy away, but I only find myself back where I
started. I realize I've already left, even though I've always
been here. A fork of light branches off the nearest tube. It
touches my leg. It's in my veins. It's burning through my
synapses. It's like winter air, emanating from my bones and
out toward my skin. I try to scream, but I already was
screaming, and I will never stop.

Then the light pulls back. It snaps back and forth in a
way that reminds me of a wounded animal. There's
something dark creeping up the forks from where it
touched me, making its way down the central shaft, joining
the others, and spreading.

Corruption.

The light is making a noise, or it always had been, and I just never thought to hear it before. It sounds like static. It sounds like waves. It sounds like screaming.

. . .

I jolted awake, which was a bad idea. It felt like somebody had replaced my bones with tin foil. There was something in my mouth, the texture of cottage cheese and the taste of undercooked steak. I spat out a wad of coagulated blood. I looked at the red chunks oozing down the front of my shirt, and threw up.

More blood.

What happened? Was there some sort of accident, or . . . ?

I was squinting into a bright light. My eyes must have turned supersensitive, because it gave me an instant headache. And that sound, like a superhighway running between my ears.

I must have been hit by a car. The lights, the sound, the blood . . . it makes sense. I remember being in one with Jackie, and we were going to—

Oh, shit.

Jackie? What have they done with her? I can't see her anywhere.

I focused on the light. There were layers upon layers inside of it, shifting independently from one another. The parallax made me nauseous, but it was the sound—that crackling chorus—that sent me over the edge.

I ignored the pain and thrashed in place, only to remember that my hands were pinned.

That's right. Still tied to the old tree where Marco started cutting me. God, it felt like that went on for hours. I lost so much blood. I remember everything fading and being kind of grateful that it was all over. Not just the pain, but the pressure, too—nobody could say I hadn't done my best to stop him. But he won. I was dead, and it was all okay.

But now I wasn't dead, and it wasn't okay.

The angel wasn't coming for me, so I guess it still couldn't see me. That was a break, at least. But this time Marco and the Unnoticeables were ready for it. Two Unnoticeables were already untying my feet, a third working on the bonds that held my wrists. I tried to focus on them, but all I got was a blurry sketch of generic features and the urge to look elsewhere. They got my ankles loose first, and didn't bother holding me down. Either they thought I was dead, or too weak to fight, or maybe just had nowhere to run to. Maybe they were right on all accounts.

The one behind me finished untying my hands.

I had meant to kick the one on the left in the face, then flee while they were disoriented. Instead, I managed to bump one in the nose with my head as I fell, limp, into their waiting arms. She said, "Ow, damn," and then got on with the process of dragging me toward the light.

The last time I met an angel, I got pulled inside of it—into a null space where my physical body didn't really exist. I found a weakness in there, and I killed it, but it took everything I had. It felt like I was using muscles I never knew existed, and had never exercised. It was like trying to do push-ups with my tongue. I couldn't even do a regular push-up right now. Seriously, I was trying. I was trying to push off the ground and kick the Unnoticeables away from my feet, but all I managed was to weakly claw at the dirt. I left five thin, snaking tracks in the dust with my right hand, six with the other.

Somebody grabbed my shoulder and flipped me onto my back.

When I was thirteen years old, I wanted nothing more than to fuck Marco Luis until my hips disintegrated. I wasn't even really sure what "fucking" was—I had the talk and everything, but it was all such a distant concept, unrelated to my actual life. All I knew was that I wanted him on top of me, and that it would be warm. When I had those thoughts, Marco would smile at me with that trademark smirk of his, raising just one side of the mouth— the side with the dimple. It was a smile that said, "I know what you want, girl, and if you're real good, maybe I'll let you have it."

Now the real Marco was giving me that same smirk. It was still saying the exact same things, actually—I just finally understood what "it" was, and I no longer wanted it.

"Hey, chica!" he said, full of inappropriate pep. "The big day's finally here, huh?"

He winked at me.

I tried to tell him what he could do to himself and how hard, but I mostly just drooled blood on myself. I reached out to try to slap him. The blow was so feeble as to be laughable, but Marco still jumped back about six feet.

What?

"You should have her restrained," he said, his voice gone flat. "She should not be able to move. She should not be able to touch me."

The Unnoticeables immediately dropped to their knees and seized my forearms. I actually did manage to laugh a little, then.

What am I gonna do, weakly paw him to death?

"Is it time," Marco asked, but there was nothing in his intonation to mark it as a question.

"Might as well be, yeah," answered a female voice.

Meryll was standing a few feet from the angel, just beside the raging fire. She glared down at her own nails with studied disinterest.

"I can't see the girl, but I figure that if you feed her to the Flare first, I can take them both at once."

"Take . . ." Marco echoed.

I saw a flash. Like a single out-of-place frame in a film reel.

"What do you mean, 'take,'" he said. "That is not in the ritual. We have performed the rites to summon a Tool of the Mechanic here so that it may solve her. To give back what she has stolen."

There it was again. Just a flicker of an image, and then it was gone. But I saw it clearly that time. There was another set of events happening, overlaid on these ones, like tracing paper over a photograph.

Here: Marco and Meryll on either side of the fire, three Unnoticeables hoisting me toward the ball of light hovering between them.

There: Marco had Meryll by the throat, the Unnoticeables were scattered, frantically looking for something. I wasn't in the picture at all.

"I mean 'take,'" Meryll said, "as in absorb. It's what I do. Don't worry—the Flare will, uh . . . live on in me or whatever. Think of it like this: We're just collecting forces. Putting the girl's and the Flare's powers in the same basket as mine."

"You mean to do what that thing did," Marco asked, pointing at me.

He was always still. No shuffling, no blinking, no breathing. But he was especially still now.

"I . . . bloody hell," Meryll said, and she ducked just as Marco snapped into motion. She was fast, but he was faster.

He had her by the throat before I could blink.

Flash. The same picture. But without me in it.

I could feel where everybody was looking. No, it was more than that. I could feel what everybody was aware of. The three holding me were focused entirely on the angel. They were staring into its depths, watching the fractals turn in there. Marco was focused on Meryll. Meryll was focused on Marco. Nobody was focused on me. Nobody was *aware* of me. And if nobody is aware of you, who's to even say where you really are?

I felt myself move sideways, and I was gone. I was still here, in the same reality, but I was now outside of theirs: The Unnoticeables were holding nothing. I was laying on the ground between them, watching them move in slow motion. I rolled to my side, hacked until my vision went blurry, then crawled toward the fire. I was hoping I'd just missed something. Maybe Jackie was lying down and I couldn't see her. But no, I couldn't see her anywhere.

Maybe they'd let her go, now that they had me. Maybe she was running down to the road right now to get help. Maybe she'd learned how to fly with the power of positive thinking and was already halfway to Neverland.

It was denial, but denial keeps you going.

There was only one thing I could do. It was madness. It would certainly kill me. But maybe it would kill them, too. Maybe that would be good enough.

Just a few more feet and I could reach the light. But I had to crawl right past Meryll and Marco first. Marco's face was blank. His fingers dug into Meryll's throat so viciously that they broke the skin. Meryll had one combat boot firmly planted in his groin and both of her hands wrapped around his wrist, just trying to support her own weight. They were barely moving right now, but how long would this last? I had no idea what I did to get here, to this other place, and no idea when or if I'd be kicked back out.

Just a few more feet.

I could almost reach the angel. My fingertips brushed its surface. It was cold and sharp, like winter wind. I pushed, and the surface yielded. Then broke. The world rushed into the angel like I'd just poked a hole in the bottom of a pool. I went with it.

. . .

White.

Noise.

White noise turned up to 11.

I was lost in sunshine that gave no warmth. It was just like the last time—a pervading, blinding void that was at once lukewarm and freezing—but this time I saw the trick. This place wasn't empty. That's what I thought the first time I went inside an angel. I thought it was the purest, most unbroken emptiness that I had ever seen. But it wasn't empty at all. It was just overly dense. There were fine, twisting strings everywhere. They were made out of light, each independent but also interlaced with one another. A million-dense thread count woven into infinity. They were communicating something—information flowing to, or from, a place that I couldn't see. I got glimpses of it when I unfocused my eyes and managed to watch all the strings at once. But it felt like an ice pick in the back of my neck when I did it. My eyes immediately focused and my thoughts shunted elsewhere, like the sight had triggered a self-defense mechanism inside my brain. But each time I looked at the whole picture, I came away with a little detail. Just tiny, unrelated pieces.

There was information that burned my tongue, information that shook my bones and pulled at my tendons. I had no framework to even start to comprehend it. My brain kept trying to knock it away, the oscillation of a star twenty-eight billion light years from here—gone. The shifting rift pattern between seventeen dimensional barriers. Gone. The infinitesimal amount of heat radiating from a colony of mold on an asteroid in—no, gone. The only things that stayed in my head were the human parts. The stuff I could find a way to relate to.

There was a string in here from a girl named Luz. The person this angel used to be. The person this angel killed to become what it is. There were little shreds of her left all over.

I saw the same sorts of things inside the first angel. I found a little piece of humanity in there, all tiny and sad and worn. The number six. It got to me—what they do to us. They simplify us, like all of our complications are things not worth having. Like our problems aren't really a part of us. And it pissed me right the hell off.

Back then, I made a fist. It wasn't really a fist—I don't think I even had hands—but the *idea* of a fist. I felt the power surge through my extra finger, and I smashed my way out of the angel from the inside.

I tried to find that fury again. I curled my imaginary fingers and I swung. Again and again. It was like punching through molasses. Like trying to run in a dream. I had no anger left in me. Just . . . exhaustion.

Good god, I want my bed. I want my twelve inches of memory foam. My two inches of temperature-sensitive pillow top. My well-washed flannel sheets. My down comforter and goose-feather pillows. My window fan blowing cool air over my too-hot body. My bed. My fucking bed. Filling the whole room. Every tiny inch of it. Everywhere I roll—and I do roll; I curl up sideways, I lay spread-eagle, I turn upside down and prop a leg up on the wall, I take every inch of that space—is part of my bed.

I miss it with every atom. And I just want to go to sleep.

I swung again.

Nothing happened.

I don't sink, I don't float, I don't sit, I just exist—all alone in this white space, just watching incomprehensible information slip by.

The pattern solar radiation makes as it strikes the dust of a nebula in a galaxy that nobody has ever seen and will never name.

The sound that entropy makes.

A brick.

What?

A memory flitted by, chilly but happy. Fireworks and the smell of rain. A bench by a well, and two little kids throwing rocks at each other.

I chased the memory, try to find the person it came from, but she's scattered, and most of her is gone.

Pieces.

A brick.

A brick in the well. It has initials carved into it.

LG+JH.

I reached out and wrapped my fingers around the brick. I worked them into the gritty spaces between the bricks. I dug away the mortar—so old it crumbled at my touch. I worked the brick back and forth, a steady grinding sound like teeth on teeth, until I drew it out.

The brick atop this one fell into the empty space. The brick beneath it crumbled. The bricks to the side faded. The strings of information unraveled. The white gave way—slowly, like it feared the dark, but it gave. It faded like a Polaroid developing in reverse.

And I was left standing on a mossy patch in a Mexican forest. It was humid as hell. Breathing felt like snorkeling. There was a bonfire to my left that had passed "out of control" an hour ago. It had jumped the bounds of its little pit and spread to a nearby bush. The little dry patches of grass all around it were aflame. There were shadows out there, just beyond the light of the fire. Some were dancing. Some were fighting. Some weren't human at all. Just shadowy humps, groaning and drifting in the dark.

Marco had released Meryll. He was holding his forearm, which had been snapped in half. Meryll was doubled over on the ground, gagging and clutching her neck.

I saw another flash. A frozen tableau: Meryll was lying facedown on the ground in a pool of blood. Marco was screaming, terrified, leaping into the flames of the bonfire. In the middle of it all, there was a blank spot, roughly my size and shape—a void in the probability.

I stepped sideways through the moments, out into the space where nobody was looking, where nobody was aware. The world resumed its normal speed. Meryll got to her feet and tried to run. Her path took her right toward me. Marco grabbed his broken arm at the wrist and twisted it back together. Somebody behind me shouted, "I got her!"

"Got me, hell," Meryll said.

A faceless kid in a black trench coat tried to grab her. She ducked under his arms and uppercut him so hard he flew out of his own shoes.

She was mere feet away from me, but still couldn't see me.

I reached out and grabbed her arm. She jumped and

turned, wrenching out of my grasp. She threw a wild punch, and missed by a mile. I shoved her as hard as I could, but she barely moved. I punched her in the side of the head, which felt like it broke my hand. I danced away from her as another blow cut through the air, inches in front of my face. It would've taken my jaw off.

She laughed. "I can't see you, and maybe that gives you a little advantage. But you sure as shit hit like a girl."

Meryll backed away, out of the firelight. I thought about tackling her, then thought about the sound her fist made as it whistled through the air.

One lucky blow and I'm a vegetable, at best.

She was going to get away. She was *getting* away. She was gone.

I lost again. First Marco, now Meryll—they all just walk away, and I can't do a goddamned thing about—

In the shadows about ten feet back from the spot where she'd disappeared, there was a flash and a loud crack.

Somebody or something was coming this way. It was roughly the size of a man, but all hunched over. Its legs dragged and its posture was all lopsided. Slowly, it emerged into the light: mangled features on a hanging head, big black spiky shoulders. The whole thing drenched in blood.

Carey had seen better days.

In his right hand, an antique pistol dangled. Barely. He was trying to raise it again, point it at something behind me. I turned, but there was nothing there.

Wait . . . where was Marco?

There was a small, dark ball near the fire. It quivered and moaned.

I took a step toward it. It groaned louder. Another step, and it unfolded.

Marco looked like he was about ten years old and had just seen the bogeyman. His eyes were wide; there were tear tracks through the dust from when he'd buried his face in the ground. Snot poured out of his nose. He was sobbing so hard he'd given himself the hiccups.

That's when I realized: There was no blast. When I killed the angel this time, there was no big explosion that took out every monstrous thing nearby. The light just went out—ceased to be—and left Marco unharmed.

Shouldn't that make him . . . less scared?

I took another step and Marco screamed. He turned and leapt into the bonfire. I lost his details in there; he was just a mad dancing skeleton in the flames, trying to sprint straight through to the other side.

No, you're not getting away again.

Without even thinking, I stepped sideways into that other space and emerged in front of Marco. He was just coming out the other side of the bonfire, already fried to a crisp, his skin gone, his charred muscles pumping as he ran. He didn't see me, because his eyes had boiled away. He was about to run straight into me, so I stepped aside and held my foot up. He tripped over it and splayed into the grass. He lay still, his fat crackling and popping like bacon frying. He tried to moan, but had no tongue.

I knew what he was trying to say.

He was trying to say "please."

I pictured one of those strings of knowledge I had seen inside the angel. One of the ones that had slipped right out of my head, because I didn't understand it. I understood it now.

I crouched down beside Marco, still whimpering and trying to crawl away from me. The grass burst into flames where his fingers clawed at it.

I opened my mouth and made sounds I didn't understand, words that didn't exist now and maybe never did. The charred sockets where Marco's eyes used to be lit up. I closed my eyes. The ground shook. When I opened them, he was gone. There was a four-foot-long charred streak in the grass.

That's all that was left of Marco. Just a stain.

Seems appropriate.

I looked around at the shapes in the dark. They had gathered closer, alerted to what was going on up here by the fire. The angel was gone, they'd noticed that much, and the ones nearest me had seen what I did to Marco. Word was spreading. A few ran. A few others considered it for a moment, and then ran.

I sat down in the warm grass. I tucked my knees up beneath me and pressed my forehead to the ground. The ground was amazing. It was ground. Just ground. Dirt and rocks. I huffed it. Smelled the earth. Smelled the promise given by that fresh, wet grass. It promised summer days, barbecues, walking dogs.

It smelled like normal.

Normal was a thing, now. It was an approachable concept. It was a fucking possibility!

It was over. Over.

I looked up and the world was blurry. It looked like everything was underwater. I blinked, and tears ran down my cheeks. I rubbed my eyes. The hunchbacked shape was shuffling toward me.

"Carey?" I said, laughing.

No answer.

"This was Marco," I said, gesturing at the smoking patch.

"He's gone. He's really, really gone."

He still said nothing.

I rubbed my eyes harder and blinked a few times.

There was a weird look on Carey's face. He looked sad, which was a strange and foreign concept for his face. Even stranger—he looked serious. He was pointing something at me. His hand was shaking.

The pistol.

"What are you doing?" I asked. I looked behind me again. Nothing. "It's me. It's just me."

I held my breath. Neither of us moved.

Then, slowly, his hand dropped to his side.

I exhaled.

"What was that all about?" I said.

"Sorry, darlin'," he said, "I took a bad beating getting here. I'm just a little confused. Probably got a concussion or six."

"Help me up," I said, and held out my hand for him.

"Help yourself up," he said. "I'm barely standing. I'll just join you on the ground."

We found Jackie unconscious in a heap. She had a wicked red welt the shape of a hand on the side of her face. It was already swelling. Carey wouldn't even help me drag her back to the car. I couldn't blame him. Even dragging Jackie, I outpaced him dramatically. I lost him in the forest, and had to wait a good five minutes for him to drag himself past the tree line and hobble to the car.

I had to drive.

Can you believe that?

After everything I did, everything I'd just been through, I still had to get in some shitty Volvo, turn on the headlights, and release the parking brake. I even signaled. Force of habit.

I pulled out onto an empty Mexican highway in the

middle of the night. I left the radio off. I rolled the windows down. I drove, and it was good to have such a simple purpose. There were no turns I had to worry about. No directions. No traffic. I was exhausted, but still not tired. I wanted to sleep, more than anything, but I guess I hadn't earned that yet. Jackie hadn't woken up yet, but I knew she would. Carey was pretending to sleep, but I knew he wasn't.

The trees to either side of me were dark. The old kind of dark. Prehistoric dark. No streetlights had made it out here. No power lines, no houses, no gas stations or minimarts. The only light they got out here was headlights and fireflies.

I supplied the former, the forest supplied the latter.

Fireflies twinkled in the dark like stars.

Like stars . . . blinking out.

"Carey," I said.

"Rnh," he said.

"I have this dream. I keep having it, over and over again. I get a little farther in the dream each time. In the dream, I'm floating in the ocean, but I think it's more than the ocean. I think it's the whole universe. . . ."

"Gk," he said.

"There's something beneath me, something bigger and older than the ocean. And there are stars above me, but they're cold, and I think they hate me. The thing below rises, and it consumes me, and together we rise up toward the stars. But as we get closer, they get farther away. Farther and farther, until they start going out altogether."

"Ngrl," Carey added, "pff."

"I think I understand the dream," I said.

Carey growled and shuffled in his seat, swiveling his head away from me.

"I think I know how to kill the angels. All of them."

I listened to the engine sputter and pout its way up a hill. I held the pedal to the floor, just trying to stave off entropy. When we reached the top, I eased off the gas and let us coast back down the other side, picking up too much speed for the rickety old car. It tried to shake itself to pieces as we descended.

"How?" Carey finally said. "How do we kill them?"

TWENTY-NINE

1981. Los Angeles, California. Carey.

I cannot roller-skate worth a god damn.

Look at all those motherfuckers, gliding about like swans out there. This one white guy with a bright red afro—the asshole actually did a spin. A full spin, all the way around.

That's just showing off.

All I can do is run as fast as possible and try to stay ahead of the inevitable shit-eating. But shit-eating will not be delayed forever. I trip over a fat kid tying on his skates and skid to a stop on the shitty roller-rink carpet. It's got bright red electric guitars on it, running over white ribbons on a blue background.

It is ugly as shit.

Uglier than me, though by the raw feeling on my chin, maybe I just got a bit uglier.

Some girls laugh at me. That's normal. I'm used to that. I look up and smile at them, and they laugh harder.

Good sign.

I can close this deal, but I need a distraction while I sneak into their hearts.

I look around for Randall. The last I saw him, he was

chatting up some black girl over by the jukebox. They were flipping through each selection, explaining to each other why that particular song sucks. But he and the chick were gone now.

That lucky bastard. Probably off boning by the Dumpsters.

The girls are already migrating away from me, to wherever girls go when they're away from me.

The population of that place must be fucking booming.

I grabbed hold of the railing and pulled myself up. I tried to make it look super casual, like I was just hanging out on the retaining wall outside the rink, waiting for the right moment—the right song, maybe—to bust out my spins. I surveyed the crowd. Tried to see if I could spot the drunkest girl with the least self-esteem.

There was a young chick across the rink from me. She was giving me the eye. Just my type, too. Short black hair with a red streak. Black lipstick, too much eyeliner, a torn-up Sex Pistols shirt hanging off one shoulder, exposing a bra strap. It was purple. And I was in love with it.

She gave me a little wave.

Shit. Meryll?

I jumped the wall and started sprint-running across the rink. It was like Scooby-Doo seeing a ghost—me just running as hard as I could without getting anywhere. A pack of girls rampaged around me, gangbanging me with giggles and elbows. I shoved through them and managed to flail halfway across the rink, when that red afro-ed spinning asshole crashed into me and sent me sprawling.

When I looked up, the girl was gone.

God fucking da—

Whatever. It probably wasn't Meryll anyway. How many chicks in LA look like her, these days? Punk died three years ago.

Now the mall rats were wearing its corpse to piss off their daddies.

In short: It was a good time to be me. I had cachet. I had potential. I had options.

I didn't have Meryll. But I didn't think about that. Much.

But I punched red afro in the balls for good measure, anyway.

ACKNOWLEDGEMENTS

The following people are awesome, and if they ever run up to your driver-side window, frazzled and out of breath, insisting that they need to commandeer your vehicle, please be assured that it is for a good cause, such as pursuing a cocaine smuggler who is escaping via helicopter, or perhaps fleeing the giant eyeball that is currently destroying the city but which you, up until this moment, had remained oblivious to. They almost certainly do not need your car just for drunken joyriding, though even if that is the reason, please give them a pass anyway. They're just that awesome. Their names are: Sam Morgan (my dynamic and powerful agent), Paul Stevens (the editor who acquired this series), Liz Gorinsky (the editor of this book), Patty Garcia (the publicist who's almost certainly the only reason you bought this book), and all the other talented and dedicated folks at Tor, Will Staehle (who designed the amazing covers and, like all of us, did not see the clown until it was too late), Robert Brockway (my dad—I don't need to thank me; I know what I did), Meagan Brockway (my loving and endlessly patient wife), and Penny and Detectives Martin Riggs and Roger Murtaugh (my beautiful, idiotic dogs).

ABOUT THE AUTHOR

Robert Brockway is a Senior Editor and columnist for Cracked.com. In addition to *The Unnoticeables* series, he is the author of two books, the cyberpunk novel *Rx: A Tale of Electronegativity*, and the essay collection *Everything is Going to Kill Everybody: The Terrifyingly Real Ways the World Wants You Dead*. He lives in Portland, Oregon, with his wife Meagan and their two dogs. He has been known, on occasion, to have a beard. You can find him online at

www.robertbrockway.net

or on Twitter
@Brockway_LLC

THE UNNOTICEABLES

By Robert Brockway

There are angels, and they are not beneficent or loving. But they do watch over us. They watch our lives unfold, analyzing us for repeating patterns and redundancies. When they find them, the angels simplify those patterns, they remove the redundancies, and the problem that is you gets solved.

Carey doesn't much like that idea. As a punk living in New York City, 1977, Carey is sick and tired of watching the strange kids with the unnoticeable faces abduct his friends. He doesn't care about the rumors of tarmonsters in the sewers, or unkillable psychopaths invading the punk scene—all he wants is drink cheap beer and dispense asskickings.

Kaitlyn isn't sure what she's doing with her life. She came to Hollywood in 2013 to be a stunt woman, but last night a former teen heartthrob tried to eat her, her best friend has just gone missing, and there's an angel outside her apartment.

Whatever she plans on doing with her life, it should probably happen in the few remaining minutes she has left of it.

There are angels. There are demons. They are the same thing. It's up to Carey and Kaitlyn to stop them. The survival of the human race is in their hands. We are, all of us, well and truly screwed.